"My hired h[elp hasn't arrived] yet. Maybe y[ou'd like to come] with me?"

Will's smile took ten years off him.

"I'd love that, if I won't be in the way."

"Not at all. In fact, I think you may actually be a help." Annie headed for a nearby cupboard. She couldn't explain why she'd been so impulsive, but the man had roused her curiosity. Handing him a tub of honey and waving goodbye was the last thing she wanted to do.

"I'll just get my suit and a cardboard box," she said.

"That's it? Just the canvas and a cardboard box?" His frown reappeared. "How can you catch a swarm of bees with that?"

Annie smiled. "You'll see."

Available in October 2006 from Silhouette Superromance

Family at Last
by KN Casper
(Suddenly a Parent)

In Her Defence
by Margaret Watson
(Count on a Cop)

And Justice for All
by Linda Style
(Cold Cases: LA)

When Love Comes Home
by Janice Carter

When Love Comes Home

JANICE CARTER

SILHOUETTE® SuperROMANCE™

DID YOU PURCHASE THIS BOOK WITHOUT A COVER?
If you did, you should be aware it is **stolen property** as it was reported *unsold and destroyed* by a retailer. Neither the author nor the publisher has received any payment for this book.

All the characters in this book have no existence outside the imagination of the author, and have no relation whatsoever to anyone bearing the same name or names. They are not even distantly inspired by any individual known or unknown to the author, and all the incidents are pure invention.

All Rights Reserved including the right of reproduction in whole or in part in any form. This edition is published by arrangement with Harlequin Enterprises II B.V. The text of this publication or any part thereof may not be reproduced or transmitted in any form or by any means, electronic or mechanical, including photocopying, recording, storage in an information retrieval system, or otherwise, without the written permission of the publisher.

This book is sold subject to the condition that it shall not, by way of trade or otherwise, be lent, resold, hired out or otherwise circulated without the prior consent of the publisher in any form of binding or cover other than that in which it is published and without a similar condition including this condition being imposed on the subsequent purchaser.

Silhouette, Silhouette Superromance and Colophon are registered trademarks of Harlequin Books S.A., used under licence.

First published in Great Britain 2006
Silhouette Books, Eton House, 18-24 Paradise Road,
Richmond, Surrey TW9 1SR

© Janice Hess 2005

(Original title *The Beekeeper's Daughter*)

Standard ISBN: 0 373 40272 4
Promotional ISBN: 0 373 60498 X

38-1006

Printed and bound in Spain
by Litografia Rosés S.A., Barcelona

Dear Reader,

There is a scene in *When Love Comes Home* where the heroine, Annie Collins, explains how honeybees learn to identify their hive by memorising the outside of it, so they can always find their way home.

That's how firefighter Will Jennings felt when he drove into Ambrosia Apiary. As if he were coming home. Not only was he revisiting a boyhood fantasy about the family of beekeepers who lived and worked there, but he was finding a new life—something he both needed and wanted.

Annie's return home to help out with the family beekeeping business, on the other hand, was supposed to be temporary—a respite from her old life in the city. Just when coming home is beginning to feel too permanent for Annie, a letter and a stranger arrive at her door on the same day, changing her life forever.

In the end, both Will and Annie learn—just like the honeybees—where home and heart can be found.

Janice Carter

PROLOGUE

WILL CLOSED the door gently behind him. His apartment was dark and stuffy with the closed-up smell of an attic in an old house. He set his duffel bag down and headed straight for the kitchen. If he was lucky, there might be a beer in the fridge.

There was, along with a quart of sour milk and an opened packet of salami that looked like something off a tannery floor. Will took out the beer, popped the tab and shut the fridge. No rush to clean it out. He had all the time in the world. The icy beer sent a jab of pain to the center of his forehead and Will clutched the back of a kitchen chair, overcome by vertigo. He closed his eyes, waiting for the room to settle down before sitting in the chair. Will breathed deeply, forcing air into his lungs. The pounding against his rib cage eased and he loosened his grip on the beer can. The moment had passed. When he finished the beer, he tossed the can into the recycling bin in the far corner and went into the living room.

Not much to get rid of in here. One armchair, one floor lamp, a small television perched awkwardly on a wooden folding table and a portable CD player with a stack of CDs on the floor next to it. He walked over to the window and raised the Venetian blinds, filling the small room with dust—and the first glimmer of daylight since the morning of the accident. Will sneezed.

He took a moment to stare down at the street, shrouded in the same pall of mist that had hung over Newark for the past few days. It was the end of April, though you'd never know it. Will checked his watch, thinking it must be later than the day looked, but it was only three o'clock. Too early for dinner—not that there was anything edible in the place—and probably too early for another drink, though he was tempted.

He withdrew from the window. He'd checked out of the hospital just that morning and had taken a taxi right to Headquarters downtown, where he'd made his resignation from the Newark Fire Department official. The rest of the day was his. And the next and the one after that. At least, until his savings disappeared, which wouldn't be too long.

He paused in the middle of the room, considering his next move. Funny how unexpected free time was so wonderful when your days were full. Now time had suddenly become a kind of monster—something to be reckoned with, demanding to be filled.

Will's mouth twisted. It was perverse really. People—doctors, the few friends he could still count on—had warned him about the importance of filling each day. Otherwise the temptation to sit idly inside his apartment would be overwhelming. He would find more and more excuses not to leave. And in spite of his resistance against taking advice, Will knew they were right.

Hence the decision he'd made in the middle of the night, days before he was discharged from the hospital. Forget taking a leave of absence. Forget the physiotherapy and the recommended counseling sessions. He'd known almost as soon as he'd regained consciousness hours after the paramedics whisked him to Emergency that his life would never be the same again.

Frank and Gino were dead and he was alive. Nothing he could ever do would change that cold hard fact. No matter what he did or how hard he tried to convince the rest of his squad that he was every bit the firefighter he'd once been, Will's gut told him otherwise. Regardless of how many people told him he wasn't responsible in any way for either death, Will knew there must have been something more he could have done.

He sucked in a deep breath. *Not a good idea to relapse your first day out of the hospital, buddy. Stick to the plan. Keep moving.* He grabbed the key to his Harley and headed for the door.

CHAPTER ONE

ANNIE TOSSED the bundle of mail onto the seat beside her and aimed the pickup away from the mailbox and down the long gravel driveway. She felt a small surge of pride at her skill in maneuvering the truck. Of course, she'd had a year's practice to finally master the trick. The scratches on the side of the aluminum mailbox were testament to her efforts.

A maroon Buick was parked in the driveway. Shirley was already here. Annie bit down on her lip and parked close to the honey barn, well clear of the car. Shirley had a disconcerting habit of failing to check her rearview mirror when reversing. Annie grabbed the mail and made for the kitchen door. Through the sagging screen she could see her father sitting at the table across from Shirley, who was jotting on a notepad.

"Good timing, Annie," he said, turning to

her as she came in. "Shirley's just writing down her cousin's address and phone number for you." In spite of the heat, her father was wearing his old navy pinstripe suit and a white shirt, unbuttoned at the neck. Annie couldn't recall the last time she'd seen him in the suit, but guessed it might have been at her college graduation ten years ago. He looked every bit as uncomfortable in it now as he had then.

"You're early," Annie said to Shirley. "I hope you wouldn't have left before I got back." She hated the reproach in her voice but couldn't help herself. Her anxiety over the past few weeks was now—on the day her father was leaving for his hip replacement surgery—at its peak. Shirley, her father's "lady friend," was driving him to Charlotte where the two would stay with her cousin while he recuperated.

"Of course we wouldn't have," Jack Collins said. He shot her an exasperated look edged with apprehension.

Annie set the mail on the table and went to the sink, turning her back on them while she ran the cold water. She wet her hands, rubbed them across her face and then filled a glass. "It's warming up out there," she said before taking a long drink of water. She placed the glass on the counter and added, "I hope it isn't going to be too hot in Charlotte."

"The hospital's air-conditioned, I'm sure," Jack said with an indifferent shrug.

Annie stared down at her father. He looked frail suddenly, and much older than his sixty-four years. Nothing like the robust man who'd swung her over his head till she'd begged to be put down when she was a child. She could still recall her shock at the change in his condition when she'd first arrived back home to help him with the business a year ago.

The past few days Annie had been so absorbed in her own worries about checking all the beeyards after the spring setup that she hadn't considered how her father might be feeling about leaving the farm. It was probably the first time in years—if not in his adult life—that he was handing over the operation of the apiary to someone else, and she suspected he was having difficulty accepting that. On top of that, he had to face surgery and physiotherapy a long way from home.

Her eyes shifted from the top of his wispy, gray-haired head to Shirley's even hazel gaze. They were both worried about Jack, Annie realized, and she gave Shirley a quick smile. "At least you'll have Shirley to watch out for you, Dad. That should make the change from country to city more palatable."

He grunted. "The sooner I get back here, the better."

Shirley's eyes flicked a message to Annie.

"Best not to rush it though," Annie said lightly. "The doctor advised you to be in good shape before coming back home."

Another grunt. "Humph. What do doctors know?"

"Well, hopefully more about hip replacements than we do."

He tilted his head toward her. "Maybe I'll take that up when I retire."

She grinned. "What, you retire?" Annie hugged him. "Don't worry about the business. I told you I've got Danny McLean helping after school and on weekends. He'll be able to come full time once school's finished for the summer."

"I hope he's got his driver's license, otherwise he won't be much help."

Annie stifled her irritation. They'd been through this already. "He does and his father promised him the use of their truck if necessary."

Shirley cleared her throat. "I think we'd better get going, Jack." She stood, collecting her purse and keys from the table.

"I'll get your suitcase," Annie said, moving toward the hallway.

"Shirl put it in the car already," he said. "We were just waiting for you to get back so's we could say goodbye."

Now Annie felt guilty about the ice cream she'd stopped for on her way out of town. She reached for her father's cane propped against the refrigerator and handed it to him as he slowly and painfully rose from his chair. She hated to see him moving like an old man. If he hadn't been so stubborn a year ago, he might have been able to have the surgery in the winter, when beekeeping came to a dead halt.

On the way out to the car, Shirley told Annie she'd call her in the morning but Annie was focusing on her father as he leaned against her. She knew the surgery was nothing to worry about and knew, too, that he was otherwise in good health. She simply wasn't accustomed to any vulnerability in a man who'd labored tirelessly and effortlessly all his adult life.

Shirley opened the passenger door and waited for Annie to help him into the car. Annie wrapped her arms around him as tightly as she dared.

"I'll keep an eye on Paradise for you," she whispered. Paradise was his nickname for their home.

"You do that," he said, patting her cheek. "Remember, those pesky bees may wander miles every day but they always come home. And I will, too."

After an awkward struggle getting his six-foot length into the car, Annie closed the door and bent to the open window for a last kiss.

"You may want to think about hiring another student," her father said. "Danny hasn't done the work before and may be a bit slow. Can't hurt to have a third pair of hands."

If only it were that simple. Getting Danny to work for her had been difficult enough. Her father didn't realize that most of the local high school kids wanted easier, better-paying jobs in town.

"And one more thing," he added, lowering his voice. "If you get a call from the people at that damn food conglomerate, tell them to go to hell."

"Jack," Shirley interjected.

If he weren't going off to a hospital for surgery, Annie might have been tempted to take the bait. They had an ongoing argument about selling the business.

"I think you've already done that, haven't you?" Annie reminded him instead. "We'll talk about it when you're back home. It won't be that long, you know. Just a few weeks."

He started to say something but Shirley quickly opened the driver's side door and climbed inside. As the engine turned over, Jack leaned out the window, determined to get the last word. "All's I'm saying is, get hold of Arnie Harris if they start pestering us again."

Arnie was not only their lawyer but her father's longtime friend. Wonderfully impartial, Annie thought, pretending not to hear him over the idling car. She slapped her palm firmly on the roof and jumped aside as Shirley shifted into reverse.

"Take care," she called out as the car headed down the driveway. Annie watched until it turned onto the highway, then went inside, sat in the chair her father had just vacated and tried not to cry.

When the moment passed, she reached for the mail. There was the usual collection of catalogues from suppliers and a handful of bills, which Annie pushed aside for later. They'd only be a reminder that time was running out for the apiary. She and her father would have to come to some agreement about selling sooner rather than later. The last item was a letter addressed to her from her father's sister in Charlotte. Annie recognized the delicate spidery handwriting of Auntie Isobel, who'd called a few days earlier to wish Jack good luck.

Annie was about to open it when she saw the end of a long white business envelope sticking out of a catalogue. Pulling it free, she saw that it had been sent to her, care of her aunt, who had re-addressed it to the farm.

St. Anne's Adoption Agency
256 Elmgrove
Charlotte, North Carolina

The envelope shook in Annie's fingers and she dropped it onto the table. Stumbling out of the chair, she got another glass of water and, as she drank, stared at the envelope. Maybe it was merely a request for financial support. A fund-raiser. Annie pushed that faint hope aside. Not likely. She'd had no contact with the agency for thirteen years and had almost obliterated it from her memory. *Almost.*

She took a huge gulp of water, moved back to the chair and sat. Finally, she picked up the envelope and tore it open before she could change her mind.

Dear Ms. Collins,
We have recently been contacted by the adoptive mother of the baby girl placed by you for adoption with our agency in August 1992. She wishes us to assist her daughter in locating her birth mother. Pursuant to the agreement in the contract signed by all parties in 1992, we are simply passing this information on to you. There is absolutely no obligation on your part to agree to this request, but should you wish to do so,

please contact me at the agency. If we receive no response from you we will—as per our agreement—consider the matter closed and advise the parents accordingly.
Respectfully yours,
Sister Mary Beatty

Annie slowly set the letter down. Taking a deep breath, she picked up the note from her aunt, which related that a letter from the adoption agency had arrived and that she was forwarding it. In typical fashion, Aunt Isobel had asked no questions nor offered any speculation about what the letter might contain. It had ended with the unnecessary reminder that should Annie need her for anything, she was always available. Annie blinked back tears. Aunt Isobel had never let her down.

In all the years since the birth and adoption, her aunt had never referred to that summer of '92. Perhaps she'd sensed that Annie didn't want to talk about it—which was true—or that the subject would be too painful for her. Also true. Yet it had been her aunt's quiet, nonjudgmental support that had spurred Annie to finish college and become a teacher. And now she had to make the tough decisions on her own.

Annie glanced at the kitchen wall clock. It was almost four and Danny would be arriving soon. Working hard for a few hours was just what she needed to take her mind off the letter. She took it upstairs, along with her aunt's note, and tucked them in her dresser drawer. This decision, she knew, wouldn't be as easy.

On her way downstairs the telephone rang and she froze midstep, caught by the crazy thought that it was a follow-up from the agency. Paranoia. It was more likely Danny, telling her he was going to be late. She dashed to the kitchen phone.

WILL GRIT HIS TEETH as he listened to the digressions that popped up like detour signs in the shopkeeper's account of how to get to Ambrosia Apiaries. He hoped the road there wasn't going to be as winding as these directions because the van was already showing signs of fatigue.

"But if it's their honey you want," the store owner said, "I can sell you a jar myself. Save you the trouble of going all the way there."

Will shook his head. "No thanks, I just want to have a look at the place." The man's raised eyebrow made him add, "I'm a friend of the family."

"Oh yeah? Jack or Annie?"

"Uh…Annie."

The man's frown deepened. Will was painfully aware of the stillness in the fine food shop. No doubt the man was wondering why, as a friend of the family, Will didn't know how to get to the apiary. Why hadn't he simply told him the truth? That he'd read about Ambrosia Apiaries in a magazine article years ago and had come looking for the place.

There were only a handful of customers inside the store, and they'd stopped talking when he'd come in. Now a couple of them exchanged whispered comments, and he felt their surreptitious glances at his scar. He ought to be used to stares by now. The problem was, every stare was another reminder.

"Thanks for the information," Will said and, every eye on him, hustled out.

He strode toward the van, parked half a block away. Of course he could have simply purchased the honey, as the man had suggested. But honey wasn't his reason for coming to Garden Valley.

The sight of a brand-new Honda motorcycle parked behind his van made him smile, nostalgic. It was an auspicious reminder of his decision to walk out of his old life and begin a new one. He paused to admire the bike, much flashier than his old Harley Davidson.

The Harley had been the last of his personal possessions to go. Will had kept putting off selling it, the symbol of a wilder, more carefree life. Before the accident.

His gaze shifted to the somewhat beat-up camper van, a far different symbol for the new direction his life was taking. The flare of nostalgia suddenly died. *No regrets.* Will climbed into the van, carefully eased out of the parking spot and, with one last glimpse in his rearview mirror, headed down the main drag of Essex, North Carolina.

It was a pretty town with a larger commercial center than he'd expected for a population of eight thousand. Though he didn't know if that figure—emblazoned on the town's welcome sign—included the outlying rural area. What he did know was that as soon as the van had begun its descent from the foothills an hour ago, he'd been so awestruck at the size and beauty of the valley that he'd had to pull off the road.

Garden Valley was a fitting name for the lush countryside that rolled away beneath him. The rooftops of Essex, clustered at the base of the hill, glittered beneath the midafternoon sun. Surrounded by verdant pastures and tracts of woodland, the town sparkled like underwater treasure. It could be a scene out of a fairy tale. It was definitely a scene out of the magazine article folded up on the seat beside him.

He headed southwest, as the store owner had instructed, taking his time. Now that he'd finally reached his destination, he had no idea what his next step was. Pull out the article and confess he'd saved it since he was twelve years old? *Yeah right.* Now that he was here, what did he expect would happen?

That was the issue, he mused as he searched the signs at each crossroad after leaving Essex behind. His ex-wife had once accused him of running away from his problems and he'd bristled at the suggestion. Yet here he was, proving her right. Suddenly he caught the sign for Dashwood Side Road, slammed his foot on the brake and turned onto the hard-packed gravel.

Five miles in, the man had said, and then make a left at somebody's orchards. Will had forgotten the name of the farm itself, but the barn behind the house was supposed to be bright red. Weren't all barns red? He was going less than twenty miles an hour and had plenty of time to make his turn when he spotted a red barn and silo immediately ahead on his left. What he failed to notice was the other vehicle coming at him like a tornado.

Pebbles and dirt pelted the van as Will cranked the steering wheel right. By the time he'd straightened out the van, the other vehicle—a mud-brown pickup—had disappeared. Damn. Country drivers were no better than city ones. Will kept going, occasionally checking the rearview mirror in case the maniac in the pickup came back.

Another three or four miles after the turn, according to the store owner, and he'd see the sign at the end of a long driveway. Will passed fields of some kind of bushy, flowery crop on both sides of the road, crossed over a narrow stone bridge spanning a strip of bubbling water, rounded a curve and spotted a yellow and black sign up ahead on his left. As he drew nearer, he pulled over and turned off the engine.

The sign, with its curlicue scrawl *Ambrosia Apiaries, J. Collins and Family,* had seen better days. It had been fashioned out of sheet metal into the shape of a picture-book-style beehive. But the apex of the hive had twisted into a rusting knot. Will guessed that the scattering of black spots was supposed to be honeybees. Or maybe the yellow paint had just worn off.

He sat for a moment. What should he say? *Just passing through from New Jersey and happened to notice the sign.* He cursed again.

He'd never really expected to find the place. The article had been written years ago and who would have thought that the apiary, with its tired old sign, would still be here? A twelve-year-old kid's boyhood fantasy. Buying honey was the plan. Besides, he couldn't leave without at least seeing the place. Maybe he'd even catch a glimpse of the girl in the picture—Annie. The girl he'd once befriended in his imagination. Someone with a family that could be traced back a few generations.

He was about to drive up the lane when he noticed a vehicle approaching from behind. Will watched as it grew larger in the rearview mirror. Seeing the square front end of a mud-brown pickup, he frowned. The same crazy driver who had almost sideswiped him? The truck slowed as it passed. Maybe he'd have a chance to give the guy a piece of his mind. Then it turned sharply into the driveway to the apiary and lurched to a stop.

Will waited, his eyes riveted on the pickup. Someone was getting out, striding purposefully toward him. Male or female? The sun was in his eyes and Will couldn't decide if the person was being confrontational or not. Trouble was the last thing he was looking for, but on the other hand…

Will realized with some relief that the driver was indeed female. Very female, he thought. Jeans and a loose shirt failed to conceal the evidence. The unbuttoned shirt flapped open in the breeze to reveal a form-fitting tank top. She marched right up to his open window.

"Can I help you?" she asked.

Her voice was confident and challenging. She was blocking the sun and as Will peered up, he realized that it was her. Annie of the magazine article. Same honey-colored hair, no longer braided but skimming her shoulders, and same heart-shaped face. And definitely no longer an eleven-year-old girl.

He cleared his throat. "I, uh, was driving by and noticed the sign. Thought I'd buy some honey. Are you the owner?"

Her golden brown eyes narrowed. She pursed her full, naturally rosy lips and didn't speak for a long moment. "Buy some honey," she repeated slowly.

Her tone made the excuse seem wildly implausible.

She scanned the side of the van. "You're not from Sunrise Foods, are you? A private investigator?"

"I'm just here for honey. And I'd love to see your apiary." He climbed out of the van and leaned against the door.

"See the apiary," she echoed, giving him the once-over.

Will sighed. He took off his baseball cap, realizing at once from the way her eyes widened that the inch of hair covering his scalp wasn't a reassuring sight. "It's actually a long story. Some years ago I read a magazine article about a family of beekeepers."

Something flickered in her eyes.

"I know this may sound crazy," he continued, "but ever since I read it I've wanted to see the place. And, uh, well, so I came." When she still didn't speak, Will reached through the window for the article on the passenger seat. As he straightened, he saw that she was looking at the scar on the right side of his face. Her eyes moved quickly back to his.

"Were you in some kind of accident?"

"Yeah."

"What happened?"

"Another long story."

"Does it still hurt?"

It was a refreshing question, not the standard two or three he usually got. "Sometimes." He stretched out his hand and she took the magazine article. She skimmed it for a few seconds, smiling.

The effect was transforming and when she raised her face again, her smile washed over him like warm water. He felt lighter somehow and the knot between his shoulder blades was gone.

"I remember when this was written," she said.

"Is that you in the picture?"

"Yes, and my dog, Skipper. Long gone now."

"And your parents?"

She peered down at the article again. "Yes, those are my parents. My mother and grandfather, next to Dad there, are dead, too. My great-grandfather was the *J* in the sign back there. John Collins. Dad was named after him." She held out the article.

Will stepped closer, relieved she didn't inch away. Up close, he noticed a smatter of pale freckles across the narrow bridge of her nose and a tiny dark mole at the corner of her mouth. A beauty spot, it would have been called once. In her case, appropriate. She had the healthy, wholesome looks of the all-American girl but there was something else in her face, too, he decided. A hint of sadness perhaps.

"I guess you should come up to the house then, and get your honey."

"I'd like that," he said. "By the way, I'm Will Jennings." He held out his right hand.

She clasped it, surprising him with her quick, strong grip. "Annie Collins—but you already knew that." Her eyes held his a moment longer and then she said, "Follow me in your van. It's about a quarter of a mile up the driveway."

Will waited until she'd climbed into the truck and fired up the engine before his fingers fumbled at the keys in the ignition. As he followed the truck up the driveway, he caught glimpses of fields through the row of trees lining the gravel road. The fields seemed to stretch out forever. When the white-framed farmhouse with its wraparound veranda and gingerbread trim came into view, Will felt as though he had come home.

CHAPTER TWO

ANNIE CHECKED her rearview mirror. She couldn't believe she'd just invited this guy up to the farmhouse for a tour of the apiary. What had she been thinking? She was supposed to be back at the Vanderhoff place to retrieve the swarm in their apple orchard. That's where she'd been heading when she'd almost forced him off the road. At least, she was pretty certain now that it had been his van she'd spotted at the last second as she'd made the turn.

He wasn't the first person to wander into the apiary in search of honey or even out of curiosity. The year after the magazine article came out, the place had been deluged with tourists. But it had been a long time since anybody had arrived, magazine in hand.

Twenty years later and he still had the article? If she were in the city, alarm bells would have been clamoring in her head. Stalkers. But this was Garden Valley, for heaven's sake. Besides, the look in his eyes and her own instincts convinced her his story—though weird—was legit.

Her father would have given the man a tour. There was nothing he liked better than talking to unexpected visitors about the habits of the honeybee and the curative powers of honey.

She took her foot off the accelerator and let the truck coast the last few yards around the side of the house to the kitchen door. No sign of Danny yet. When she'd seen the size of the swarm at the Vanderhoffs', she knew she'd need help to get it down and had come back for Danny.

Annie was unlocking the door to the barn when Will Jennings climbed out of his van. He paused to look around the yard and his smile wiped out any doubts she'd had about bringing him up to the house.

"This is…" He stopped, as if he couldn't find the right words. "You were very lucky to grow up in a place like this."

"Hmm." *More or less.* She was about to ask where he'd grown up but something in his ensuing silence warned her off.

"Come on inside," she said, pulling the door open. "This is the honey barn. Years ago when my great-grandparents were alive, this was still a working farm and they kept animals in the barn, as well as storing grain and hay. They only had one or two hives back then. It was my grandfather who made the transition from farming to beekeeping." She flicked on the lights and watched his reaction.

Will didn't say anything at first, just made a slow turn, taking it all in—the huge gleaming stainless steel extractors, the settling tank, shelving units filled with various beekeeping essentials, frames for supers neatly stacked in corners and two long, sturdy wood tables. Counters ran along two walls beneath windows obviously not original to the barn. Will stretched to peer out one of the windows. "There was a picture of rows of hives in a meadow in the article," he said.

"When the article was written, my father and grandfather were still planting crops in the back acreage. We have a few hives in a buckwheat field my father plants every year but most of them are on neighboring farms."

"Why? Don't you have to rent the land from them?"

"No. They're happy to have our bees because they pollinate their orchards and crops. Plus, we give them honey."

"How many hives are there?"

"We used to have about three hundred, but after Pete retired a couple of years ago we've been gradually reducing the number. I think we've got about two hundred and thirty now."

He whistled. "What's this?" he asked, leaning over the extractor.

"A honey extractor. It's electric, but they used to be hand-crank. The frames from the supers—those white boxes over there—are slipped into these slots—" she pointed "—the extractor spins and the honey falls into the well and comes out the spigot. It all works by centrifugal force." She bumped against him as she turned away from the extractor. "Sorry."

Annie lost her train of thought. She felt her face heating up and she turned aside, gesturing to one of the shelves. "After extraction, we transfer the honey into a settling tank where all the debris rises to the top. Then we pour it into buckets. It's a pretty simple process."

Annie stopped, her voice echoing in the

spacious barn. She was babbling, she suspected. But then wasn't that understandable when the guy's only response was to fix his blue-gray eyes on hers?

"Look," she said, unsettled by his level stare, "I've got to remove a swarm of bees down the road. I'll get you some honey and then—"

She broke off when she saw him frown, obviously disappointed. "Oh, sorry," he said quickly. "Well, uh, thanks for showing me around. As I said, I've been curious about this place ever since…since I read the article."

Again, Annie relented. "My hired help hasn't turned up yet. Maybe you'd like to come with me? It won't take long and I could show you the rest of the place after."

His smile took ten years off him.

"I'd love that, if I won't be in the way."

"Not at all. In fact, I think you may actually be a help." Annie headed for a nearby cupboard. She couldn't explain why she'd been so impulsive, but he'd roused her curiosity. Handing him a tub of honey and waving goodbye was the last thing she wanted to do.

"I'll just get my suit and a cardboard box,

check for phone messages to see if Danny's called and then we'll be off."

"Danny?"

"He's a high school student who's going to work for us this summer. Why don't you wait by the truck while I pop into the kitchen?" When she came out less than five minutes later, he was standing by the truck, looking around him as if he'd just landed in some exotic locale. "All set?" she asked.

"That's it? Just the canvas and a cardboard box?" His frown reappeared. "How can you catch a swarm of bees with that?"

Annie smiled. "You'll see."

WILL CONSIDERED Annie's deft handling of the pickup as she maneuvered it around the potholes in the gravel road and realized that, in spite of his first impression of her driving skills, she knew what she was doing. "Was the swarm the reason you almost collided with me at the corner up there?"

"So that *was* you I almost mowed down." She grinned. "Not really. I mean, I should get the swarm as soon as possible before it moves somewhere else, but I was expecting Danny any minute and I was rushing to assess the situation and get back before he arrived. I didn't notice your van till the last second. Sorry about that. Dad's always on my back about my driving but I'm not really as reckless as I look."

Will thought about how she hadn't noticed a van on an otherwise empty country road, but decided not to belabor the point. He stared out the window, spotting the red barn and the farm at the junction ahead. "So, three of you manage all those hives?"

"Actually it'll just be the two of us for a few weeks. Dad's gone to Charlotte for a hip replacement. Afterward he's supposed to be taking it easy, though I'll probably have to tie him to a chair to stay put."

Turning, he caught her wide grin. With the splash of freckles across her nose, she looked like a teenager.

"Have you always lived and worked here?"

"I grew up in Garden Valley—as you know. But I left to go to University of North Carolina in Charlotte and after graduation I taught high school in New York. Queens."

"A long way from home," Will said.

"Yes," she said, "a long way."

He tried to picture her in front of a class of

street-smart adolescents. "That must have been tough—teaching high school in New York."

She shrugged, keeping her eyes on the road. "At first, but by my fifth year I was a pro."

"How long did you teach altogether?"

She glanced his way. "Almost six years before I came back to the Valley."

"Because your dad needed you," he repeated.

"Yessss," she said, drawing out her reply. "And...I was ready for a change."

She shifted her attention back to the road. So there was another reason as well.

As she neared the junction, Annie slowed down to turn into the driveway of the farm with the red barn.

"This place looks familiar," Will commented.

"I bet you didn't get more than a glimpse of it through the dust cloud I spun." She looked across at him and grinned.

Definitely not feeling defensive, he thought.

"The Vanderhoffs live here," she went on. "They keep a lot of our hives in their orchards. The swarm's in one of the apple trees out back, past the barn. It's about a five-minute walk." She reached behind the seat and pulled out the canvas. "I'll get the box and my suit from the back, but could you bring the two supers? I always carry a couple in the truck in case of a swarm or if I need to set up a new colony. I'll let Marge know I'm here. Oh, and there's a hand saw. I'll need it, too."

Will watched her walk up to the back door of the farmhouse. He had an odd sense of familiarity, as if he'd helped her with a job like this many times. Perhaps it was the casual way she accepted his presence—her assumption that he'd be right behind her, doing his part.

His eyes narrowed when the screen door opened and what could have passed for a small bear bounded out and lunged at Annie. Will pressed down on the door handle, about to rush to her rescue, when he realized it was a dog. Annie dropped the box to hug it as a woman appeared in the doorway. Annie turned and gestured for Will to join her.

He hesitated. He wasn't much for social conventions since the accident. Getting out of the truck, he went around to the back for the supers. The dog raced toward him, barking, and Will froze.

"Bear!" shouted the woman.

I called that one right, Will thought, as the dog bounced back to its owner. He hefted the supers out of the truck and walked toward them.

"Marge, this is…uh…."

"Will Jennings," he quickly filled in. She'd already forgotten his name.

The woman smiled politely, waiting for some addition to the introduction. But when none came, she said to Annie, "I'm sorry Ted isn't here to help out."

"Will and I can manage. I just wanted you to know why the truck was here. And thanks for letting me cut the branch."

Will followed her across the yard, past the barn and into an orchard so large he couldn't see the end of it. "Quite a place," he said as he caught up to her.

"They keep a good third of our hives here. Listen," she said, stopping him, "I hope you don't think I forgot your name back there. I was just trying to think of what to say about you. I mean…" A red stain crept up her neck. "You know how people always tack on something about the person they're introducing? Like, this is—"

"I know what you mean," he said, cutting her off. "You could have said I stopped in to buy honey."

The stain deepened. "I have a tendency to babble awkwardly," she finally said with an embarrassed laugh that made Will regret his bluntness.

They continued walking. There was a cool breeze in the dappled rows of trees laden with pink-and-white blossoms and Will greedily sucked in the fresh perfumed air. He could have been on another planet, the place was so far removed from Newark. A muted hum drifted toward them on the breeze and grew increasingly louder the farther into the orchard they walked.

Annie dropped the box and saw onto the ground and stared up into a tree a few feet away. Will swallowed hard. Thousands of honey bees clung together in a massive, pulsing pendulum hanging from a branch. His first impulse was to vacate the area immediately.

Without taking his eyes off the swarm, he whispered, "How're you going to get them down from there?"

"It's tricky," she said, "but not complicated. The swarm came from one of those hives." She pointed to half a dozen towers of white supers about a hundred yards away. They were stacked in groups of four to seven, with bees flying in and around them. "Once the bees have left a hive with the queen, they won't return. The hive has likely been taken over by a new queen. I have to get the swarm to go into a new hive, which I'm setting up with the two supers you're holding. Come on."

Will gave the tree a wide berth.

"The swarm won't bother you," she said, smiling. "The bees are in what my dad calls a state of bliss. Before they leave with the queen, they fill themselves with honey. They're really docile right now."

"But won't they want to protect the queen?"

"They are. She's in the middle of the cluster. Here, I'll take the supers." She set them one on top of the other onto a wooden stand about five feet away. Then she picked up the canvas tarpaulin and unrolled it, spreading it on the ground directly in front of the supers.

Will was fascinated by her unhurried manner. Obviously, she'd done this many times before. He watched as she climbed into a white jumpsuit made of some kind of canvas material. The bee suit. Zipping it up, she reached down for the helmetlike hat with its mesh curtain and a pair of gloves.

"Okay," she said, "now for the fun part. This is where you get to help."

Uh-oh. He didn't want to risk a reply, in case his voice gave him away. Swallowing, he traipsed behind her as she headed back to the tree with the swarm where an aluminum ladder was propped against the trunk. Annie picked up the hand saw.

"I'm going up the ladder to cut off the branch holding the swarm. It's not very thick, so it won't take more than a few seconds. You're going to stand right below the swarm with the box. When the branch is cut through I'm going to lower it very carefully into the box."

"That I'm holding," he said.

"It's going to be heavy," she warned.

"Uh-huh. So how come I don't have one of those outfits, too?"

The obvious concern in his voice drew a smile from her. "Don't worry. You're the box man. I have to hold the branch with one hand

and saw with the other. Besides, as I said, the bees are in a—"

"State of bliss. Right. And what if they quickly shift into some other state? Like a state of attack?"

Her smile widened. Will had the uncomfortable feeling she was enjoying this. "They won't, trust me. I started helping my dad collect swarms when I was about ten years old."

"Won't they just, uh, freak out and take off?"

Annie shook her head. "They want to stay with the queen." She positioned the ladder closer to the branch with the swarm and began to climb, saw in hand.

Will felt his heart speed up. He was certain the swarm would either attack her or head immediately for him, and wondered how much protection the cardboard box would offer. Instantly, he had an image of his hapless cartoon self being chased by bees into a river. Annie began to saw at the branch.

"Okay," Annie said quietly. "I'm almost through. All set? By the way—"

Here it comes, Will thought. The disclaimer that puts a lie to every assurance she's just given me.

"Sure you're okay?" She was frowning down at him. "You look a bit pale."

I'm a firefighter for God's sake, he wanted to say. *I've tackled far more dangerous jobs than this.* But nothing came out.

"I was about to say that after I lower the branch inside the box, all you have to do is carry it over to the tarpaulin and set it on the ground. *Gently.* As I said, it's going to be heavy so don't let the sudden weight catch you off guard. Okay?"

He nodded and managed to inch closer to the branch. He raised the box until it was poised a mere four or five inches away from the tip of the pendulum of bees. His sweaty hands gripped the cardboard.

Annie made one last cut with the saw, which she then dropped to the ground. Will knew at once what she'd meant by weight. He could hear her breathing heavily as she struggled to slowly lower the branch into the box.

Will's grasp gave slightly at the heft of the swarm. He heard Annie clamber down the ladder but his eyes were fixed on the top of the box as he headed for the canvas.

"You're doing great," she called out behind him.

He'd have made some glib remark about hollow praise but was trying not to trip. Annie was standing at the edge of the tarpaulin by the time he reached it, smiling encouragement as he set it down.

"Okay. I'll take it from here."

Will watched her carefully tip the contents of the box onto the canvas. Then she moved back to where he was standing and took off her hat and gloves. "Thanks."

He smiled, unable to take his eyes off the bees. The swarm began to break up, moving across the canvas tarpaulin toward the opening in the bottom super.

"So they're just going to go inside now?"

"Yep. It won't take too long. Maybe half an hour. I might have to brush some of them off the branch to hurry them along."

"And they'll start up another hive in there?"

"That's right. Look, there's the queen. She's the large oval-shaped one with the three stripes on her back."

Will leaned over the tarpaulin and, after a few seconds, spotted the much larger queen.

"She looks like royalty," he said, "the way she's marching across the canvas."

"Yeah. Dad says it's the equivalent of the royal wave." She placed a hand on his forearm. "It's natural to be wary of a swarm. I guess many of us remember getting stung as kids. And of course, some people are allergic." Her face clouded over. "God, I never thought to ask if you were allergic."

"It's okay. I was stung once and nothing much happened so I guess I'm not." She'd removed the bee suit and the front of her tank top clung to her in a large, damp V. Will glanced at her hand on his arm, instantly regretting it when she pulled it away. He'd liked the feel of her warmth against his bare skin.

His eyes drifted to her face, still flushed with the exertion of bringing down the branch. A drop of perspiration clung to one eyebrow and a strand of hair was plastered to her forehead.

Abruptly he turned his attention back to the swarm. "You were right. They're almost all inside."

"Safe and sound." After a moment, she

added, "How about a cold beer when we get back to my place?"

Will felt his tension begin to unwind. "I'd like that. Thanks." *Well worth snaring a swarm of bees.*

CHAPTER THREE

ANNIE RAN THE TIP of her finger along the edge of her empty glass, peering down at it as if she found it far more interesting than the man sitting across the table from her. But she wasn't fooling herself and likely wasn't fooling him, either.

The strange fact was that even though she'd known Will for less time than it usually took her to grocery shop in Essex, she felt as though it had been years.

"You said your father's surgery was tomorrow morning?" he suddenly asked.

"Hmm?" She raised her head. "Yes."

"When do you expect him back?"

"Maybe not for a couple of weeks. His friend, Shirley, is hoping she can persuade him to take a bit of a holiday afterward. But knowing Dad, I don't think that's going to happen."

He nodded thoughtfully. "I was thinking

of looking for work myself. Maybe...in town."

Annie stared at him. Was he asking her for a job on the farm?

She was debating whether to be frank and tell him straight out that they could barely afford to hire another part-time student when he added, "Just that I thought I might stick around the valley for a bit before...well, heading out on the road again. If you know anyone looking for someone to do odd jobs, I'd appreciate it."

"What kind of work?"

He shrugged. "Anything really. Yard work. Basic carpentry. Whatever."

"What did you do in New Jersey?" As soon as the question popped out, Annie felt the temperature in the kitchen drop.

There was a quick interplay of emotions in his face, as if he were having an argument with himself. He stared at his empty beer bottle. "I was a firefighter."

"Oh." She hesitated for a second before blurting, "Is that where—"

"Yeah. An accident."

"Oh." She couldn't think of anything much to say. "The long story."

A trace of a smile crossed his face. "The long story," he repeated. After a moment during which Annie wished she'd never asked the question, he added, "Part of a burning roof collapsed on me."

A simple statement, but enough to etch a vivid picture in her mind. "So are you on sick leave now...or holidays?"

"Actually, I quit. And that's—"

"Another long story," she finished.

"You got it." There was a slight pause. "Maybe I should confess now how badly I wanted to run from that swarm."

Annie bet he wasn't the type to admit to a real weakness quite so nonchalantly, but she played along. "Could have fooled me."

"Why do I get the feeling you're mocking me?"

He sounded stern but she caught the look in his eyes and smiled. Then she realized that she was practically flirting with a stranger in her kitchen. She looked down at her empty glass again.

"I guess I should be heading out," he said after another long silence. He pushed his chair back and got to his feet. "Thanks again for the honey, but you should let me pay for it," he said, reaching for the small plastic bucket on the table.

"No way. As I said, I really appreciated your help."

She followed him to the kitchen door and out into the yard. The sun had disappeared behind the honey barn roof and the yard, now in shade, was cooler. A faint breeze carried with it the delicate fragrance of the tulip poplar in full bloom at the corner of the house.

Will paused by the driver-side of the van and raised his face into the breeze. "Smells like spring."

"Spring's been here for a few weeks now. We're a long way from New Jersey."

"Yeah." His expression was unreadable. "A long way," he repeated softly, before abruptly opening the van door.

Annie peered over his shoulder into the van. "Looks like you've made yourself a cozy living space."

"It works for me." He set the honey inside. "That bench folds down into a bed and there's a small fridge and propane burner for cooking. I stay at campsites wherever possible for the shower and laundry facilities."

"There's one not far from here," Annie said impulsively. "Off the main highway back toward Essex. Rest Haven Camp, about ten miles outside the town limits."

"Thanks for the tip. Maybe I'll head there now and check out the job situation in the morning. And... thanks again for your hospitality, Annie." He extended his right hand. "You took a chance asking a stranger with a story like mine into your home. I appreciate the opportunity to finally see Ambrosia Apiaries."

Annie placed her hand in his. Touched by the gratitude in his eyes, she was tempted to invite him to stay for supper, but common sense prevailed. Still, she had to admit to a definite spark when his hand folded around hers. Even the way he said her name made it seem exotic, as if it belonged to someone else. Someone far more daring. She stepped back from the van.

"It was my pleasure, Will. All the best with...your road trip."

He nodded and turned the ignition key. The engine's rumble made any further talk pointless. Annie waved as he reversed, made a neat three-point turn and lurched forward.

Will's left hand tipped a quick goodbye. Annie watched until the van drove out of sight. When the last dust settled, she headed for the kitchen door, wondering why she felt so inexplicably deflated.

She cleared the table in silence and sat in the chair Will had just vacated, trying to see the room through his eyes. So ordinary really, lacking the flash of a modern kitchen. Yet there had been such awe in his face when he'd followed her inside that his odd story about the magazine article had rung true. His interest in the apiary was clearly serious and focused. She hadn't wanted to admit that while he'd been dreaming of Garden Valley and beekeepers as a child, she'd been planning her escape.

Ironically, he'd more or less realized his fantasy while she...well, that was another story. A long one. Annie glanced instinctively upward to her bedroom and then closed her eyes. Once upon a time she'd thought by going off to college she could escape Garden Valley and for a while, she had. Until reality caught up with her in the form of an unplanned pregnancy.

Annie sighed and rose shakily to her feet.

Tucking the letter deep into her dresser drawer had merely put it out of sight. When she reached her bedroom, she first piled her dirty laundry into a basket to take downstairs, retrieved soiled towels from the bathroom and, on the way, paused to peek into her father's room. He'd made his bed and, as if he were coming home that night, had left his pajamas folded on top of his pillow. Annie teared up at the sight.

Finally, she opened her dresser drawer and took out the letters.

Sitting on the edge of her bed, she read them again, starting with her aunt's brief note. Annie knew that her aunt would expect her to call, especially with news of her father's surgery. Although she appreciated Aunt Isobel's wisdom and common sense, Annie also knew that this was her problem. Her aunt had done more than enough for her. Taking a deep breath, she opened the letter from the agency. Was Sister Mary Beatty the woman who'd counseled Annie? She remembered a woman whose quiet, non-judging manner had soothed Annie's fears and guilt.

She lay back on the pillows at the head of

her bed, letter still in hand, and stared up at the ceiling. She could simply toss it into the garbage and go on with her life. The agency wouldn't bother her again. She closed her eyes, her thoughts flying back to August 12th, thirteen years ago, and the day she gave birth to a tiny baby girl.

And now that baby girl—a teenager—wanted to meet her. In spite of Annie's curiosity about the person that baby had become, she wasn't certain she wanted to relive an event from her past that still evoked guilt. The thought of coming face-to-face with… her daughter…was almost terrifying.

Daughter. The word sounded foreign to her, a concept she couldn't connect with, even though she was a daughter herself.

If her mother were still alive, what advice would she give her? If her mother hadn't set out for Essex on that icy winter morning, what would Annie's own teenaged years have been like? If Annie hadn't drunk so much the night of that frat party, what would she be doing that very moment instead of lying on her bed con-templating a meeting with the daughter conceived that night?

If, if, if. A useless word. Almost as pointless as the phrase *I wish.* She sat up, tossing the letter aside, and reached for a tissue on the night table. The clock radio told her it was almost six-thirty. Auntie Isobel had likely finished dinner long ago and was now dozing in front of the television. Annie hesitated, index finger poised above the phone. Then, before she could change her mind, quickly tapped in the number.

Annie could tell from the disoriented tone in her aunt's greeting that she had indeed been napping. "I, uh, wanted to tell you that Dad and Shirley got away just before four and that Shirley will call you tomorrow after the surgery."

There was a slight pause. "I know that, dear. We made those arrangements last week. Remember?"

Annie cleared her throat. "Oh, right. Well, I also wanted to tell you that I got your letter and…the one from the adoption agency."

"So quickly! I just mailed them the day before yesterday."

The ball's back in my court. "I was surprised. No, more than that. Well, maybe closer to shocked."

"I thought you might be, dear."

Annie closed her eyes, knowing Auntie Isobel wasn't going to ask the question. "The letter was from a Sister Mary Beatty. She said that the...that is, my...uh, daughter wanted to make contact with me."

When her aunt finally spoke, she sounded almost sad. "I thought that might be the reason for the letter. I couldn't think why else they'd be writing after all these years."

"The thing is...I don't really know what to do."

"Of course you don't. How could you possibly? Take your time, Annie. There's no rush, is there?"

"No, but I... It's just that Dad will be home in two or three weeks and..."

Auntie Isobel's voice was soft. "You haven't told him, I'm assuming."

Annie waited for the pounding at her temples to ease. "No. There never seemed to be a good time and then—frankly—I left it so long I couldn't bring myself to do it."

"I know you're worried about his reaction, dear, but you're an adult now. He won't be disappointed in you."

"I never thought he would be. But he might

feel hurt that I never told him in the beginning. And now all this time has passed and—"

"Your father may come across like a gruff man, Annie, but we both know he's not really."

"Telling Dad is the least of my... I just don't know what I want.... Do you remember this Sister Mary Beatty? Was she the one who was so nice to me?"

"I can't recall, Annie." She paused. "I suppose this has brought back all the memories."

"In a huge overwhelming flood."

"Would you like me to come for a visit?"

"No, that's okay, Auntie Isobel. I'll be coming your way soon."

"Do you think your father will give in and stay with Shirley's cousin?"

"Hard to say. You know Dad."

"Are you managing without him?"

"I'll be fine."

"That's good. So you'll let me know when you're coming? You might have a chance to pay a visit to the agency while you're here."

Annie felt as if time was squeezing her. Obviously she'd have to make a decision soon. "I guess so."

"Just a suggestion, dear." Her aunt must have picked up the tone in her voice. "Don't feel pressured to decide before you've thought everything through very carefully. Otherwise, how're things? Anything new in your life?"

Annie had a vision of Will Jennings waving goodbye from his camper van. "Not really," she said. "Sorry, but I've got to run. I'll talk to you in a couple of days." When she hung up, Annie wasn't certain if the call had helped or made her feel worse.

As he headed into Essex, Will scanned the paved road ahead for a sign indicating that campsite Annie had mentioned. When he spotted a small arrow-shaped sign, he let the van coast to a stop. Rest Haven Camp, a mere five miles away. Worth a look-see, he decided, and turned onto the gravel road. It was an unusual location for a campsite. How many tourists wandered this far off the highway?

Three miles in, he suddenly understood. Cresting a hill, Will jammed the brake and stared openmouthed at a jewel of a pond ringed by trees. It was the centerpiece of a stretch of green pasture at the bottom of the hill. The roof of a farmhouse reflected the setting sun. Beyond it, about half a mile to the north, were three shedlike constructions in a stand of trees and the wooden framework of a larger, rectangular building in progress. A dirt trail wound around the buildings out to the gravel road and the entire area was bordered by a split rail fence. The late-afternoon sun cast the scene in a rich gold that Will had seen only once before, in a book of paintings. He eased his foot off the brake and drove down the incline.

As he passed he saw that the farmhouse on his right was boarded up. The roof of the weathered gray barn behind the house had collapsed and the front yard was overgrown with tall weeds. Will gave the van more gas, anxious to check out the campground ahead. The sign fronting the entrance to Rest Haven was newer than the first one Will had seen from the highway. He turned onto the dirt lane. The van bumped and jostled along the potholed surface as Will drove toward the building with the *Office* sign.

He parked in front and climbed out. Except for the clamor of birds in the trees, the place was silent. There were no vehicles as far as Will could see and when he called out a hello, no response. Standing in the open clearing, Will made a slow circular turn and decided that the place either hadn't opened yet, or the manager had been called away on urgent business. The office door was locked, as he'd suspected. Cupping his hands against the reflection, he peered through a window next to the door.

Squinting, he could just make out a telephone on an otherwise empty desk. Two or three chairs loomed in the shadows and he thought he saw the outline of a filing cabinet. If the place was open, it obviously wasn't enjoying a busy season. He called out once more but when there was still no reply, he got back in the van and started up the engine.

Ten minutes later he was back on the highway leading into Essex. He had the money for a motel, but hated to spend it unnecessarily. What was there to keep him in Garden Valley? Annie's face popped into his head as clearly as if he were still sitting across the kitchen table from her.

The small upturned nose with its sprinkle

of golden freckles. Eyebrows arched quizzically at him above her large, tawny eyes. She was all golden light, he realized, like the painting he'd been reminded of moments ago, only drawn in clear, strong lines. There was nothing delicate or ephemeral about Annie Collins.

Face it, man. You don't want to leave. His mind made up, he continued toward Essex. But long before the town limits, Will saw something he'd hoped not to for a long time. An inky black column of smoke spiraled up from a thicket of trees about a quarter of a mile ahead, on the left. Maybe a farmer was burning trash. As he drew nearer, Will saw a farmhouse and behind it, the burning roof of a barn.

He pulled over onto the gravel shoulder at the end of the driveway leading to the farmhouse. The fire was roaring unchecked, flames darting through the open barn doors and out the ground floor windows. Likely filled with hay, it was already a goner. Will couldn't see anyone trying to douse the fire and unless help came quickly, the house was in danger too.

Sweat broke out on Will's forehead and he

felt suddenly nauseous. There wasn't much he could do by himself. He had to get into the house and telephone for help. Surely there was at least a volunteer fire hall in town. If the valley wasn't linked with a 911 system, he could probably raise an operator.

Still he sat, wasting precious seconds. What if he just kept on driving? No one would ever know he'd been there. Except, of course, he would. Will took a deep breath, jerked the door open and jumped down from the van.

CHAPTER FOUR

ADRENALINE GOT HIM to the side door of the farmhouse, pounding and shouting above the fire. But something else held him there, seconds longer. *Fear.* Sweeping up from deep in his gut, bursting out in beads of sweat. Turning from the locked door, Will looked at the barn.

Was it his imagination, or did he really hear voices over the roar? He squinted into the thick, billowing gray smoke and his heart almost stopped. Was someone or something moving in there? He'd automatically assumed there were no animals in the barn because he hadn't heard any cries. Could he have been mistaken? Will rubbed his eyes, smarting from the acrid smoke in the air. Nothing there. He forced himself to stay calm. This wasn't Newark. He was at a barn fire in North Carolina. And if he was lucky, he wouldn't have to step one foot inside it.

Fortunately the slight breeze was coming from the right direction, wafting the sparks away from the house toward the clearing on the far side of the barn. He could at least try to delay the fire's spread until the trucks arrived. That is assuming someone had spotted the smoke and called in the alarm. If nobody arrived momentarily, he'd have to break into the house and call himself. Meanwhile, there should be some kind of garden hose.

Hand over his mouth and nose, he ran along the side of the house until he found the hose attached to a tap in the stone foundation. He cranked the faucet to the max, grabbed the hose by the nozzle and began to spray the section of house closest to the barn. The intense radiant heat of the fire could easily scorch and perhaps even ignite the house as well. The paint was already beginning to blister and the spray from the garden hose wasn't going to be terribly effective. But until help arrived, it was all he could do.

Will was deciding which window to smash when he heard something behind him. He craned his neck, hoping to see an engine and tanker coming up the driveway. Instead, a bright yellow school bus idled beside the house and a stocky, barrel-chested man was running toward him.

"What the—?" He stopped, gasping for breath and staring at the barn, panic in his face. Then he snarled at Will, "Who the hell are you?"

It wasn't quite the reception Will had been expecting. He didn't think the man was looking for an introduction either. "If you live here," he replied, raising his voice against the fire, "call the fire department. Now!"

But the man had already unlocked the side door and was disappearing inside before Will completed his sentence. The smoke was thickening. Will's eyes stung and sweat dripped from his forehead. He doused his head and face with the hose, though the relief lasted no more than a few seconds. The man suddenly reappeared at his side and lunged for the hose.

Will let go, but when the man swung around to aim the hose at the fire, he grabbed his arm. "Forget the barn. Save your house!"

He stared at Will, his eyes wild. For a tense moment Will was afraid it would erupt into a fight, but the man suddenly directed the spray back to the house.

"Where's the nearest fire hall?" Will hoped the guy wasn't going to say Essex.

"Not far. It's a volunteer brigade. They're on the way." He looked behind him at the barn. "Got an antique harvester in there."

"Nothing else? Animals?"

The man shook his head. Will could see pain and frustration in his eyes. It was a look he'd seen many times after fires had wiped people out. Homes, possessions—not to mention lives.

"Let me do this," Will said, moving his head closer to be heard. "You better move the bus out of the way before the trucks get here. Then start taking anything out of the house that you want to save."

"You think it'll spread to the house?" The man's voice cracked.

"Just in case." Focusing on the house would distract him from the barn and the antique harvester.

Hesitating for no more than a second, the man tossed the hose to him and vanished into the smoke. Will turned to check on the barn and saw that the roof was ablaze. No possibility of saving it now. He just hoped the guy had a good insurance policy. He also hoped the meager spray from the hose would be enough to keep the house from scorching before the trucks arrived.

A familiar sound rose above the roar of the fire—the muted wail of sirens. Will felt the tension ease out of him. An engine rolled up the driveway, followed by a tanker truck. Will squinted. Figures in heavy bunker gear and yellow helmets were jumping from the trucks and quickly unraveling hoses. One man stood apart, wearing a red helmet and shouting instructions. Noticing Will, he strode toward him.

"Who're you? Where's Warren?"

"If he's the guy who lives here, he's inside the house. I happened to be driving by and saw the smoke."

The man stared at the hose in Will's hand. "Leave that. I'll get a couple of my men over here. There's a shed behind the barn that needs cooling down, too." He glanced behind him. "Too late for the barn." He started to head for the tanker truck. "Stick around. I want to talk to you later."

Will turned off the tap and stood aside as two men dragging a hose ran toward him. Responsibility was now on someone else's shoulders, which suited him just fine.

He watched while two others began assembling the metal frame of a portatank to hold the water from the tanker truck. Once the tanker dumped its water it would go back for a refill at the nearest water source. Will estimated there'd be seven minutes for the truck to race back before the portatank emptied. Hopefully, a reservoir or water tank serviced the farms in the valley and it was close enough.

The owner of the house was now outside, talking to the captain. The two looked quickly at Will, then away. Discussing who he was, he figured, and how he'd so coincidentally happened on the scene. He'd expected questions. It was no secret that arsonists often hung around to witness their work. But there were more pressing matters at the moment. The captain began to help another firefighter lug a hose around the side of the barn. Probably saving the shed.

The farm owner walked over to Will. His face was flushed and he was breathing heavily. He held out his right hand. "Name's Warren Lewis," he said. "Wanna thank you for helping out."

In spite of his words, Will saw wariness in the man's eyes. *Not quite sure what to make of me?* Still, he clasped the outstretched hand. "Will Jennings."

"Scotty—that's the captain, Scott Andrews—said you did the right thing by cooling the house." He lapsed into silence, watching the firefighters hosing down the house and the shed. The barn blazed unchecked. "If they had more men and another tanker truck, they could've saved the barn," he muttered.

"For what it's worth, the barn was already at peak when I got here."

"Yeah?"

Warren's curiosity prompted Will to add, "I…uh… used to be a firefighter."

"So why aren't you helping them?" He turned his head at a sudden shout from the firefighter at the portatank.

Will swore under his breath. He'd blown it. The portatank was probably full and the tanker would be leaving for a refill. They'd be a man short.

Lewis turned back to Will as the tanker

began to reverse out of the driveway. "Where's he going?"

"For more water. Is there a lake or something nearby?"

"There's a reservoir about two miles down the road."

Will nodded. They stared at each other for what seemed a long time before Will relented. "Guess I'll see if they can use my help." He jogged toward the man monitoring the portatank. Without protective gear, there was no way the captain would let him do anything nearer to the fire anyway.

The guy at the tank frowned when Will shouted that he'd watch the water pressure and do the refill when the tanker returned. Will could hardly blame him, knowing that firefighters seldom wanted civilian help. "It's okay," he said, raising his voice, "I know what I'm doing. I used to work for the Newark Fire Department."

The other man shouted back, "The truck'll be back soon and the tank'll need refilling right away. We got about three minutes of water left here."

A tight time frame. Likely one of many drawbacks to rural firefighting. Still, it seemed that the guy had no sooner dashed to help the hose men working on the house than Will heard the tanker returning.

As soon as the truck pulled up alongside, Will had already extended the chute and pressed the electronic switch. Water gushed into the tank. Except for a brief look of surprise, the firefighter who had driven the truck accepted his presence. They worked silently and quickly until the tank was full again. The man motioned that he was going for another refill and climbed back into the tanker.

As the truck left for more water, Will looked across the smoke-filled yard at the barn. In spite of what he'd said to Lewis, he knew if they'd been in a city where water was handy, the men would have made some attempt to save as much of the barn as they could.

Time was suspended as the repetitive pattern of emptying and refilling continued. At one point, the captain appeared a few yards from where Will was working and watched briefly before disappearing around the side of the barn. Will could see that he was directing a couple of the men to work on the barn now that the fire there had peaked. Probably wanted to hurry the burn-out so that they could finish the job and go home. It was already dark. The pale yellow glow from an outside light above the side door of the house was barely visible through the smoke.

Suddenly a car roared up the driveway and pulled over next to the school bus. A woman climbed out, her face toward the barn. She had the dazed, disbelieving look of someone waking to a nightmare. Then she spotted Lewis and ran to him. They wrapped their arms around each other and somberly watched the last of their barn crumble.

Most of the men were working on the barn, hosing down the embers. Wafts of steam mingled with the smoke and the men shifted in the thick night air like wraiths in a horror movie. Except for the hiss of water on fire and the crash of falling beams, the yard was quiet. Will heard the tanker coming. The last run, he figured. The big job now would be mopping up and hanging around to make sure the embers didn't reignite. He helped the tanker driver load up the portatank and when they finished, the man thanked him.

Will nodded. He'd have liked to get back in his van and head to town for a shower and a cold beer. Except the captain, directing the mop-up, kept glancing his way. He sighed. The evening wasn't going to end any time soon.

But things moved quickly once the remaining embers had been doused. The firefighters worked silently as they put away their equipment. Will recalled all too well the mood after a fire. The first rush of anxiety on arrival at a blaze led rapidly to a routine polished by practice and real-life runs. Save lives, then save property. Afterward, the relief was always muted by the realization of loss and suffering.

The captain finished his conversation with Warren Lewis and his wife and headed in Will's direction. He'd removed his helmet and the balaclava beneath it, his face and forehead slick with perspiration. He leaned against the tanker truck beside Will and, taking a handkerchief from his coat pocket, wiped his face. Then he withdrew a pack of cigarettes, offering one to Will.

"No thanks."

Lighting up, the captain took a long draw, releasing the smoke slowly before speaking again. "I'm Scott Andrews, by the way."

"Yeah. Warren told me."

"Appreciate the help, Jennings. Especially manning the portatank." He took another drag on his cigarette before adding, "Warren said you're a firefighter."

"Was," Will corrected. "In New Jersey."

"Uh-huh. Well, I gotta say, I figured you knew something about fires. Most civvies would've been trying to put out the barn with the garden hose."

Will didn't say anything.

"Sorry for the initial suspicion," Andrews went on, "but we've had a few barn fires in the area lately. Any stranger needs checking out—especially one so conveniently on the scene."

"I'd have done the same, in your place."

Andrews looked at him. "On a leave of some kind?" His eyes flicked from Will's eyes to his scar.

"Nope. Quit."

"You get that in a fire?"

No beating around the bush with the guy. Still, his bluntness was refreshing. It reminded him of Annie's question earlier in the day. He nodded. "Yeah."

Andrews fell silent, finishing his cigarette. Will waited until the other man finally asked,

"Where were you coming from? This road is hardly a main highway."

"I was visiting Ambrosia Apiaries, not far from here. Then I went to some campsite—I don't remember the name—to see if I could stay there for the night. No one was around so I was heading into Essex." Will took a deep breath. "Mind if I go now? It's getting late."

"You a friend of the Collins family?"

Will sighed. The guy had obviously missed his calling. He should've been a cop. "I'm on a road trip and was driving through the valley when I saw the apiary sign. I was curious. I had a tour of the place and as I was leaving, Annie told me about the campsite."

Andrews stared at him for a long tense moment. "Like I said, I appreciate your help. And so does Warren. He had an antique harvester in there. Good thing you were around to keep him from getting hurt going after it."

The compliment must've meant he'd decided to accept his story. Will rubbed his face, wondering if it was as sooty as the captain's. "Look, if you don't mind, I should be finding a place for the night. Right now a shower and a cold beer are all I'm interested in."

Andrews smiled. "You'n me both. As a matter of fact, one of my men owns that campsite. He's at home sick today, but I can give him a call."

Will considered the offer for a moment, but hot water and a frosty ale were too irresistible. "Thanks, but for tonight I'd rather be in town. Maybe I could get his name and number from you though, in case I decide to stick around?"

"Sure. Hang on for a sec. I need to talk to Warren." He walked to where the couple stood staring at their ruined barn.

Will waited by his van. He was worn out. Just pumping out the tanker had left him exhausted—a sign he had yet to recoup his strength since the accident. He saw the captain gesture toward what was left of the barn as he spoke to Warren. No doubt the local fire marshal would have to come take a look, especially if there'd been an outbreak of fires in the area.

He frowned, thinking of Annie Collins running the apiary alone while her father was away. Then he shrugged the thought aside. Whatever was happening in Garden Valley was no business of his. Anyway, more than likely the perp was simply some troubled or bored teenager.

Andrews came back, a grim expression on his face. "Warren was just telling me he decided to drop the insurance on the barn a few months back. He was using it basically as a storage shed and the premiums were getting higher every year so…" He shook his head. "Damn bad luck."

"So you think it was arson?"

"Oh yeah. One of my men found an empty gasoline canister in the bushes over there that Warren says isn't his."

"The same person who's been setting the other fires?"

"We won't know for sure till the marshal's had a look around, but my guess is a yes. *Why* is another big question."

"Someone obsessed with fires?"

"Possibly, but *here?* In Garden Valley?"

Maybe Andrews considered the valley some kind of Eden but personally, Will was a bit more skeptical. Life so far had convinced him paradise existed more in the imagination than the real world. "So what other reasons have you been tossing around?" he asked.

Andrews absently patted down his jacket pocket before pulling out his pack of cigarettes again. He offered one to Will, who shook his head. "Oh yeah, sorry. Forgot. I have to quit—so the doctor says. I've been having some angina." He took a long draw, blowing out the smoke in a satisfied sigh. "I promised the wife this would be my last pack."

"That you bought? Or borrowed?"

Andrews gave a sheepish grin. "Right. I've been working on that. Anyway, at first we thought the fires were part of some kind of insurance fraud thing. Couple of the farmers were really down and out—on the verge of bankruptcy. But then about a week ago, one of the most prosperous outfits in the area lost its hay barn." He took another drag on the cigarette. A sprinkle of embers from its tip flew into the air with the evening breeze.

Will had a sudden vision of calling back the trucks, this time to put out a blaze started by the captain. "No pattern to the victims then?"

"None we can see. Except all of the barns and sheds have been used for storage or whatever. No animals."

Interesting. The perp has a heart? "When did the fires begin?"

Andrews shrugged. "About three months ago. It took a while for us to realize we had a serial arsonist at work."

"Serial arsonist? That doesn't sound like teenagers."

"Could be, though. You know—one with serious problems." Andrews finished off the cigarette and carefully ground the butt into the earth with the heel of his boot. "You ever encountered a serial arsonist?"

"Can't say I have. The only arsonists I've met were hired."

"I thought of that, too, along with the possible insurance fraud. But the one thing every victim had in common was a different insurance company. Or, like poor Warren here, no insurance at all."

"Poor guy," Will muttered.

"No kidding. Anyway, knowing folks in the valley, there'll be a barn-raising organized before the end of summer. Okay, that's it for me," said Andrews with a loud sigh. "I'm beat. You wanna follow me? There's a pretty decent motel about five miles this side of Essex."

"Sounds good," Will said.

"Motel's got a sports bar attached."

"Better still." He turned to open the van door, but caught Andrews's appraising stare.

"Too bad you're not planning on hanging around a bit. I could use some big-city expertise on this."

This meaning the fires, Will assumed. How could he let the captain know fighting fires was the last thing he wanted to do? Did the man think the sheen of sweat on Will's face had been put there by the fire's heat?

Something in Will's face must have been answer enough for Andrews. "Oh well, can't blame a guy for trying." He signaled to one of his men, who began to climb behind the wheel of the fire engine. "Give us a sec to turn the truck around and we'll lead you right to Traveler's Way Motel."

Will could just as easily have found the motel himself, but the gesture was meant to be hospitable. He got into the van and watched the engine reverse until its nose was aimed toward the main road. As he followed, Will glanced in his rearview mirror. Warren Lewis and his wife were still standing arm in arm, staring at the black, crumbled beams and timbers that had once been their barn.

ANNIE'S RELIEF was palpable. Jack had just been wheeled out of surgery and everything had gone well.

"I know he'll be asking me when you're coming to visit," Shirley said on the other end of the line. "Have you decided yet?"

"Soon," Annie said. "I called Auntie Isobel after you left yesterday and I'm going to stay with her. Did the doctor mention how long Dad might be in the hospital?"

"There's a rehabilitation center nearby that will have a bed for him in a couple of days. The doctor said maybe a few days there to get started on a program and then he'd be able to go home." Shirley's sigh resonated along the phone line.

"Are you worried if he comes home too soon, he'll want to get right back to work?"

"Of course. You know how stubborn your father can be, Annie."

Tell me about it. "I thought you planned to stay on a bit longer in Charlotte—to visit your cousins."

"That was the plan but last night Jack was

hinting quite strongly that he wanted to get back to Garden Valley as soon as possible." Another sigh.

"He may not feel the same once he tries to get up on his feet. I'm sure you can persuade him to stay a few days after the rehab center."

"I hope so. Anyway, dear, can I give him some kind of timeline?"

Annie hadn't thought that far ahead. She had to call Danny McLean to let him know she'd be away and to discuss the work he'd be doing in her absence. "I'm not sure. I'll call you later tonight or tomorrow morning to let you know. Give Dad a kiss for me, okay?"

After hanging up, Annie sat staring at the phone. Since receiving the letter yesterday, going to Charlotte had suddenly taken on a whole other meaning. Auntie Isobel would be expecting her to have made a decision about contacting the adoption agency while she was there. Her father likely wanted her to come as soon as possible, bringing mail as well as news about the business and Garden Valley. The walls were closing in.

She pushed her chair back and took her

empty coffee cup to the sink. The day promised to be bright and sunny, but she couldn't work up any enthusiasm for it. She'd impulsively given herself a deadline of the next morning at the latest and saw no way out of it. Going to Charlotte also meant having to make a decision about her daughter.

If she started down that path this early, she'd never get through the day. There was shopping to do in town and she wanted to check on the new hive she'd set up in the Vanderhoff orchard yesterday.

Was it only yesterday that the firefighter from New Jersey had arrived on her doorstep? She smiled to herself. Will Jennings had flashed across her mind enough last night to make her want answers to several questions.

Such as, what was her attraction to a quiet, almost solemn man with a scarred face and an obviously traumatic past? Was her life so empty that she was compelled to fill it with some crush on a complete stranger? Annie grimaced. She had no answer for the first question but the second—well, how much longer could she delude herself about the so-called life she'd had since returning to Garden Valley?

In the beginning, the plan had been to stay long enough for her father to find a replacement worker for Pete, the hired hand who'd retired. Annie had been grateful for the excuse. It sounded a whole lot better than admitting to friends and colleagues in New York that her fiancé had jilted her. In fact, she'd quickly come up with the line that her wedding to Jim had to be postponed because of family reasons. And Annie knew the very best place to recuperate from the pain of the breakup was Garden Valley.

What she hadn't realized until she'd come home, was how badly her father needed help. She still couldn't believe how quickly a few weeks had rolled into a year. Her life in New York—teaching, her friends and even Jim—was now a distant memory.

Inexplicably, and against all reason, she hoped Will Jennings had stayed. Seeing him one more time just might guarantee a better day.

CHAPTER FIVE

Annie was about to climb back into the cab of the pickup when Marge Vanderhoff's voice halted her midstep.

"Heard that friend of yours helped save Warren Lewis's farm last night." At the farmhouse back door, Marge loomed on the other side of the screen mesh.

"Huh?" Annie asked, her eyebrows raised.

"That fella who came with you yesterday to get the bees."

She was talking about Will? "What happened?"

Marge stepped out onto the small porch. "Fern Lewis said the fella—what was his name again?"

"Will Jennings."

"Seems he told Captain Andrews that he'd been visiting the apiary, so when I heard that, I put two and two together and figured it must've been him they were talking about.

Anyhow," Marge went on, "this Will Jennings was driving by the Lewis place when he noticed smoke coming from the barn."

"Was anyone hurt?"

"No, thank heavens. The fella told Warren he was a real firefighter and Captain Andrews said he did all the right things."

What must it have been like for him to have to deal with another fire? She glanced up, realizing that Marge was waiting for her to respond. "Does the captain think it's the same person who's been setting the other fires in the valley?"

"Word's out until the fire marshal investigates."

The idea of someone creeping about the valley setting fires unnerved Annie. This blaze was too close to home. It wasn't the best time to leave the apiary untended.

"By the way," Marge said, "have you had news of your father yet?"

"I talked to Shirley about half an hour ago. He's fine. Everything went well."

"That's great. Any idea when he'll be coming home?"

"Tomorrow, if he had his way."

Marge laughed. "That'd be your dad all

right. But they don't keep them in the hospital long anymore, do they?"

"No. Shirley's hoping she can persuade him to take some vacation time in Charlotte."

Marge's laugh deepened. "Good luck to her!"

Annie's smile felt forced. She pictured herself and her father driving back together, while Shirley stayed in Charlotte. If he got wind of this latest fire, so close to the apiary, he wouldn't even consider recuperating longer.

Marge must have made a similar connection. Suddenly sober she asked, "You going to be okay staying at the apiary on your own?"

Annie gave a dismissive wave. "Of course. Besides, the thing with all of these fires is that no people or animals have been hurt." She paused, adding, "It's almost as if the places have been chosen for that very reason."

"Still, accidents can happen."

"Hmm," Annie murmured, thinking of Will. "Look, I have to go into town. Want me to pick up anything for you?"

"Thanks, dear, but I have to go in later myself. You take care and give our love to your daddy when you're talking to him."

Annie promised and climbed into the truck. As she turned over the engine, she realized she hadn't mentioned she might be seeing her father in a day or two. If she had to leave the apiary, it would be good to have the Vanderhoffs keep an eye on it. On the other hand, it might also be better if no one knew she was away and the apiary untended.

On her way into town, it occurred to her that if Will had spotted the fire, he must've been heading away from the campsite. Presumably he'd decided not to stay there after all.

No doubt Will Jennings was driving out of the valley at that very moment and that was a good thing. *Wasn't it?*

THE CAMPER VAN stuck out like a parent at a high school prom. It sat in a far corner of the parking lot behind the Red and White Grocery Store, surrounded by an assortment of cars, SUVs and pickup trucks. Annie spotted it as soon as she turned into the lot and almost sideswiped an exiting car. Her heart rate surged, which she blamed on the near accident rather than the sight of Will Jennings' van.

As she pushed a grocery cart through the store, Annie automatically scanned the customers, although she knew he could be anywhere in town. Most people parked in the Red and White lot, situated in the center of the main street shopping area. Annie strode up and down aisles, looking for Will rather than the items she needed to buy. By the time she'd reached the opposite end of the store, she was disgusted. *You really do need to get a life, Collins.* Then she sighted him at the end of the express checkout.

He was staring absently into his shopping basket and didn't glance up until she was standing right beside him, her cart angled away from the next checkout line.

"Hey." He smiled.

"Hey yourself." She paused to calm her breathing. "So you found the best shopping place in town."

"Heard it was the one and only," he said, his eyes fixed on hers.

"Almost. You won't need to buy honey, anyway."

"No."

The man was definitely no master of small

talk, as he'd said yesterday. "I heard you helped save the Lewis place last night."

His face flushed. He winced and gave a half shrug. "The fire brigade did that."

She could see that he didn't want to discuss it, but she couldn't think of anything else to say. "Still, it would have been a disaster for Warren and Fern if they'd lost their house, too."

"It wasn't at serious risk," he muttered. "Word travels fast here."

"Oh, yeah. The Garden Valley Grapevine. I almost missed it when I was in New York." Someone jostled Annie from behind and she turned sharply. When she looked back up at Will, his gaze hadn't wavered. So now what? Annie wondered. *Nice to see you again? Have a good road trip?*

"So, are you heading out of the valley?" she asked.

"Uh, no. Captain Andrews gave me the phone number of the fellow who owns that campsite you mentioned. I've arranged to meet him there at noon."

Annie hoped her voice was calmer than her insides. "It's a beautiful place. I think you'll like it."

"I drove through it yesterday, but there was no one around."

"Ah. That's when you spotted the fire."

He nodded, then noticed it was his turn at the cashier and moved forward. Annie peered into her cart. She had enough for the express line but still hadn't completed her shopping.

"It's early yet," she said. "Want to go for a coffee?"

A trace of a smile crossed his face and he said, "Sure."

WILL STIRRED his coffee slowly, trying not to be too obvious about staring at her. Her hair was tied back in some kind of knot that made her look a bit older. Or sophisticated, he amended, except for the jeans and sleeveless cotton blouse.

"How's your father?" he suddenly thought to ask, careful to angle his body so she wouldn't have to look straight at his scar.

"He's fine. Everything went well."

Will nodded. He took another drink of his coffee, glancing at her again as he swallowed. She didn't look any more comfortable than he was feeling. Was it the scar? He didn't blame her. He couldn't stand to look at himself in the mirror. Reminded him of too much...

The problem was he really wanted to talk about Annie. How she spent her leisure time. Or more to the point, with whom. She was far too pretty not to have someone.

Don't even go there, Jennings. You could hardly expect her to be attracted to you. Not like this.

"I'll probably go to Charlotte in the next day or so," she added.

He thought immediately of the arsonist on the loose in the valley. "What about the apiary? Will someone be looking after it?"

"The McLeans—Danny, our student help, and his father—will check on the place for me."

"Will that be enough?"

"Enough?"

"Of a deterrent."

He saw something in her face. He couldn't tell if it was annoyance or anxiety. "Of course. Why wouldn't it?"

He shrugged.

"Is there something else?" she asked, her forehead lined with worry. "Something you found out at the Lewis place?"

"No, no," he said, clearing his throat, trying to think of a way to get past the roadblock he'd just set up. "The captain—"

"Scott Andrews."

"Yeah. He thought the fire might have been set by the same person responsible for the others in the valley but he doesn't know for sure yet."

"So there you go," she said, pursing her lips. "For all we know, the fire could have been caused by somebody driving by the place and tossing a cigarette butt out a car window."

Except for the gasoline can, he thought. "Sure. It happens." They looked at one another long enough for Will to realize she guessed he was saying that to ease her mind. But the chances of the arsonist striking so soon and so close to the Lewis farm were small. How many fires had actually been set—something like four in a three-month period? Nah. The odds were in her favor. "No point in panicking," he added.

She continued to stare at him before finally picking up her coffee mug and sipping from it. When she set it down, she asked, "What time do you have to meet Sam Waters?"

The unexpected change of subject took him aback. Obviously, she didn't want to keep talking about the fires and any potential danger to the apiary. What options did she have? She had to visit her father and there wasn't anyone else at home. He looked down at his watch. "In about five minutes."

Her eyes widened. "Guess you'll have to go."

He wished now he hadn't set a time with Waters. The coffee break might have segued into lunch. He pushed back his chair and got to his feet.

As he glanced down at her upturned face, he thought he saw disappointment. Maybe his intuition had been right yesterday after all, when he'd felt a connection with this woman. It was something he hadn't felt in a long time. "Thanks again for the coffee."

She rose from her chair. "I should be going as well. Lots to do before I can head for Charlotte."

He followed her out to the street, his mind teeming with images. The way the sun picked up strands of amber, chestnut and honey in her hair; the scatter of gold in her eyes. Her skin reflected a glow of good health. Next to her, he felt old, wrung-out and far too worldly.

"Well," she said almost breathlessly, "if you need any more honey, you know where to get it."

"And if you need any help with swarms, you know where to find me."

That made her smile. She turned, walking away from the Red and White Grocery.

The old Will Jennings—the one before the accident—would never have let a beautiful woman slip away like that.

He was still mulling over this transformation when he turned onto the gravel road at the campsite entrance. The sunlight-dappled trees, sparkling stream and distant hills confirmed the wisdom of his decision to leave Newark.

There was a Chevy Blazer parked in front of the office and when Will pulled up alongside it, a burly man in faded jeans and plaid shirt who looked to be in his late thirties ambled out to greet him.

"Jennings?"

"Yeah," Will said as he climbed out of the van.

"Sam Waters. Nice to meet you," he said,

shaking Will's hand. He cast his eyes across Will, lingering a fraction of a second on the scar before switching to the van. "Haven't seen one of those in a long while. Right out of the sixties."

"It's a later model, but you're right. Not many around."

"Too bad. I bet they're better made than most of the new vans."

Will thought of the struggling transmission but just nodded.

"Scotty said you were interested in hanging around the valley for a few days. Were you planning on doing any fishing or hunting?"

"Maybe some fishing and hiking."

"Okay. Just asking 'cause there's trout in the stream but the season's not open yet. As for hunting, not much around except white-tailed deer and season's not on for them either. Unfortunately." He paused for a moment. "If you do go hiking, wear long pants. Lots of ticks in this area."

"Sure. Uh, how much is it for the night?"

The man scrunched up his face in thought. "Tourist season isn't quite open yet so... How does twenty bucks a night sound to you?"

"Fair enough."

"Do you want a cabin, or are you going to bunk in the van?"

"Is the cabin twenty bucks?"

"Maybe double that."

Will had the feeling the guy was making up the prices as he went along. He peered around at the otherwise deserted grounds. "I assume there are facilities, if I stay in the van."

"For sure. Even got hot water. The washroom and shower lodge is over there." He pointed to a cabin halfway between the office and the stream. "Me and my brother are working on a laundry right now. That shed there," he said and jerked his head to a wooden structure the size of a small garage several yards to the left of the office. "The place is in a bit of a turmoil right now but…"

Will wondered for a moment if he might be better off going back to the motel. But then he caught sight of a large hawk skimming over the trees. The ambience was a heck of a lot more relaxing here than the sports bar adjacent to the motel.

"No problem," he said.

"Great. Well, c'mon in and get registered.

I'll show you around before I have to leave for work."

Will followed him into the office. The desk wasn't so tidy today. It looked as though most of the contents of the filing cabinet had been dumped onto it. Waters waved a hand at the mess.

"Don't mind that. The one piece of paper I need seems to be missing. Isn't that always the way?" He opened a drawer and fingered through it, coming up with a pair of keys. "Here. The small one opens the padlock on what we call the wash house—toilets and showers. I keep it locked when I'm not around. I don't want any teenagers vandalizing the place."

"There's the arsonist, too."

Sam's eyes flashed back to Will. "Damn right. By the way, congratulations on a great job yesterday. The Cap was telling me about it."

Will was getting tired of the fuss. He knew, without a trace of false modesty, that what he'd done had been miniscule. "So I heard this is your first season. Think people will find the place, given that it's not on the main highway? Not that it's any of my business," he swiftly added at the cloud that fell over the other man's face.

Waters grimaced. "Never mind. That's exactly what the bank manager asked when I applied for the loan. My brother and I plan to run a fishing and hunting lodge eventually. One of those places that offer one-on-one guides along with gourmet meals. My sister-in-law's a great cook and my brother knows all the best fishing holes."

"Sounds great," Will said, trying for a note of encouragement. Personally, he thought rich people might want to fish and hunt for more exotic game in more exclusive surroundings. Still, he'd already put one foot in his mouth. There wasn't room for the other.

"Yeah, I hope it will be. We have the vision anyway," Waters said, chuckling. "All we need to do is finish the work." He handed Will the keys. "I'll show you where things are. You'll have your pick of sites, but I recommend the one closest to the wash house."

Will followed him outside and looked at the log cabin beneath a giant sycamore tree about two hundred yards from the stream. Exactly the place he'd have chosen himself.

ANNIE HAD a bad feeling as soon as she saw Danny climb out of his father's pickup truck. He didn't make eye contact with her until he was almost two feet away and even then his gaze was directed at some point beyond her right shoulder.

"You look like something's troubling you," she said. "Have you come to tell me you can't work for me today, either?"

"No…uh…I mean, I can work for you today and probably tomorrow but the thing is…"

"What?" she asked, more sharply than she'd intended.

"Annie, I'm real sorry but I just found out that I'm failing English and I have to have the course to get into the college I want to go to in Charlotte. My teacher said I can go to summer school and that starts next week. Mom and Dad are real pissed—sorry—ticked off at me and say I have to have no life but school until it's over."

"And when will that be?"

"It's only for six weeks. End of July."

"But I really need you now, Danny. By the end of July my father will be back on his feet to help."

He blushed. "I don't know what to say, except I'm sorry. Maybe you can find someone else from school."

"Well, since you're here we might as well head out to the buckwheat field and check the hives there," she muttered. "Why don't you follow me in your dad's truck? We can load both trucks at once and save some time. I've got a lot of spring honey coming in over the next few days."

"Like I said, I'm real sorry."

"It's okay, Danny. Not your fault. At least, except for failing English. How did that happen?"

"I dunno. I don't like writing essays and stuff about poems and that. Kinda boring. And my teacher and I didn't get along."

She'd heard echoes of that last sentence countless times over the past few years from students. But she wasn't a teacher anymore, and he was simply her student in the beeyard.

"Well, good luck with summer school. C'mon into the honey barn and try on my dad's bee suit."

Danny's eyes flashed. "Are we, like, gonna be in those white space suit thingies?"

At least he was excited about it. "You bet. Complete with hats and netting."

While he was getting suited up, Annie's mind raced, trying to think of someone—anyone—who might be available for even a week. It wasn't until Danny had left, almost three hours later, that Annie came up with a name.

She shied away from the idea at first but by the time she turned out her bedside lamp, she knew Will was a good possibility. She just wasn't certain how good it would be for her, to have the attractive ex-firefighter in such close proximity.

CHAPTER SIX

SHE COULD HAVE WAITED another day, Annie was thinking as she turned onto the gravel road leading to Rest Haven Campground. Danny had promised to keep working until she found someone else. But what if Will decided to leave the valley before she had a chance to offer him the temporary job?

The irony of the situation hadn't escaped her. When he was sitting in her kitchen just the day before yesterday, asking her about available work, she'd been afraid he'd been hinting for a job at the apiary. If she was worried about her take on her invitation to coffee yesterday, what was he going to think when she showed up offering him work after all?

Annie blew air out her pursed lips. Too bad what he thought. She was desperate for help and he was an available, able-bodied man. That's all that really mattered. As her truck curved past the office, Annie spotted Will's van parked at the edge of the stream beyond the dirt road linking the campsites.

She pulled up behind his van and waved her fingers at him, where he stood by a picnic table. He walked toward her, holding a spatula in his hand. Annie opened the door and jumped down to the grass.

"This is a surprise," he said. "I was just cooking some breakfast. Have you eaten yet?"

"Cereal."

He gestured with the spatula to a small propane stove on the picnic table. "Feel up to bacon and eggs?"

She hesitated, reluctant to make her visit seem like a social one. On the other hand, the food smelled delicious. "Sure."

"Great. Coffee's in the thermos jug on the table."

"You've camped before, I see," she commented, studying his preparations at the table. "Looks pretty organized."

"Camping was a good cheap holiday years ago, when I first joined the department. After I got married, I gave it up." He paused to flip the eggs sizzling in a cast-iron pan.

Married? Did he just say married?

He turned the eggs onto a plate, added two pieces of bacon and passed it to her. "There's another fork, in that plastic container next to the coffee."

She waited for him to clarify the married remark but he seemed in no hurry. After he cracked open another two eggs and dropped them into the pan, he glanced her way and said, "Go ahead. They're no good cold."

Annie popped the lid on the plastic container and withdrew a fork from the assortment of cutlery, knives, can opener and bottle opener. She halfheartedly broke into the eggs which, in spite of her lack of appetite, were delicious. Crisp on the edges, runny inside and lightly salted and peppered. She was mopping up the eggy residue with pieces of bacon by the time he sat opposite her with his own plate.

He looked at her empty one and arched an eyebrow. "More?"

"No thanks, but they were yummy."

"It's the air," he said between bites. "Anything eaten outside at a picnic table tastes better."

She watched him eat silently and quickly, as if he knew she'd come for some purpose other than an impromptu breakfast. When he finished, he pushed his plate aside, reached for his coffee and took a long swallow. Then he set the mug down, placed his elbows on the table and asked, "What can I do for you?"

Annie felt herself color. "Am I that obvious?"

"Well, Rest Haven isn't exactly on the road to Ambrosia Apiaries."

"Something's come up," she began.

"Nothing about your father, I hope."

"No, no. But remember how I told you that Danny McLean was going to work for me for the next few weeks?"

"The high school kid?"

"Yes. It turns out he has to go to summer school and his parents won't let him work. At least, until summer school's finished."

"When's that?"

"End of July."

"So basically for the next six weeks you're on your own?"

"Yes, until Dad gets back from Charlotte."

"Though he may not be able to get right back into things for a while."

Annie nodded. She hoped the expression on her face wasn't as bleak as she was feeling.

"And you were wondering if I'd be interested in helping out?"

"Just for a day or two," she quickly said, not wanting to make the favor seem to be an imposition. To her relief, she saw no sign of reluctance in his eyes.

"Sure," he said. "I'd be glad to. When do I start?"

"Now?"

"Fine by me. Do I have time to wash up the dishes?"

"I'll do that. You made breakfast."

"How about if you head back to the farm now and I'll join you there in about half an hour? Give me time to shave, too."

"Great." Annie stood. "And thanks so much, Will. I really appreciate it."

As she walked back to the pickup, Annie noticed a fishing rod leaning against the side of his van. She felt a twinge of guilt, that she might be spoiling his plans for the day.

But on the way back to the apiary, Annie kept seeing the look on Will's face when she'd asked for help. As if she'd given him an unexpected gift.

KIDS TEND TO romanticize things. A twelve-year-old boy would certainly love to wear a bee suit. But Will gave the white canvas cloth jumpsuit Annie handed him a skeptical once-over. "I don't think it's going to fit."

"Dad's a bit shorter and not as bulky as you are, but we can fill in the gaps with socks and gloves."

"Yeah? Will that work?"

Her smile was somewhat indulgent. After stepping into it, he pulled his arms through and, sucking in his stomach, tugged up the zipper. About four inches of jeans hung below the cuffs of the bee suit and at least three inches of shirtsleeve below the wrist band. Will tried not to imagine how he looked. Annie was averting her eyes.

"Here," she said, handing him a large pair of long, woolly socks. "Pull them up over your jeans and the cuffs of the suit. Dad's boots will probably fit. He has big feet."

"Will I be able to run in these?" he asked, once he'd squeezed his feet into the tall rubber boots.

"Run?" Annie stopped to look at him, her own bee suit halfway up her legs.

"In case the bees attack."

To her credit, she continued pulling up her suit before replying, "Running won't do you much good, Will. The idea is to prevent anything from happening that would make you want to run."

Sweat trickled down his armpits. "Such as?"

"You're going to stay behind me and do everything I tell you, for one thing. The bees aren't dangerous, but they will be angry when we start disturbing their hives. That's why I have the smoker. Some of them will buzz around you, but as long as there are no gaps in your suit, you'll be fine."

She zipped up her own and shoved her feet into her boots. Then she handed him a pair of gloves before grabbing hers. "You won't need to put these on until we're at the beeyard. Don't forget your hat," she said as he turned to leave without it.

Will glanced at the pith helmet-style hat with its curtain of fine mesh. Somehow the outfit didn't look as glamorous as he remembered. He eyed the metal smoker with its accordion-like bellows. It looked pretty damn small. "Does that produce enough smoke?"

"Yep. Besides, it's a sunny day. Most of the worker bees will be out of the hives searching for nectar. The smoke will make any still inside think their hive is on fire. They'll fill up with honey and fly down to the lower supers. When I give the word, you place this bee excluder on top of the second super from the bottom." She held up a flat metal grid with a cross-hatched pattern that resembled something that might fit on a barbecue.

Will couldn't resist a skeptical look.

She smiled. "It'll stop them from coming back up into the top part of the hive to get at the honey."

"What about the queen? What's she doing while all this is going on?"

"The queen and her brood are in the bottom two supers."

He wondered how many bees would decide to stay behind to guard the honey instead of joining the queen. When he glanced at Annie, she was grinning. "Do I look that funny?"

She shook her head. "Not at all. You look

like a real beekeeper. Well," she added, "a real nervous beekeeper."

Exactly, Will was thinking, as they got in the truck and drove out to the colony at the back of the property. Although it was a mere fifteen-minute walk, they'd need the truck to bring back the supers full of honey.

"I've never seen or tasted buckwheat honey, but I read somewhere that it's very dark," he said as they drove by the buckwheat field.

"Dark and bitter. It's an acquired taste. Most of our customers prefer the pale clover honey, but surprisingly there's still a good market for the buckwheat."

"So the honey we're collecting today, is that from the buckwheat or what?"

When she didn't answer right away, he turned her way. She looked amused.

"No. This is the spring honey," she said.

"Yeah…I get that part."

"The buckwheat doesn't bloom until summer. This honey's from spring clover or fruit blossoms."

"Oh." His eyes flicked back to the tall green plants for a second. "Right. Should have thought of that. Must be the city boy in me."

"Newark can't be all asphalt and concrete."

"The section of the city where I grew up only had a few green areas. I remember some people turned an empty lot into one of those community gardening projects. I spent a lot of time in it. It was a place I could relax in, feel at peace. It got me through a lot of bad times."

Her face sobered and Will instantly regretted the comment, realizing that it opened the door to a conversation he didn't feel like getting into right then. She looked like she was about to ask him something but they'd reached the end of the trail. The truck lurched to a stop.

Annie looked over at Will. "Just follow my lead and do what I say. Everything will be fine."

As a firefighter, he'd been the one to give orders. How life had changed!

"You okay?"

Will blinked. "Yes, just drifted off for a second there."

She raised an eyebrow and smiled. "So long as you don't drift off while I'm waiting for you to lower the excluder."

"Right."

Will helped her remove the equipment from the back of the pickup and they carried it the few yards to the hives, stopping a few feet away to put on their hats and gloves. Will had a sudden flashback to his fire training days, when he was still trying to figure out the various snaps and flaps on his bunker gear.

"All set?"

He couldn't see her face clearly through the mesh, but her voice was edged with doubt. "Just waiting for you," he said, louder than necessary but with as much confidence as he could muster.

She took the smoker and headed for the first hive, removing its top cover. Will watched as she squeezed the bellows and gently puffed smoke across the exposed super. A cluster of bees flew up at her and instantly Will stepped back. Annie continued working the smoker, apparently oblivious to the bees swarming around her head.

A pulse drummed at Will's temples. He forced himself to take a slow, deep breath.

"Will?" Annie raised her head from the

smoker. "Can you lift this super when I give the word?"

Bees, he told himself. Tiny honey bees and smoke from a handful of wood chips. That's all this is. He walked slowly toward her. In spite of the smoke, there appeared to be an awful lot of bees still circling.

Annie squeezed the bellows a couple more times. "Okay."

Will set his gloved hands into the slots on either side of the super and pulled. It was heavier than he'd expected and he made a kind of dipping motion, raising and lowering it before managing to heave it completely off the hive. A cloud of bees flew up into his face, brushing against the mesh of his hat.

A surge of adrenaline sent blood rushing to his head and for a moment, he was afraid he was going to pass out.

Annie puffed more smoke onto the super and said, "Take that as far as you can carry it. The bees will leave you alone after a few seconds."

He didn't quite make it to the truck, but was forced to lower the super onto the ground midway. When he stood, he waited until the vertigo left him. He suspected his face was bright red beneath the dark mesh and was glad Annie couldn't see. When the sense of panic eased, Will went back to the hive.

Annie was waiting for him, seemingly oblivious to what was happening. Except that just before she stopped smoking the second super, she asked, "Feel up to finishing this now, or do you want to take a break?"

"Let's keep on," he said, stooping to lift the other super.

"Okay."

They worked silently for another hour, removing supers, setting the bee excluders down and replacing the supers back on the hives.

"It takes a few days to get all the bees settled at the bottom of the hive," Annie said. "Then we'll come back for the honey. Dad and I have already set bee excluders in those over there." She pointed to a cluster of hives with stones on their covers. "We marked them so we'd know which hives to take honey from on the next round. We'll do them just before we leave."

Will was prepared for the next hive. He took a deep breath as he raised the cover and clenched his teeth when the first cloud of bees flew up in his face. By the third hive, his heart rate scarcely budged and by the time they set the last excluder, he was feeling like a pro.

"Now we take the honey. The supers will be heavy, but there won't be many bees to bother us."

Will wondered if she was smiling underneath the dark gauze of her hat. But she was right about the honey part. His heavy breathing was purely from hard labor this time. When they were finished, they both sagged against the side of the pickup, ripping off their hats and gloves to let the slight breeze cool them.

"So what did you think?" Annie asked.

Will hesitated. "Harder work than I expected," he began, "and I admit to feeling some panic when that first super came off. I was expecting them to go down to the bottom right away."

"There are always a few that get angry rather than frightened." She closed the rear end of the truck. "How about a sandwich and a cold drink back at the house?"

"Great," he said, tossing his hat on top of hers in the back of the truck and climbing into the passenger side. "So what's on the agenda after lunch?" he asked after she slid behind the steering wheel.

"More of the same?"

"Okay. I'll be an expert by the end of the day."

"Definitely," she said, glancing across at him. They both laughed at the same time.

They were almost at the house when she asked, "It's none of my business really, but did you have some kind of spell back there?"

"Spell?"

"At the beginning, you seemed to freeze up."

After a slight hesitation, he muttered, "I had a small panic attack."

"Yeah? Like, some kind of flashback to... you know... the fire?"

"I guess so. It wasn't a big deal."

"You think the smoke triggered it?" She looked more curious than concerned.

He shrugged. "Maybe. Who knows."

Will felt relieved when she dropped the subject. "Do we go back to that same colony this afternoon?"

"I should check the hives at the McLean place."

"Is Danny still able to look in on your place when you're in Charlotte?"

"I think so. His summer school course doesn't start until next week."

"Well, it's already Wednesday," Will said. "When were you thinking of leaving?"

"Tomorrow or the day after."

"So maybe as late as Friday."

She heaved a sigh. "I guess I'll have to give him a call when we get back to the house. Sometimes he races his dirt bike on the weekend." She slowed down, letting the truck coast the last few yards to the parking area at the back of the farmhouse.

Once inside, Annie directed Will to the bathroom. "You go ahead. I'll wash up here at the sink and get some lunch stuff out."

She was setting packets of cold meats and various cheeses on the table when Will returned. His hair was damp as if he'd stuck his head under the tap.

"Have a seat," she said, glancing up from where she squatted in front of the fridge. "Do you like Dijon mustard? I know there's a jar in here somewhere. And what do you want to drink?" She glanced back at him. "There's beer."

He shook his head. "Maybe at the end of the day, when we've finished."

It was the answer she'd hoped he'd give. There was still much to do. She shut the fridge and sat across from him at the table. He didn't wait for her to tell him to go ahead, but began to make a sandwich for himself. She liked that. As she assembled cheddar and Virginia ham, she wondered if she ought to ask him more about his panic attack, but sensed he didn't want to discuss it.

Annie bit into her sandwich and watched him munch on his across from her. The silence in the kitchen was odd, considering they hardly knew each other. But here they were, passing each other mustard and pickles, as if they'd done the lunch thing hundreds of times. As if she were sitting with her father.

Her father. She'd promised Shirley to let her know today when she was coming to visit. "I should call and see how my dad is."

"And you were also going to call Danny."

Annie tried not to smile.

"Are you worried about your father?" he suddenly asked.

"I know he's okay. I talked to Shirley yesterday morning."

"I meant, worried that he wouldn't want you to be on your own here—without Danny."

It was exactly what had been bothering her for the last twenty-four hours. "If he hears about the Lewis fire…"

"How would he feel if you told him that you had someone working for you in Danny's place? Someone who could stay until he was really ready to come home?"

"Who?"

His face colored. "Well, me, for instance."

It was the perfect solution. He was bigger and stronger than Danny and was also offering to work full-time right away. On the other hand…Annie looked down into her empty glass. Having Will Jennings around twenty-four seven was going to be complicated. She couldn't deny the spark between them and—unless she tried her best to quell it—it would make working side by side difficult.

"I'd still stay at the campsite, of course and go back there for my meals. Not that I don't appreciate the sandwich—" he grinned

"—but you'll want your privacy and I… well…uh…have other things to do as well."

"We can't pay you much more than we agreed to give Danny." Her eyes cut back to his. She didn't want to look desperate, even if she was.

"Fine by me."

His face was as impassive as a poker buff's, but Annie had a feeling he was smiling inside. "Okay, it's a deal," she said.

"A deal." He started to clear the dishes. "I'll wash up while you make your phone calls," he said. Without waiting for an answer, he walked to the sink.

Annie stared at his broad, stiff back and wondered for half a moment if she'd lost her mind. A day after asking Will out for a coffee, she'd offered him a job. *I'm going to have to do a lot of editing when I tell Dad how Will Jennings ended up working for us.*

"Feel free to phone from another room," Will said, running water into the sink and squirting detergent into it as he spoke.

Tiny hairs rose at the back of her neck. He was obviously feeling right at home. She waited a few more seconds then reached behind her for the receiver of the wall phone and, adjusting her chair so she didn't have to stand, tapped in the number Shirley had given her. It rang several times before someone picked up. Annie asked to speak to Shirley.

"Hi, Shirley. How are things?"

"Fine, Annie. I just got back from the hospital. Your father wasn't in a good mood today so I decided to give him some space."

Annie smiled. "Is he up to having a visitor?"

"He's up for anything that'll get his mind off hospital food, nurses who insist on giving him pills and taking his temperature or blood pressure and...what else has he complained about? Oh, the night staff are keeping him awake."

Sounds like Dad. It also sounded like Shirley already needed a break. How much more of Jack Collins would the poor woman be able to take? "Well, I thought I'd drive down to see him, uh, tomorrow," she said, glancing sharply over at Will, who was still washing dishes.

"Lovely, dear. When can we expect you?"

"I'll leave right after breakfast so I should get there just before noon. I'll go straight to the hospital."

"Your father will be very happy to see

you." She added, in a lower tone, "They're encouraging him to get up on his feet right away, and he's certainly making a great effort, but the problem is—"

"He may want to come home with me?"

"You said it." Shirley sighed. "They want him to go to a rehab place for two or three days after he's discharged but he's already protesting."

"But he'd have to go into Essex for physio. He might as well get started there."

"That's what I've been trying to tell him."

"Well, the two of us will have to present a united front," Annie said. "Take care, Shirley. Give Dad a kiss and tell him I'll be there for lunch tomorrow. Tell him I'll bring him a hamburger and fries."

"Maybe you'd better hold off on that. He's on some special diet right now. See you soon, Annie."

As Annie replaced the receiver, Will turned around, drying his hands on the towel from the rack beneath the sink. "Things are well?"

She gave a quick recap of her conversation. "Shirley can be as stubborn as Dad, so we'll see what happens."

"Does she hold a lot of sway over your father?"

"Sway?"

"I mean, does he listen to her?"

"Not always, but I've noticed more and more that he ends up by listening to some of her advice. Grudgingly, of course." Annie laughed. "Dad isn't attuned to the social niceties of courtship, I'm afraid. He met Shirley through a mutual friend but still can't bring himself to say they're dating or that she's a girlfriend. Not that he's fooling anyone."

There was a small silence until Will murmured, "Maybe he feels a need to protect you."

Annie frowned. She wasn't interested in discussing her family dynamic with someone she hardly knew. She got out of her chair. "Thanks for doing the dishes. Now, ready for more work? I've got to check the colonies at the McLean place and there are two other locations I should have a look at before I leave for Charlotte. On the way, I'll fill you in on what you can do for me while I'm gone."

He didn't answer for a second. "Sure.

Were you going to talk to Danny when we get to his place?"

"Of course." Annie grabbed the truck keys from the counter nearest the door.

"What about your suit? Aren't you taking it?"

"Right." Flustered, she went back to her chair and snatched it up. On her way to the truck, she was already questioning her decision to hire him. *Was he always this bossy? What happened to the taciturn, solemn man who was lousy at small talk?*

AS SOON AS Annie's pickup pulled away from his campsite, Will blew out the pent-up frustration he'd been holding in check for hours. Something had happened between them, right after her phone call to Charlotte. He'd been mulling it over all afternoon but still hadn't come up with an explanation that made any sense.

They'd worked well as a team in the morning, except for his humiliating few seconds of panic when she'd opened the first hive. He'd found the work totally different from anything he'd experienced before. And in a good way. It was definitely harder physical work than he'd imagined, but that was okay, too.

No, what was really bothering him was his need to hang around the valley. He'd satisfied his curiosity about Ambrosia Apiary and, as physically appealing as Garden Valley was, he figured there were plenty of equally beautiful places. He'd only begun his road trip, after all. So why was he acting as if this place were the end of his journey, rather than the start?

He watched Annie's truck round the curve out of Rest Haven. *Face it, pal. She's the reason you're lingering.* He could admit that much, but shied away from the bigger question. *What do you expect can possibly come out of it?*

Will unlocked the van and took out a cold beer from his fridge. There'd been the offer of one at her place after they'd visited the McLean beeyard. She seemed more relaxed than she had after the phone call. He'd known as soon as she'd hung up that she was ticked off at him. Maybe she was regretting her decision to hire him. He hoped not, but at least she hadn't changed her mind. *Yet.*

Must have been something he'd said. The

thing about her father? Nah. How sensitive could she be? It had been the most innocuous remark a person could make. He snapped the tab on the can of beer and went outside to sit at the picnic table. Still, her mood had altered dramatically after his comment about Jack Collins wanting to protect her. The observation had slipped out without any real thought. He wasn't sure himself what he'd meant by it. Now, in retrospect, he realized how presumptuous the comment had been. He didn't really know her or her father.

He swallowed another mouthful and felt his muscles begin to relax. He hadn't worked quite so hard since the accident. It felt good, mentally and physically. He missed his regular gym workouts with some of the guys from the fire hall.

But there was no reason to assume that working temporarily at Ambrosia Apiary was going to significantly change things for him. Perhaps the most he could hope for was respite from the loneliness that engulfed him.

CHAPTER SEVEN

ANNIE DROVE INTO the parking lot adjacent to the hospital and found a space near one of the entrances. She hadn't used her Ford Focus in ages. Since her exodus from New York, the car had sat in the shed behind the barn. Will had seemed surprised when she'd handed him the keys to the pickup, perhaps assuming she'd be stranded.

Back to Will again. She'd spent most of the drive from Garden Valley replaying the events of the day before. By the time she'd reached the outskirts of Charlotte, she'd forced herself to admit that she'd overreacted to his comment about her dad. He'd meant well, even if she didn't expect his two cents.

The instant she saw her father sitting in bed, staring morosely at the tray in front of him, everything else vanished from Annie's mind. She paused in the open doorway, watching him. He looked even frailer than he had the day he'd left the valley. He picked up a fork and prodded at something on the tray, then tossed it aside in disgust.

Annie smiled. Frail but still feisty. She tapped on the door frame. His craggy head swung her way, his smile illuminating the room.

"Annie!"

"Hi, Dad." She crossed the room and bent to kiss him. It was an awkward greeting with the tray in the way. There was an intravenous line in his left arm and he hadn't had a shave yet that morning. Large dark circles underlined his eyes and the furrows in his cheeks seemed deeper than usual. He looked like an old man. The image saddened her and she fought back tears. She was overwhelmed with an impulse to swoop him up and take him home.

"Shirl said you were coming. How're things at the farm? Did you check that hive at the Vanderhoffs'? The one I told you might swarm?"

Annie's face heated up. Hold that urge. "Yes, I did, Dad. Not to worry." She moved around the bed to a chair next to the window.

"Well, did it swarm or not?"

"It did—but I got it," she added quickly when he frowned.

"Set up a new one in the same area?"

"Yes, Dad. I know the drill. But how are *you*? Shirley said you were up walking yesterday."

"No rest for the wicked in this place. It's worse than an overpopulated beehive. People coming and going—all wearing those green outfits with stethoscopes dangling from their necks. Like being in one of those medical TV shows."

"The kind you never watch?"

He leaned forward to make a point. "I don't think I've seen anyone over the age of fifty. They all call themselves doctors but most of them haven't even begun to shave yet. The men, I mean." He fell back onto the pillow. His chest was heaving through his hospital gown. "When are we leaving?"

Annie felt breathless listening to him. "I don't know. What did your doctor say?"

His thick eyebrows furled together. "I've only seen him once, for crying out loud. The man's hiding from me, I think."

Annie stifled a smile. *Probably.* "Shirley

said they have a place for you at the rehab center. There's a chance you might be going tomorrow or the day after."

He glared at her. "What's the point of going to a place where they give you a bunch of exercises? I can do that at home."

"You can be supervised to make sure you're doing them right."

"Bah." He waved a hand in her direction. "Besides, there's no exercise like good honest work."

She tried not to roll her eyes. He'd trotted out this line on a number of occasions. "And Shirley thinks this is a great opportunity for the two of you to spend some time together—away from the apiary," she stressed.

He gave her a wounded look, as if she were playing dirty bringing Shirley into the equation. "Ah cripes," was all he muttered.

Annie seized her chance. "Anyway, things are shipshape at home. I've got someone new at the apiary."

"What?" He slowly pulled himself up against the pillows and pushed aside the tray. "*Who?* What about Danny?"

She'd given the story some thought on the drive from the valley and had decided to focus on the magazine article, knowing how proud her father had been to read about Ambrosia Apiaries in an international publication. "Remember after that magazine article came out and all those people started showing up at the farm, wanting to see the apiary and buy honey?"

"Yeah. Get on with it, girl. I've no time for long stories."

Annie scanned the room as if to point out that he wasn't going anywhere. "Well, the other day a man appeared with a copy of the article. He'd read it as a boy and had never forgotten about it. He...uh...was on a road trip through North Carolina when he decided to make a detour and see if the apiary was still in business."

Jack's eyes narrowed. "Bit off the beaten track, wasn't it?"

"I think it was an impulse, to satisfy his curiosity. Anyway, I showed him around and get this—he even helped me with the swarm at the Vanderhoffs'. Then when I found out that Danny couldn't help out after all—"

"Why not?"

Annie's rehearsed script began to slip away. "He has to go to summer school. It's not a problem, though, because Will—that's his name, Will Jennings—was looking for temporary work in the valley. I spent most of yesterday showing him around and—"

"You saying there's a stranger running the business? Someone we don't know?" His voice pitched.

"Dad, trust me on this, okay? I'm a pretty good judge of character. Besides, the McLeans are just next door."

He opened his mouth to speak just as Shirley entered the room with a man in hospital scrubs. Annie gave her a hug and whispered, "Good timing."

Shirley glanced sharply at Jack. "I've had a word with his doctor in the hallway."

The doctor—who'd nodded at Annie—was speaking in a low voice to Jack. "Would you ladies mind stepping outside while I have a look at Jack's incision?"

Once in the safety of the hall, Shirley explained. "I told the doctor that the family didn't want Jack to rush back to work and he was in complete agreement. He also said that they detected a slight heart arrhythmia while they were prepping Jack for the surgery."

"Arrhythmia?" Her own heart seemed to have suddenly stopped.

"It's not serious, Annie. Just that he may have to see a cardiologist for some kind of testing."

"Can he do that here, in Charlotte?"

Shirley nodded. "That's what I was asking the doctor about, before we came into the room. He said he can arrange it but wants to talk to Jack first." She paused before asking, "How did you find your father?"

As bossy as usual. Cautiously she said, "He looks tired, but he's just as vocal as ever."

The other woman smiled. "Well, language has always been one of his strengths."

Minutes later the doctor called them back into the room. Before leaving, he encouraged Jack to walk as much as possible and told him that he'd be moved to the rehab center in the next couple of days. Annie kept her eyes down at this, not wanting to make eye contact with Shirley and have her father think there'd been a conspiracy at work.

There was a long silence after the doctor left. Neither of them wanted to look at Jack. He'd need a few seconds to adjust to the disappointment that he wouldn't be heading for home right away. She and Shirley made small talk about the drive from Garden Valley and about staying with Aunt Isobel.

Finally, Jack spoke up. "That young whippersnapper told me I have to see a cardiologist before I go home. Seems there's some irregularity in my heart."

"I know, Jack, but he also said as far as he could tell it was nothing to worry about."

"What would he know? He probably just got his MD a year ago." No one spoke. "Humph. Guess this plays right into your plans, doesn't it?" Jack glared at Shirley.

Annie was about to protest but Shirley merely said, "Sometimes the gods look favorably on me, Jack. Just as they did when I met you."

He seemed to melt right before Annie's eyes. His face turned bright red and the smile he cast at Shirley was one Annie had never seen. From her dad…or anyone else. She looked with new respect at the woman who'd been dating her father for the past two years.

"I should go to Aunt Isobel's now, so we can have a bit of a visit before dinner." She patted her dad's hand. "Want me to come back later, after dinner?"

"No, that's okay. Isobel will appreciate your company. When are you going back?"

So it's *you* now, instead of *we*. "Maybe the day after tomorrow," she said. "I'll come back and see you tomorrow." She bent to kiss him goodbye, then kissed Shirley, too. "Thanks for everything." She squeezed the other woman's forearm and made for the door.

Just before she reached it, Jack piped up, "Don't forget to call home tonight. See how that fella's doing. And get Bob McLean to go round to the place, check things out."

Annie smiled but didn't turn around. "Will do, Dad. See ya."

WILL REMOVED THE LAST FRAME from the extractor and turned the spigot, allowing the viscous pale honey to flow into the stainless-steel bucket beneath. After spending an entire afternoon extracting the honey from the frames they'd collected late yesterday, he decided that the novelty of holding a fingertip beneath the spigot to catch the first globular drip was beginning to wear. A bit like working in a candy store.

The extractor spun twenty-four frames at a time and squeezed out roughly sixty pounds of honey, Annie had told him. He'd been impressed by the amount, until she also told him that the average worker bee produced only one-twelfth of a teaspoon of honey in its six-week life span. Which explained why every colony had millions of bees.

It had taken him the morning to scrape off the wax covering each of the individual cells of the honeycomb. Decapping, Annie called it. Then he'd taken a brief lunch break, using the key she'd given him to go into the house to wash up. Although she'd told him to help himself to anything in the fridge, he just poured a cold glass of water from the tap. Well-water had never tasted so good. He didn't linger inside—it felt too weird being in someone else's house when no one was home—but ate his sandwich sitting on the fold-down step of his camper van.

Cleaning up at the end of the day, he felt as though he had a good sense of what the job entailed. He also had a keen appreciation for what Annie and her father did. He could see why Annie was in such good physical condition. Will wondered how her father would manage all the lifting and carrying with his new hip.

Still, that was their problem. For now, he was content to hang around the apiary and soak up the tranquility. He hadn't slept so well in weeks. In spite of his thin foam mattress, once he'd dropped off to sleep, not even a six-alarm fire could have roused him. He decided to shower at the campground and, at the same time, make sure that Sam Waters had found the note he'd left early that morning. Will had paid a week in advance, but he didn't want Sam to think he'd suddenly up and left for no reason.

He double-checked all the locks, even though he'd be coming back to spend the night there. As he drove to the campground, he thought of Annie's sudden change in mood at his remark about her father yesterday. He hadn't intended to butt in, but he could understand why she might have taken offense.

Will slowed to make the turn onto the side road. He took another look at the rundown farmhouse tucked into the trees about a hundred yards or so off the road. Sure looked deserted. Suddenly he thought of the arsonist. If the guy was someone who simply liked setting fires—as many arsonists did—then this place would be the ideal target. He craned his head as he passed it, but didn't detect any sign of life.

When he pulled onto the gravel road to Rest Haven, a Chevy Blazer was heading his way. Will shifted to the right, tapping the brake as the Blazer rolled to a stop.

"Got your note," Waters said. "Hope you don't want a refund 'cause—"

"I don't," Will interrupted. "Just didn't want you to let my site go to someone else. I'll only be gone for a couple of days, and I want to come back and forth here anyway, to use the facilities and for meals."

Waters nodded. "So you're working up at the apiary. I'm sure Annie can use the help."

Will didn't say anything. He hadn't mentioned working there. Someone in the area must've already sent the news around. What had Annie called it? The Garden Valley Grapevine? As much as he liked his privacy, it might be a good thing if people knew he was on the apiary premises.

"Thanks for setting out the barbecue," Will

said as Waters was about to continue on his way. "I noticed it this morning. It'll make a change from the propane stove."

"No problem. See ya around."

After a hot shower Will sat at the picnic table with a cold drink and wondered—not for the first time that day—how Annie was doing. He hoped she'd been successful in persuading her father to stay in Charlotte. Mainly because he'd have a reason to stick around the apiary a few more days himself.

That is, if Annie decided to keep him on. He set the empty can on the table and wearily rubbed his face. *Face it, Jennings. The only thing that legitimizes staying in Garden Valley any longer would be a decent, full-time job—which means firefighting.*

And he wasn't ready for that yet. Will stood and stretched. He felt restless and no longer quite so hungry. It would be a while before dusk, so he decided to hike along the stream to check out the property.

The walk under the canopy of willows and poplars edging the stream was cool and the air redolent of marshy plant decay mixed with perfume from the tulip poplar blossoms. Shadowy outlines of fish darted in the water and a mallard family flew squawking out of the tall grasses as he passed.

He stopped once to take a few deep breaths of clean air. In spite of the day's labor, he felt rejuvenated. If he'd been home in Newark, relaxing after a hard day would have meant a beer in front of the television rather than going for a walk. The idea prompted a grin. Where would he walk to? Seemed as if he drove his motorcycle everywhere, even the gym. Which kind of defeated the whole purpose of going in the first place. But that's what people did in the city. They drove, rather than walked. Unless you were into jogging and that had never appealed to him.

The sun hovered above the foothills to the west when he finally came to a clearing, or what seemed to be overgrown pasture. The remnants of an old barbed wire fence at the far end of the acreage suggested he was on private property. He hadn't seen any farms in the area except for the abandoned place a mile or two down the road, so Will assumed this land was part of that spread. Curious, he walked across the pasture and carefully ducked under the barbed wire. Now that he was closer, he could see the back of the house and the barn with its sagging roof. He paused, wondering if he ought to be trespassing, but decided abandoned places were fair game.

The yard behind the barn was littered with empty and rusting metal objects—cans, buckets, farm implements. Part of an old harvester or combine was almost hidden by tall weeds. As Will bypassed the barn, he was struck by the earthy odor of moldering hay and paused to peer in one of the broken windows. It was dark and shadowy inside. Something fluttered from a rafter and he jumped back. Then he laughed at himself. Probably a bat or bird of some kind.

He kept on walking and, rounding the corner of the barn, stopped suddenly. There were two large chicken-wire coops filled with pigeons. Pigeons of every kind, totally unlike the ubiquitous gray ones in his Newark neighborhood. They were perched on the roofs of bird houses inside the coops and also on an arrangement of various lengths of wooden poles, nailed crudely together to form a kind of avian climbing equipment. There must be at least fifty birds in there, he was thinking, and then realized that the place was obviously not deserted.

That realization came a tad late. A gravelly, aggressive voice bellowed behind him. "Stick up yer goddamn hands."

CHAPTER EIGHT

WILL DIDN'T ARGUE. He raised his hands, feeling more than a little foolish, and slowly turned around.

The man at the other end of the shotgun was in his midseventies. His face was grizzled from weather and age. Long, wispy gray tendrils of hair dangled at various angles from his small head, as if he'd been abruptly wakened. He was so scrawny that Will wondered how he managed to keep the shotgun level. Sort of, Will amended, noticing now that the barrel wavered frighteningly from left to right.

"This here's private property, buddy. Whadda ya think yer doin'?"

"Can I put my hands down?" Will asked.

"Go ahead, but I'm keepin' this gun aimed right at you."

"I'm staying at the campground. Thought

I'd have a look around, that's all. The place looks abandoned from the road."

"Well it ain't abandoned, as you can damn well see. So just hightail it back to Rest Haven."

"Sure. Maybe you could put that shotgun down, then?"

The man glared at him, but slowly lowered the gun.

"Mind if I go back the way I came," Will asked, "or would you prefer me to take the road?"

"Whatever you want. I'll be watching either way."

In case I run off with a pigeon or two? "Then I'll go back by the stream."

Something flickered in the man's eyes. "You a fisherman?"

"Not really, but the owner of the campground—"

"Waters," the man snarled.

Will paused. "Yeah. He said trout fishing season's not open yet, but there were other fish."

"There are. Some nice sunfish and catfish, too. Small, but you can get a meal from a few of them."

Will bet the guy was speaking from experience. Still, in spite of the rundown appearance of the property and the house, the pigeon coop was in tiptop condition. "Nice pigeons," he said. "Do you race them?"

The man's eyes narrowed. "Used to, don't anymore. Too damn difficult carting them around the countryside for the events. You know anything about racing pigeons?"

"I read a book about them when I was a kid. How long have you been keeping them?"

"About thirty years." He paused a moment, adding, "Got a buddy over t'other side of Essex who has pigeons. We send messages back and forth and sometimes trade birds, keep the breeding stock good."

Will stared at the coop. "Built that yourself, I suppose. It looks pretty sturdy."

"Darn better'n a lot of ready-made things."

Will had run out of things to say. "Okay, well I'll be off. Nice to meet you. I'll be staying at the campground for a week or so, if you need any help with anything here." He cocked his head toward the pigeon coop. "I'm helping out at Ambrosia Apiaries for a bit," he added.

That got the man's interest. "Oh yeah?" He frowned. "Guess Jack's gone off to Charlotte for his operation." A short pause, then, "He's a good man, Jack Collins."

Even the local eccentric has access to the grapevine.

The man suddenly shifted the shotgun to his left hand while extending his right one. "The name's Henry Krause."

Will shook his hand. "Will Jennings."

Krause nodded, staring frankly at Will's face. "Get that injury in some kinda accident?"

"Yep." Will held the man's gaze a moment longer before saying, "I'll be off then." He started in the direction he'd come but was halted a few yards on.

"Anytime you want to come see the pigeons, just give a loud knock on the side door there."

Will smiled, half turned around and said, "So long as you keep your shotgun inside."

That raised a sheepish grin. He turned his back on Krause and continued on his way, not daring to relax until he was back at the campsite. There'd been a numbing moment when he'd been certain the old geezer's bony finger was going to pull on the shotgun bolt—accidentally or otherwise.

While his steak was sizzling on the portable barbecue, Will perched on the edge of the picnic table, his thoughts wandering back to Annie and her apparent ambivalence about the trip to Charlotte. At least, he assumed that had been the cause of her ill humor that morning while she was showing him how to run the honey extractor.

At one point he'd finally asked, "Are you sure you're okay with me handling this? Should I try to get Danny McLean or his father to come around after all?"

It was the first time she actually looked him in the eye. After a slight hesitation, she'd said, "I trust you."

Those three words were surprisingly elevating, until Will saw her expression—kind of a "so don't let me down" look. But he was okay with that. She ought to be cautious, considering she'd known him less than forty-eight hours.

Will sniffed the air, noticing belatedly that his steak was flaming. He jumped from the picnic table and quickly turned off the barbecue. After forking the now well-done strip loin onto a plate, he rummaged in his tiny fridge for the premade salad he'd purchased. In spite of the imperfections of the meal, he enjoyed every bite. Food always tasted better outdoors. He cleaned up, made sure the propane barbecue was shut off and got into the van.

As he approached Henry Krause's place, Will slowed down. Nightfall was just an inch of scarlet horizon away, dark enough for regular people to turn on lights. But no illumination filtered through the shutters on the Krause farmhouse. Either Henry was already asleep—a good possibility—or was conserving energy.

Eccentric personalities were everywhere and Will had met many in his thirty-two years, though none holding a shotgun on him. He wasn't certain if he wanted to chance another visit. What if Henry didn't remember inviting him?

The Ambrosia Apiaries sign was a shadowy outline by the time Will reached the driveway. He hadn't passed another vehicle all the way from Rest Haven. Except for a few farmhouse lights twinkling here and there like fireflies against the inky backdrop of sky, the valley was dark and quiet. Rural life. *Early to bed, early to rise.*

He drove the van into the yard alongside the house and extinguished the headlights. Darkness fell like a blackout curtain. For a few disconcerting seconds, Will couldn't even see his hands still resting on the steering wheel. As his eyes adjusted, the house took shape on his left and the barn straight ahead. Everything seemed normal but he'd get the flashlight and have a walk around before settling in for the night.

Garden Valley might look like paradise, but with an arsonist on the loose and a recluse toting a loaded shotgun, appearances were definitely deceiving.

By the time he'd made his rounds and read another chapter in his book about the Civil War, Will was ready for an early night. The last image he had before dropping off to sleep was Annie's pinched face as she waved goodbye that morning. Nothing ambiguous about the misery in her large eyes.

ANNIE MIGHT HAVE FELT some guilt as she crossed the hospital parking lot a mere hour after she'd first pulled in if her father hadn't nodded off to sleep. Shirley had pointed to the door and whispered, "Go. I'll call you if anything new develops." Knowing there was little more for her to do anyway, Annie had gratefully taken her cue.

She'd arrived at the hospital in time for the consultation with the cardiologist who had assessed the various tests Jack had undergone the previous afternoon. Nothing to worry about, he'd assured them. He arranged a follow-up appointment just before Jack was to return home and advised maintaining proper diet and appropriate exercise. When he'd suggested that Jack might want to ease up on the heavier tasks involved in beekeeping, Annie had given a skeptical sniff. *Right.*

Her father had made a last attempt at skipping the rehab program and the planned holiday but an unexpectedly stern look from Shirley had stopped him in his tracks. Sensing that she now held the balance of power, Shirley was no doubt making up for previous lost opportunities.

Annie sat behind the wheel of her car for a few moments, putting off her next move a bit longer. The plan she and Auntie Isobel had come up with during their late-night talk was that Annie would see her father before going to the adoption agency. That way, whatever the emotional fallout from the agency visit, Jack would be unaware of it. It wasn't fair to burden her father with her problems until he was home and able to give her the support he would want to give.

And now, thought Annie, clutching the steering wheel, the time was here. No more postponements. She started up the car and proceeded out of the lot, following the directions Sister Beatty had given her. As she turned off the expressway to the quiet, residential area where the agency was tucked discreetly into a strip plaza, a surge of familiarity rose up from memories held at bay for thirteen years.

She remembered driving into the small parking lot, Aunt Isobel perched birdlike behind the wheel of her Lincoln Continental. Annie had wedged herself into the corner of the passenger seat as if the last thing in the world she intended to do was get out of that car. But she had. And now, taking a deep breath, she grabbed the handle and opened the car door again.

It all came back as soon as Annie walked

into the air-conditioned office. The walls were a different color, but the basic layout was the same. A young woman sat staring at the computer on the desk.

"Can I help you?"

"Uh, I have an appointment with Sister Beatty. Annie Collins."

The young woman's fingers played over the keyboard. She read something from the monitor and raised her head back to Annie. "Oh yes. Please have a seat, Ms. Collins. I'll let Sister know you're here."

Your last chance, Annie. Get up and leave quickly before it's too late. But though the spirit was willing, her mind refused to pass the order along to her legs. She clasped and unclasped her damp, cold hands on her lap. The main door suddenly opened and closed behind a couple who stood hesitantly, staring first at the empty receptionist desk and then at Annie. The woman murmured something to her partner and, after waiting a few seconds, they sat in two chairs at right angles to Annie's.

They appeared to be in their mid- to late-thirties and, as they whispered to one another, occasionally glanced toward her.

Annie felt her face warm up. She had a flashback to thirteen years ago, when she'd first stepped into this office.

Heads abruptly raised, eyes aimed at her face and then—or so it had seemed to Annie—at the slight swelling of her waist.

She laced her fingers together and squeezed hard. *Get a grip, girl. They're not thinking about you.* She stared at the floor, straining to hear the sound of footsteps. Which she heard, mercifully, seconds later.

Right on the heels of the receptionist was a petite, brown-haired woman whose smile dispelled all the irrational thoughts from Annie's mind. It was the same nun who'd been so kind to her.

"Miss Collins? So wonderful to see you again." She reached for Annie's cold hand and held it in hers.

Everything was going to be just fine, Annie thought, as warmth flooded through her.

"Come in," Sister Beatty said and led Annie along a short hallway into an office at the end. She gestured to a chair across from a desk and, rather than sit at the desk herself, pulled up another chair directly in front of

Annie. She wore a plain but crisp pale-blue cotton dress with a delicate silver cross pinned to its collar and simple black pumps. She could've been any suburban matron at a casual social event.

"I've thought about you from time to time," Sister Beatty began. "Tell me a bit about how things are going."

Annie felt herself begin to unwind, as if she were meeting with a long-lost friend. "Where do I begin?" she asked, her voice unfamiliar, soft.

"Wherever you like, Miss Collins."

"Please, call me Annie. It's not as though we're strangers."

The other woman smiled, tilting her head slightly, and waited.

"I, uh, went on to get my degree at the University of North Carolina."

The sister's smile broadened.

"Then I worked in Central America for a few years, volunteering."

"Wonderful."

"Teachers' college after that and teaching high school in Queens, New York, for about five years."

"I imagine you're a great teacher."

Annie blushed. "My aunt forwarded your letter to me."

Sister Beatty's smile faltered. They had come to the purpose of Annie's visit. "Thank you for responding so promptly. I suspect the letter evoked the gamut of emotions."

Nicely put, Annie thought, but said nothing.

Sister Beatty moved to her desk and picked up a file folder. "I received the request approximately three weeks ago. We were in the middle of some small renovations here—painting and such—so I didn't get the letter out to you for ten days or so. If you're interested in making contact, I can give you some information about your daughter. Otherwise, I must respect the confidentiality agreed upon when we signed the contract with her adoptive parents."

Annie nodded. Auntie Isobel had reminded her of the details of the agreement last night. *As if she'd forgotten.* "She can contact me if she still wants to," she said.

"I see that you're prepared for her to change her mind and of course, she might well do that." Sister Beatty returned to the chair opposite Annie, the file folder in her hand. She opened it and withdrew a five-by-seven inch photograph. "She sent this with her letter," she said, passing it to Annie.

Annie hesitated a nanosecond before taking the photograph. She blinked several times before she realized Sister Beatty was handing her a tissue.

"It was taken just this past Christmas," the nun was saying while Annie stared down at the adolescent girl standing in front of a Christmas tree. She was wearing black slacks and a periwinkle-blue sweater that was a perfect foil for her flaming red hair. Although there was no frame of reference, Annie guessed she was tall. Certainly slim, with budding breasts evident beneath the sweater. Her smile was slightly lopsided, as if she'd been about to change her expression just as the picture was taken.

The trembling in Annie's hand eased as she continued to stare long and hard at her daughter. *Her daughter!* The smile, in spite of its crookedness, was her own smile. The hair she recalled instantly. His. Adam's. She squinted, noticing the freckles to match it.

"What's her name?" Annie asked, her voice cracking in the silent room.

"Sorry. I ought to have mentioned that first. Cara."

"Cara." The name rolled around on her tongue, unfamiliar yet pleasant at the same time. "A nice name."

"Yes. I think it means 'dear' or 'sweetheart' or something like that."

Or precious. Something close to the heart. Suddenly, Annie liked the adoptive parents a whole lot more. She took one more look at the photograph before holding it out to Sister Mary Beatty.

"No," the woman said, shaking her head. "It's yours. Cara specified in her letter that if you agreed to make contact, she wanted you to keep it."

So my daughter is thoughtful and sensitive. Unexpected pride welled up inside her.

"When you leave, I'll give you Cara's home and e-mail address. I spoke to her on the phone and she understands that meetings can't be rushed. Sometimes, it's best to take these things slowly."

Annie scarcely heard what Sister Beatty was saying. "I…uh…have to talk to some people first," she stammered.

"Of course you do, Annie! I should have asked, but are you married or engaged?"

Annie shook her head.

"Just that sometimes other relationships present challenges."

Annie immediately thought of her father. She looked at the photograph again and knew he would be enchanted.

"Cara is also looking for her birth father, but so far hasn't had much luck. His name is on the birth certificate, but there's nothing else on file. I don't suppose—"

"I have no idea where he is. We...split up as soon as I learned I was pregnant."

Sister Beatty frowned. "That's often the case."

"It's not what you're thinking. He never knew I was pregnant. His father had a heart attack a few weeks after we...well...after Cara was conceived and he left university. We never contacted each other again."

"Oh dear. I know Cara will be disappointed if she can't locate him. What was his name again?" She opened the file folder.

"Adam Vaughn," Annie said quickly. "Perhaps through the Internet?"

Sister Beatty closed the file and shrugged. "Perhaps. The thing is, well, I can't tell you too much but Cara has a deep need to find her birth parents. She's had such a tragedy already in her young life."

Something caught in Annie's throat. She swallowed hard and asked, "Something to do with her parents?"

Sister Beatty nodded. "Her adoptive father is dead. He was murdered, actually, almost a year and a half ago."

The information stunned Annie. "Oh my God," she whispered. She was overwhelmed with the urge to protect this young girl she didn't know at all and yet shared a deeper connection with than any other person alive.

"The family lives in Raleigh. Perhaps you read about the case. Their last name is Peterson."

"No, no. I was still in New York then." She tried to digest what she'd learned, but with the image of Cara—now a real live person with a face—she could assimilate nothing more.

"Cara didn't say, but perhaps the tragedy spurred her search for her birth parents. I don't doubt that the affair has shaken her sense of security and with just her mother and herself…" There was very little either could find to say after that.

After a few minutes, Sister Beatty rose from her chair. "I'll let Cara know you'll communicate with her. I know she'll be thrilled. What would you prefer? E-mail? Telephone?"

Annie's mind was swirling. "Uh, maybe e-mail? The next few weeks are busy ones for us at the apiary—my father's farm, where I'm now working—and there won't be anyone to pick up the phone. I wouldn't want her to get discouraged by constantly hearing voice messages."

Sister Beatty smiled. "How good of you to consider that. Here's Cara's address but I think the next move has to be up to her now, don't you think?"

Annie got up slowly. "Oh, yes. Of course." She hadn't taken it all in yet, but reached out for the piece of paper, her other hand still clutching the photograph. Dazed, she said goodbye and suddenly found herself behind the wheel of her Ford Focus, staring blankly through the windshield.

She eyed the dashboard clock. Two o'clock. If she left for Garden Valley now, she could be there by dinnertime. Home was the only place she wanted to be. Even more peculiar was the realization that Will was the one person she looked forward to seeing.

AT SOME POINT IN THE LONG DAY, Will wondered when Annie would be coming home. Not that it mattered, because there weren't any other job prospects on his personal horizon. And besides, he was actually enjoying working with the bees. He no longer felt so claus-trophobic wearing a beekeeper's white jumpsuit and hat and the adrenaline that shot through him every time he lifted up the cover of a hive was manageable.

He'd spent the entire morning setting bee excluders in the hives or colonies, as Annie called them, on the McLean acreage. Bob McLean drove up once to check things out, more out of curiosity, Will thought, than suspicion. He'd been surprised at how quickly the other man had accepted not only his presence, but his work. *Either I've finally got a grip on this job or McLean knows even less about it than I do.* Then he drove back to the Vanderhoff colonies to extract the frames he and Annie had set up.

He was beginning to see how beekeeping involved basic tasks endlessly repeated. He spent the afternoon trucking supers laden with honey back and forth to the barn, running the extractor, then returning to collect more. During one of these trips, Marge Vanderhoff had popped out of her kitchen with a glass of cold lemonade for him.

By six o'clock he was locking up the barn and contemplating a shower and a cold drink—the order of which he hadn't yet determined—when he heard a car coming up the driveway. When he saw the glint of silver, he was filled with such pleasure it startled him. Will waited for Annie to climb out. Ever so slowly, the door creaked open and she stepped out.

He saw right away that something had happened. There was uncertainty in her face and she moved almost in a trance. "Annie?" he asked, closing in on her. "Are you okay?"

She made a funny half laugh and half sob, before bursting into tears. Will swiftly wrapped his arms around her, tucking her against his chest, placing his palm on the top of her head to keep her there for as long as necessary. Her face fell into the crook of his arm and her arms tightened around his waist.

Will closed his eyes, wishing he could make everything better for her.

Pulling away was difficult. Annie could have stayed wrapped in Will's embrace for hours. When she did pull back, his hands remained on her shoulders while he studied her face.

Finally his hands dropped to his side. "Tell me that wasn't about the traffic," he said, his voice oddly hoarse.

She shook her head. "It's a long story," she said, struggling to smile.

After a light pause, he asked, "Have you eaten yet?"

"No, I drove straight through."

"I've got some food here in the van. How about if I cook us a light supper, as my mother used to say?"

"Are you sure? I hate to use your supplies. I'm sure there's something in the freezer."

"Hey, I've got eggs, tomatoes and cheese. Do we need anything more than that to whip up a great omelet?"

Annie knew he was trying to lighten the mood and played along. "Can't think of anything except maybe a glass of wine."

"Got that, too. You go on inside while I

rustle up some victuals." He started toward the van. "See? I'm getting into the local lingo now that I've been in the valley for a couple of days."

Annie smiled, indulging him. She wasn't certain where his lingo actually belonged, not having ever heard it in the valley, but let him keep his illusions. By the time she'd finished in the bathroom and changed her clothes, she could hear cupboard doors and drawers being opened and shut in the kitchen. She paused in her bedroom doorway. Was he whistling?

When she reached the kitchen, the table was set and two wineglasses were already filled with white wine. He turned from the stove. "I had a nice bottle of Sauvignon in the van, waiting for the right occasion."

The fact that he considered making her supper an occasion was both flattering and disconcerting. She picked up her wine and sipped. She was home, in her own kitchen. An attractive man was cooking her dinner. Or supper. A wave of emotion threatened again and she blinked back tears.

He came over to the table with the frying pan and carefully slid the fattest omelet she'd ever seen onto her plate. It was golden brown, crisp around the edges. Tomatoes and melted cheese oozed out from the fold. The rich aroma that wafted up from her plate made her realize how hungry she was. She watched as he set a bowl of salad on the table. Annie smiled, recognizing the crockery mixing bowl from the cupboard.

"Salad, too?"

"Had a bag of that premixed stuff from the grocery store. Good thing you came along. I'd never have been able to eat it all myself before it went off." He served his own omelet, plunked the frying pan on the counter and settled into his chair. He picked up his wineglass and, holding it aloft, said, "Cheers! Welcome home."

Annie clinked her glass against his. It was, she thought, one of the best homecomings she'd had.

They ate without talking. Annie was grateful for his silence. It gave her a chance to let her visit with Sister Beatty shrink to something she could think about without tearing up again.

She pushed her empty plate aside and moaned. "That was the biggest omelet I've ever eaten! And delicious. Hardly what I'd call a light supper. Is that what your mother would have called it?"

Will set his fork down. "No. It was an expression she used for the few days before every pay. Her idea of a light supper was usually crackers and peanut butter, or sardines on toast."

"Was there just the two of you?'

"Yep. Never met my dad. I believe he took off sometime in the nine months before I was born."

"And your mother?"

"She passed away a few years ago. Breast cancer."

"Oh. I'm sorry." She didn't say anything for a long while. "It must have been difficult for your mother being a single parent."

"It was. She didn't have a college education and few skills. Most of her jobs were waitressing or working as a cashier. That type of thing. But she made do."

It explained something about his fastidious ways. He'd even rinsed the plastic wrap from the package of cheese and hung it over the faucet, to reuse later.

Would she have been the same kind of

struggling mother, if she hadn't given her baby up for adoption?

"Hey."

She raised her head, her watering eyes scarcely focusing.

"What happened?" he asked, his voice soft.

Annie took a deep breath. She knew it wasn't his problem, but she was desperate to tell someone. Besides, she'd promised to call Auntie Isobel as soon as she got home to give a full report and if she didn't have a run-through, she knew she'd simply dissolve again and would be totally incomprehensible on the phone.

"I...uh...something happened while I was in Charlotte," she began.

"I gathered as much from your arrival. Your father?"

His concern took her off-guard, but also gave her the courage to go on. "No. It has to do with me. A long story." She gave a faint smile.

"I can relate to that. We've got all night."

Annie ran her fingertip along the edge of her plate. "When I was in my first year at the University of North Carolina—in Charlotte—I was very foolish one night. Had too much to drink and—" she paused "—got pregnant."

She glanced at him, but his face was impassive. She continued, giving him a summary of that August as if it had all happened to someone else. When she finished with the details of her visit to the adoption agency, she detected a change in his expression. A softening.

He waited a moment before asking, "What about the baby's father?"

"We'd only dated a few times."

"So he didn't want the baby?"

"I never got the chance to tell him."

"So he doesn't know that you got pregnant?"

Annie stared into the empty wineglass clutched in her hand. She shook her head. "Around the time I found out, he was called home for a family emergency. I tried to contact him, but didn't have much success. Finally, I left him a note, but I never got a response."

He nodded thoughtfully, then asked, "How do you feel about your daughter making contact with you?"

"I'm not sure yet. Obviously I made the decision to open up that door, but to be honest, I've no idea how I'll feel if and when it happens. The whole thing is still pretty overwhelming."

"Of course it is." He stretched his arm across the table and gently released the wineglass from her grip to take her hand. "It sounds like you've got a supportive family when the time comes."

"That's just it. My father doesn't know. There never seemed to be a good time. After my mother died—"

"When was that?"

"I was fifteen. She was in a single-car crash. On the highway going into Essex." Annie stopped.

"So when you found out you were pregnant, there was some distance between you and your father that made it difficult—"

"Impossible," she interjected. "After my mother died, my father and I went our own ways. I stayed with my aunt the summer I had the baby." She paused again, thinking of her aunt's worried face as she'd driven off that morning. "She's been wonderful. And don't get me wrong. I know my father loves me more than anyone else in the world. He's a lot different now, especially since he met Shirley."

"When are you going to tell him?"

"I know he'll fret and have a ton of questions and likely feel bad that I hadn't told him years ago. It'll be easier when he's home."

"So I guess you have no idea when your daughter is going to call."

"No." Annie withdrew her hand, tucking it under her chin and resting her elbow on the table. She suddenly felt drained of all energy and emotion.

"Why don't you go to bed while I clean up here?"

Her eyes cut to his. There was no innuendo or invitation in his face. Merely a friend offering some help. "Thanks. I'd like that." She rose shakily from her chair. "How did things go, by the way?"

"Great. I think I've passed into Beekeeping Part Two."

"Up for another day or two?" She held her breath, praying he'd say yes.

"Definitely. I'll be around at eight and fill you in on what I did while you were gone."

"Could we make that ten? And thank you

for staying here, Will. The trip would have been twice as difficult if I'd had to worry about the apiary."

"Get a good night's sleep."

As she changed into her nightie and brushed her teeth, she was aware of cleaning-up noises from below. Crawling into bed, she thought about how comfortable she'd felt talking to him. Being in his arms. Feeling that someone cared. She closed her eyes and didn't hear him leave.

CHAPTER NINE

SHE'D SAID TEN, but he'd been awake since six, after tossing and turning most of the night. Finally at daybreak, he got up to make a pot of coffee. He was just stringing his fishing rod when a car drove into the campground and parked in front of the office. It wasn't quite eight-thirty and Waters was nowhere around. Will worked on the fishing line, but kept an eye on the car. No one got out, and after a few seconds the car made a sharp left turn and headed his way.

Will had no idea who it was until the driver stepped out of the car. He propped the fishing rod against the picnic table and sauntered over to greet Scott Andrews. As he drew closer, he saw that Andrews had had a rougher night than he'd had.

"Morning," he said.

Andrews nodded, shaking Will's hand absent-mindedly. "See you found the campground all right."

"Yeah. Thanks for steering me to Waters."

"Speaking of...seen him around this morning?"

"No, he doesn't come in this early."

"Coffee smells good," Andrews said, tilting his head to the propane stove Will had set up on the picnic table.

"Have a seat," Will said. "I'll get a mug from the van." When he came out, Andrews was mopping his forehead with a well-used handkerchief.

"Tough night?"

The fire captain didn't reply until he'd poured milk and stirred a heaping spoonful of sugar into his coffee. "Could say that," he muttered as he blew across the mug. Andrews took a long, careful sip.

Will waited, knowing he'd get to the point eventually. He sensed the man was ticked off about something.

"Arsonist struck again last night. Only it was a shed this time, instead of a barn. Place about ten miles south of here."

"Anyone hurt?"

"Yeah. One of my men. There were some

cans of paint and paint thinner in the shed, along with a few jerry cans of gasoline the owner forgot to tell us about until the whole damn thing blew up."

"How is he?"

"Burnt. He'll be in the hospital a few weeks." He stared at Will's scar. "You know all about that."

"Think it's the same guy?"

"Oh yeah. Ninety-nine percent it is. 'Course the fire marshal's gotta have a look-see but given his report on the Lewis fire, it's gonna read the same."

"So the Lewis barn was set by the valley arsonist? That's what the marshal decided?"

"Yeah." He drank from the mug, obviously savoring the brew. "Heard you were working at Ambrosia."

"Word gets around."

Andrews grinned. "Hey, it's Garden Valley. What more can I say? Anyhow, I came by for two reasons. One, to find out where Sam Waters was last night when all hell was breaking loose and second, to find out if you planned to stay in the valley. Thought you might, since you were working for Jack and Annie."

"Can't help with the first one, but I'm here until Jack gets back from Charlotte. Why?"

"I'm a man short and with this arsonist running around, I can use some help. You interested?" He added, "It's volunteer work, but I might be able to find some money in the budget for you. It wouldn't be what you'd get back home, but enough to pay the rent here and keep you in food and beer."

"How would you get in touch with me?"

"I'll give you a cell phone. We all use them. When a call comes in on the emergency number, it goes directly to all of our cells. You have to keep it on all the time, though."

Will wanted to help the guy out, but the thought of fighting fires again made his stomach churn.

"Look, maybe this is all too much for you. I don't know exactly what happened to cause that—" he gestured to Will's scar "—but if you're not working now because of..."

Will turned the scarred side of his face away from the other man.

"Well, could you at least think it over and let me know by tomorrow evening?" Andrews got up from the table and pulled a billfold out of his trousers. "Here, take this." He handed Will a business card. "Call me. Not the number in red. That's the fire alert line. Okay?"

"I can't promise anything."

"Fair enough. If you see Waters anytime soon, ask him to give me a call. He's not answering his cell phone." Then he got back in his car and drove off.

Will looked at his watch. It was a little after nine. No time for fishing now. Although Will had plenty of mixed feelings about taking Andrews up on his offer, one thought shone through. Volunteering would give him another excuse to stay in Garden Valley. Another excuse to see more of Annie Collins.

ANNIE WAS TOWEL-DRYING HER HAIR when she heard the tapping at the kitchen door. It wasn't locked, but obviously the city boy in Will Jennings was reluctant to simply walk inside. She dashed down the stairs to let him in.

"Hi!" she said, somewhat breathlessly.

He smiled, his eyes skimming from her bare feet, up over the cutoff denim shorts and T-shirt to her damp head. "Am I early?"

She moved aside for him to come in. He'd recently showered himself, she decided, detecting the fragrance of some kind of soap. Not flowery, but spicy. And his hair—what there was of it—glistened in the sunlight pouring through the screen door. As he stepped past her, she saw a fleck of shaving cream at the edge of his jaw near his right earlobe and for some reason, she found the oversight touching.

"No, right on time. I slept in."

"Catching up on a sleep debt?"

"A few days' worth." He just nodded. She was relieved they weren't going to have to dredge up last night's conversation. In fact, she was feeling almost embarrassed about unburdening herself so readily to someone she'd known such a short time.

"Shall I make coffee while you...uh—" he glanced at her hair "—finish with...?"

"Sure. The filters are in the drawer next to the sink and the coffee's—"

"In the canister on the counter."

He didn't miss much. "Okay then. Be right back. Have you eaten?" She paused midway to the door.

"Toast."

"Help yourself to anything," she said as

she left the room. Taking the stairs two at a time, she made for the bathroom. A few minutes of blow-drying and she was all set. Although makeup was something she used infrequently and only for special occasions, she took a second longer to smooth skin cream over her face and apply a trace of eyeliner. She gave herself a once-over in the full-length mirror on the back of her bedroom door, tucking an elastic into her pocket for a ponytail later, when it was hot.

Pausing in the hall outside the kitchen, she wondered why she was behaving like a teenager on a first date. Pheromones. That's all it is. Bees have them and so do humans. *So calm yourself, girl. There's work to be done and it can't be done if you're fantasizing about your employee.*

Mugs of steaming coffee sat on the table next to a stack of toast on a plate. His face lit up as soon as she came into the room. Pheromones, she reminded herself, as she sat across from him and reached for her mug.

"I didn't know what you'd want with the toast," he said, studying her face. He gestured to the tub of cream cheese and the jars of jam and peanut butter.

She picked up a knife and began to smear on cream cheese. "This is a treat," she said. "I usually grab a bowl of cereal and eat it standing by the sink. When Dad's here, he's always humming and hawing by the kitchen door, wanting to know why I don't get up earlier."

Will laughed. "He sounds like a character."

"Oh he is, trust me. If you pass the Jack Collins test, you can win over anyone."

"Even his daughter?" His voice was teasing but his eyes were dead serious.

Annie choked on the toast. "Ha ha," was her lame response after she managed to swallow.

"So what's on for today?" he asked, getting down to business.

"What did you finish while I was gone?" She drank her coffee while he talked.

"I set up the bee excluders on all the colonies at the Vanderhoff place and I collected about half of the supers at the McLeans'."

"Not bad for a beginner."

"Like I said, I'm in Part Two now."

He had a nice grin. She wondered what kind of person he'd been before the accident.

Already she'd noticed a change in him since the day he'd arrived at the farm.

"The plan for today?" he prompted.

Annie felt her face color. "Get the rest of the supers from the McLeans' and extract them. Have you been putting the honey into the settling tank?"

"Yes. Wasn't that the right thing to do?"

"Yes, of course. Just that one of my regular customers is a commercial bakery in Essex. They don't care if their honey has bits of wax floating in it because it's used for baking."

"So we leave it in the buckets for them?"

"The sixty-pound ones. They'll send a truck to pick them up when we call."

"And the honey in the settling tank?"

"That goes into jars for retail sale. We've got several customers in Essex and the valley. Some shops in Charlotte. Plus, a few locals pick them up to sell at farmers' markets."

"Much business competition here?"

"Lots of people keep hives, but we're the largest apiary in the valley and beyond Essex. Our biggest competitor is a commercial outfit called Sunrise Foods. They supply to the major grocery chains—the Red and White in

Essex carries their produce—and to most of the other commercial bakeries. But because we don't pasteurize our honey, we pick up a lot of the health-food business."

"Sounds like business is good."

Annie swallowed the last of her coffee. "It is and it isn't. The problem is that on one hand, we have more customers than we can supply. We've had to reduce the number of our colonies the past two years because Dad and I couldn't handle three hundred hives. Right now we've got about two thirty, and can scarcely manage those without extra help. That's why we had to hire Danny." Her heavy sigh underlined her point.

"We're kind of on the cusp. Too big for the standard Mom-and-Pop thing, and too small to keep up with the demand. We seldom advertise anymore because we can't physically handle any more customers. Yet we don't have the cash flow to upgrade the way we should or to hire more help." She paused, adding as an afterthought, "Even if we could *find* the help around here. Most people—unless they're farming—want to work for those big box stores or factories outside the valley."

"Well I'm available, if you need me."

He played with the spoon on the table next to his coffee mug. The thing was, she did need him. But she wasn't quite so ready to admit that she liked his presence. She liked the way he fit right in, making himself at home. She was beginning to like too much about him, which made working together complicated.

"The pay isn't great," she said.

"But the perks are."

That grin again.

He scanned the kitchen, his eyes lingering briefly on her before dropping to his coffee. "Breakfast, maybe a lunch or two in quaint surroundings… Scott Andrews came by early this morning and offered me temporary work with the volunteer unit. Seems one of his men is out of commission."

He doesn't want me to see what must be in his face. What he feels about fighting fires again. She wished she could offer some sentiment that would reassure him. Not knowing exactly what had happened to him would make anything she might say incredibly trite.

"Whatever you decide, I'd be very happy to have you stay on here." She stood to clear the dishes.

"I'll let you know." He carried his mug over to the sink where Annie was rinsing the dishes. "Thanks," he said, without looking at her.

She nodded, unsure what exactly he was thanking her for. "I'll meet you in the honey barn in about five minutes. Okay?"

"See you there." Without another look her way he sauntered out the screen door.

Annie watched him go, fighting the impulse to call him back, tilt his head to hers and whisper in his ear that everything would be just fine.

THE SUN BEAT DOWN and seemed to permeate right through to the bone. Annie had to stop several times to blink away sweat dripping from her hairline under her hat. The bees were in a foul mood, too, which didn't help. She'd smoked them twice and they still clustered around, dive bombing at the mesh around her face. She glanced over at Will, bent over the hive across from her, and wondered if he was experiencing the same difficulty. Judging by the way he kept bobbing his head back and forth, he was. Still, he hadn't complained.

He was a decent person and sensitive, too. And not in the sappy "new age man" kind of way, but truly aware of what others might be feeling. Considerate. A sense of humor. Sexy. Yes, she had to admit he was sexy. The scar didn't do anything to diminish his good looks. If anything, it made his appearance more interesting. And....one caveat. *Married?*

That tidbit, dropped two days ago, lurked in the back of her mind. Was he still? She doubted it. He wasn't the type to cheat. Nor the type to run off. So there had to be some kind of separation. And she prayed it was permanent.

Annie stuck her gloved hands into the slots on either side of the super and tugged hard. It was heavy with good clover honey. She could smell it and so could the few dozen bees that hadn't escaped into the bottom of the hive. They flew in frantic circles around her head and hands.

Gasping, she bent her knees under the weight of the super and duck-walked to the pickup, a few yards away. She propped the end of the super against the lowered flap of the truck and, with as much energy as the heat and the end of the work day allowed, pushed the super against the others.

Before she had a chance to catch her breath and move aside, Will was right behind her. Although he slid his super onto the truck with relatively more ease, she saw that it was a struggle for him, too. Spring weather conditions had been perfect and there would be a good harvest this year. *If only they could get it all in.*

She hadn't understated their situation the other night. Jack would rebound after his convalescence, but he'd never be the man he was even ten years ago. And given his unexpected heart complication…

When she'd come home a year ago she'd made it clear to her father that the move was temporary. She'd needed a break from teaching and city life. At least that was the superficial reason, but escaping the painful reminders of Jim Fraser was the main one. So it seemed Ambrosia Apiary's days were numbered. The question of what Annie would do with her life when that point in time arrived was one she'd deferred answering.

She leaned against the back of the truck

and glanced at Will. The notion of a future that might include him was appealing.

Will whipped off his hat, wiping his brow with his forearm. "That it?"

Annie nodded, her mouth too dry for speech, and tossed her hat and gloves in with the supers. She opened the passenger door and took out the small cooler, handing Will a bottle of water, and started guzzling hers while unzipping her bee suit. Kicking off the last leg, she stepped clear of the suit and, after another long swallow of water, poured the rest of it over her head. When she looked up, Will was doing the same.

"What I wouldn't do for a swim about now," he said, raising his wet head her way. With water beading down his face, he looked like a twelve-year-old boy.

The warmth that flowed through Annie had nothing to do with the sun. "I'm with you," she said wistfully, mopping her face with the end of her T-shirt. She picked up her suit and threw it into the truck.

"Seriously, is there some place around here to swim? The stream at Rest Haven isn't very deep."

"Actually there's a small lake at the end of

it. Well, that's what we've always called it but it's really just a big pond."

"No kidding? I walked along the stream quite a ways and never saw it. But wait a sec. I saw that pond from the top of the hill on the highway to Essex. Just before the turnoff to Rest Haven." He climbed out of his suit, splashed more water on his face and placed everything in the truck.

"How far did you go along the stream?"

"To that farmhouse that looks abandoned but isn't."

"Henry Krause's place?"

"Made the mistake of wandering onto his property without an invite."

"Did old Henry come roaring out with his shotgun?"

"Guess you know the drill."

"He's the valley eccentric. Since his wife died about fifteen years ago, he's isolated himself more and more."

"Him and his racing pigeons."

"You saw the pigeons? He doesn't usually let people get that far. Must be getting old." Annie scanned the ground for any tools left behind and opened the driver's door. "Ready to go?"

"Sure." He got in and, after Annie turned over the engine, said, "Let's go for a swim in his pond."

She glanced across at him to see if he was joking. "You serious?"

"Why not?"

"Because I don't want to get shot?"

"He's harmless. Just a bit paranoid. Besides, he told me to come and visit his pigeons anytime."

"No way."

"Yeah." He stared out the windshield. "Looks like we've got company."

Annie turned her head, still trying to register the fact that Will had apparently won over Henry Krause. She saw a man on horseback riding their way. "Bob McLean. He's probably making his rounds. He likes to ride his land, then if he spots some problem he goes back for the truck."

"A nice life."

Annie glanced from him back to Bob. She knew the life Will was referring to wasn't as romantic as it seemed, though the idea of riding horseback around your property must be appealing. "Well, it gives him the chance to exercise his horses and he can avoid using the truck, cut back on gasoline."

"I was thinking more in terms of the peace of mind it must give him."

Annie felt her face warm. She'd lived in the valley too long to be able to look at things from any perspective other than practical.

Bob rode up to her side of the truck. "Morning, Annie. Will. How's it going?"

"Great. You'll be getting some good honey this year, Bob."

"The family will be happy about that. Sorry about the business with Danny." He shook his head. "Boy's got to learn to organize himself and finish a job. Anyway, he's lucky to have the chance to pick up the course he needs for college at summer school. I hope your plans haven't been tossed about as a result. 'Course—" he ducked his head to aim a smile at Will "—you've got some good help here. Even if he is a city slicker."

Annie's smile felt forced. She hoped Will didn't object to the term. "Yes, I do," was all she said, not daring to look at Will.

"How's your dad doing?"

"Fine, thanks. He'll be back in a couple of weeks, maybe sooner."

"Knowing him, it'll be sooner." Then his smile disappeared and he leaned forward in his saddle. "Did you hear there was another fire last night? A place south of Essex. One of the firefighters was injured."

Annie turned sharply to Will, who was staring straight ahead. Why hadn't he mentioned the fire to her? Was that the firefighter Will would be filling in for? "No, I hadn't heard," she said.

"Not a lot of property damage, but the fact that someone was hurt changes things a bit, doesn't it?"

"Yes," she said, distracted by Will's silence. Why didn't he speak up?

"Well, I'll let you go. You folks look hot. See you," he said, tipping the peak of his baseball cap and wheeling the horse around. As he and horse headed toward the pasture on the other side of the beehives, Annie let the pickup coast along the rutted path.

Unable to keep the question inside any longer, she half turned to Will. "Why didn't you tell me there was another fire last night?"

"I didn't want to worry you," he said, his tone casual. "Was that wrong?"

"Well, no," she blustered defensively. "But obviously the reason Scott Andrews asked you to work for him is because of the man who was injured. Wasn't it?"

"Yes."

He really was maddening, she thought. Just when he seems to be more open and almost chatty—for him—he pulls a number like this. "I don't need protecting, Will. Even if I seriously thought this arsonist might be a threat to our place, I wouldn't be scared about it." She realized at once how silly that sounded. Weren't people supposed to be frightened of threats?

His reply made her feel even more foolish. "From what I've seen of you, Annie, I hardly think you need protecting. I simply thought you didn't need anything to add to your concern about your father and...uh...you know."

She flushed at his less-than-oblique reference to their conversation last night. *I knew it was a mistake to confide in someone I don't really know.* The talk ended there, until Annie pulled into the yard at the apiary. She turned off the engine and was about to climb out when he placed his hand on her arm.

"I was going to tell you, Annie. I just got

sidetracked by other things." His eyes held hers. "Let's go over to ask Henry if we can use his lake or pond or whatever it is right after we've finished here. Okay?"

Did she really want to make an issue out of such a small point? "Sure," she said, trying to sound indifferent.

An hour later she was driving behind Will's camper van and wondering if she was doing the right thing or not. Did swimming together after work cross the employer-employee line? She knew something was changing between them. Or maybe she was kidding herself to think they'd ever had a standard work relationship. Bosses don't cry on their employees' shoulders. Or go swimming in an isolated spot with an employee who's attractive and sexy.

You've already crossed the line, Annie Collins, just thinking like that.

CHAPTER TEN

THEY'D AGREED TO PARK vehicles at Will's campsite and walk to Henry's place along the stream.

"Give me one sec," Will called out as he got out of the van. "I'll get my swimming trunks."

Annie climbed out of the truck and stretched. She was reaching inside the cab for her towel when Will stepped out of the van, wearing a pair of dark blue boxer-style swim shorts with a T-shirt.

"All set?" he asked, flicking his towel over one shoulder.

When he reached a grove of willows where the path widened, he waited for her. "Don't worry," he said. "When we get to Krause's property, I'll go ahead. I'm a bigger target."

"Ha-ha," she said. "I just hope for your sake he's wearing his eyeglasses."

"He wears glasses?" Will's voice pitched.

Annie grinned. "Just kidding."

"Have you ever swum in the pond?"

"Oh, yeah. Henry used to let people park in his driveway and tramp through his field to get to it. That was when his wife was still alive."

"Maybe after she died he couldn't handle seeing other people's happiness."

She'd never considered that. But then, fifteen years ago her own world was falling apart. Maybe she and Henry had something in common.

"When I was a teenager," she said, "we used to have bush parties at Rest Haven. It wasn't a campground then, but the Waters family still owned it."

"Yeah? I got the impression from Sam that it was a recent acquisition."

"New to Sam and his brother, Mike. His father died a year ago and they inherited the land. That's when they began to turn it into a campground. I've heard they have big plans for the place."

"Some kind of exclusive fishing and hunting outfit. I don't see it myself. The place is in the middle of nowhere. They'll be lucky to get regular campers."

"Sam will have to put in a swimming pool, too, because the stream's no good for swimming."

"What about the pond?"

"It's on Henry Krause's property and there's no access to it except through his fields."

Will stopped to wipe his forehead with the end of his towel. "Too bad. This stretch along the stream is the coolest spot in the whole campground. It'll be great for trout fishing at least."

When they reached the barbed wire fence around Henry Krause's back pasture, Will held it apart for Annie to climb through. They walked through the pasture, overgrown with weeds and wild grasses.

"Henry used to keep goats and sheep years ago. The farm was actually quite nice." She stopped when the barn and rear of the farmhouse came in sight. "Mrs. Krause would never have allowed the place to go downhill like this."

Will walked a few yards ahead of her and stopped, cupping his hands around his mouth to call out, "Henry? You there?"

There was no answer. Will signaled her to

follow. She glanced sharply at the barn with its collapsed roof and halted at the sight of the pigeon coops. "I wonder if he's still racing them."

"Not anymore." Will turned around to wait for her. "He said he has a friend on the other side of the valley and they send messages back and forth. That's about it."

She stared at Will. "You've been here less than a week and already know more about Henry than I do."

"Hardly. Just that. Nothing about his past." He cupped his hands and hollered again. This time, the screen door at the side of the house creaked open.

Annie squinted against the sun. Was that the barrel of a shotgun? Her heart pumped a bit harder. But when Henry shuffled out, his hands were empty.

"Henry? It's Will Jennings. From the campground. I've got Annie Collins with me. We were wondering if we could go swimming in your pond."

Annie winced as the old man drew closer. Unkempt and in need of a shave, he looked a lot older than his seventy plus years. But his face brightened in recognition.

"Annie Collins! How are you, dear? How's your father?"

"He's fine, thank you, Mr. Krause. How're you doing? I haven't seen you in a long time."

"Not since the day before you went off to college," he said. "Still alive and kicking. I'm doing okay."

She doubted that. With an unexpected surge of guilt, she recalled how she and a gang of friends trespassed one night as they went skinny-dipping in the pond. It was shortly after his wife had died and Henry had come roaring after them with his shotgun. Some of the kids had taunted him as they'd left. Annie had ducked behind another girl, not wanting Henry to see her and tell her father she'd been there.

He looked at Will, then back at her. "Well, you two go right ahead. The path's overgrown, but I guess you'll manage."

"Thanks, Henry," Will said.

As they turned to leave, Henry said, "Don't forget to come around to visit my birds. I'll introduce you to them. Every single one's got a name."

"You can count on it," Will said, smiling.

He waved goodbye and, placing his hand on the hollow of Annie's back, gently guided her ahead of him out of the yard.

"Henry sure has changed."

"Yeah?"

Although he didn't say anything more, Annie had an idea what Will was thinking. Maybe she'd never bothered to look at Henry in any other way, except as the valley's cranky recluse. She pondered that, along with the fact that Henry remembered the last time he'd seen her while she'd completely forgotten.

Will forged ahead, pushing his way through a mass of dogwood and bramble until he suddenly came to a halt. "Wow," was all he said.

Annie joined him at the water's edge. It is pretty, she thought, gazing out across the pond she hadn't seen for several years. "When I was twelve," she said, turning to Will, "I swam across this. Dad followed behind in Henry's rowboat for backup."

"No kidding? How far across is it?"

"Not very far. Maybe a quarter of a mile."

"Far enough for a twelve-year-old."

"I think there's a sandy beach to the right,

beyond that stand of willow trees." Without looking back, she pushed through the undergrowth and came to a small strip of sand. By the time Will reached it, she'd already stepped out of her shorts and peeled off her T-shirt. When she turned around to see if he was following, she saw that he was watching from the shore.

"What?" she asked, puzzled by the odd expression in his face.

He shook his head. "Nothing." He pulled his T-shirt over his head.

Annie felt naked in her skimpy bikini. It had been an impulsive purchase in the winter, when she'd planned a trip to the Caribbean. The trip didn't happen and she'd never had a chance to wear the suit. Back at the house, she'd considered wearing her demure one-piece, but some demon had prompted her to choose this. Likely the same demon that had convinced her that going for a swim with Will Jennings was an innocent excursion.

"Beat you in," he challenged as he dashed past her into the clear bluish-green water.

She kept her eyes on his broad shoulders as he leapt out to where the water was deep enough for plunging. He was grinning when he came up, shaking his head free of droplets. "You're not even wet," he called out.

Annie waded toward him. "I'm one of those inch at a time people. And don't even think about splashing. I hate splashers."

The water was at her hips when she heard him say, "Oh, I'm not thinking about splashing." His gaze rested midway between her neck and her navel.

She sank, submerging herself to her neck.

"Darn," he murmured, grinning. "I thought you said you were an inch at a time girl."

"Not when I'm being ogled."

"Ogled? I think admired is more appropriate." He began to breaststroke to her.

Annie flipped onto her back and floated out of his reach. He swam up to her, his head at her left shoulder. "Admired? That's a word used to describe a view," she said, lifting her head slightly out of the water.

"I was indeed admiring the view. A very small bikini."

She rolled back onto her stomach and swam farther away. But his front crawl was stronger than hers and he obviously didn't intend to give up their little game of cat-and-mouse. As he caught up to her, he reached out and held onto her upper arm, preventing her from swimming off. Treading water, she was about to duck free of his grasp when he pulled her against his chest. With his free arm, he back-paddled, taking them closer to the shoreline.

Now is the time, Annie was thinking, to try to preserve that old employer-employee status. Or myth, she amended, as she lurched backward in the shallow water, landing gently in his lap. He was sitting on the bottom, the water level with his waist, and slowly turned Annie around so that now she was straddling his lap.

"The view from here," he whispered, "is even better." He held the back of her head and drew her face to his.

One last chance, Annie thought, as his mouth came down on hers. But all thought gave way to the taste of his lips. She placed her palms on either side of his damp face, holding it against hers. The buoyancy of the water tugged them gently apart and Annie clamped her thighs against his hips, flowing with him as he fell back into the water. He raised his head just enough to keep it out of the water but not to separate their kiss.

Heat flowed through Annie from head to toe. She stretched her legs out so that she was lying on top of him, water rippling softly across her back. His arm tightened across her shoulders as the other plowed backward in the soft silt of the bottom of the pond until they were lying on the sand at its edge. Then he rolled her over onto her back, his mouth tracing a line down the side of her neck, to the hollow at its base.

Fire shot through Annie. She arched her head back, raising her hips up against his. He wanted her and she wanted him. But his hands unexpectedly loosened their grip and he rolled Annie off, to lie beside him. She didn't know what had happened or why he'd stopped. She wasn't even sure if she was relieved or disappointed that he had. All she knew was that the desire had ebbed away. For what seemed a long time the only sounds were their synchronized heavy breathing and the muted lapping of water.

Will finally sat up, passing a hand across his face as if wakening from a bad dream. "Sorry," he said, his voice hoarse. He didn't look at her. "I got carried away." His attempt at a laugh sounded more like he was choking. "Must have been the view."

But something else had crept into her mind. "You said you were married…."

He looked at her then. "I *was* married. Past tense. It ended more than a year ago. Is that what you…?"

"Best not to tamper with the employer-employee relationship anyway," she said quickly, with half a laugh.

"Your…*employee?*"

Tongue-tied, Annie watched as he got to his feet and made for the shore. He picked up his towel and began drying himself.

"It's getting late," he said. "We'd better get back. Work to be done tomorrow."

The rebuke stung. She wanted to say something about how ridiculous this whole exchange was, but he'd closed up like the shutters on Henry Krause's house. Annie scrambled to her feet and got back into her clothes without bothering to dry herself. He'd already headed off.

Her clothes stuck uncomfortably to her skin as she stumbled behind him. Her embarrassment quickly shifted to anger. Why was he upset with her? One minute they were about to make love and the next he's not only rejecting her—he's mad at her. None of this made sense.

When he reached the campground, Will turned for the first time since they'd left the pond. He hesitated, as if he wanted to say something. She clenched her teeth and held her ground. No way was she going to make anything easier for him. But all he said was, "I'll be a bit late in the morning. I promised I'd give Scott Andrews a call."

Not trusting herself to speak, she brushed past him to head for the truck. She climbed in, slamming the door behind her. Reversing, she caught one last glimpse of Will standing next to his van. *You are a complete idiot.*

HE STARTED TO CALM DOWN by his second beer. The whole pond thing had been a farce and he blamed himself.

He'd lost control and, after the accident, he'd sworn never to let that happen again. Maybe it was the sun beating down on his back or Annie's moan as she clung to him. But the sudden rush of memory—heat, smoke and piercing cries—was dizzying. He'd had to move away from her.

Then she'd made that "employee" comment. Was that how she viewed him? A hired hand seducing the boss's daughter? Like some kind of B movie.

Will set the empty beer can onto the picnic table. He knew he was making too much out of it, but she just didn't get it. She didn't understand at all that coming to Garden Valley, connecting with her, had been like coming home, when you never really had a home before.

CHAPTER ELEVEN

HE WAS BREWING A POT OF COFFEE at about eight in the morning when Sam Waters drove up to the office.

"Morning," Will said, as the man walked over. "You're early today."

"Yeah, got some workers coming in to finish the laundry shed. If you stay on, you can do your washing there." He nodded at the T-shirts and boxer shorts hanging from a tree branch.

"Great. Beats rinsing stuff in a plastic basin. By the way, Scott Andrews came by yesterday morning. He said if I was to see you, to tell you to give him a call. Apparently he couldn't reach you on your cell phone."

Sam frowned. "Damn thing went dead on me when I was in town. Cap got me at home later. He said he came round here to see you."

His tone was leading, Will thought, as if

he wants me to tell him why. More juice for the Garden Valley Grapevine? For some reason that got his back up. "He told me about the fire the night before." He paused a beat. "Asked if you'd been around."

Waters turned red. "The wife and I were celebrating our anniversary."

"Well, just passing on a message."

Waters thought for a minute, then said, "We're down a man. Did Scotty ask you to fill in for the guy?"

"Uh, yeah, he did, as a matter of fact." He bent his head, avoiding the other man's stare while he poured a mug of coffee. "Want some?"

"No. Thanks. I already had coffee this morning. So…uh…what did you tell him?"

"Nothing yet. I haven't quite made up my mind."

"There's no money in it."

"Guess not."

"Pretty small stuff to what you've probably been used to."

"Yeah, but that's what makes it ideal. No real pressure." He grinned at Waters.

"If that's what you want. Temp jobs here and there. Heard you were still helping out at the apiary. Any idea when Jack'll be back home?"

"Maybe in a week or so, Annie thinks."

"How's she holding up?"

Will jerked his head up. "Fine. Why?"

"Just wondering. The wife and I were talking about her the other night. Annie and my brother Mike were in the same class at high school. We all go way back."

Will got the message. "Oh yeah?" He tried to sound casual. Were the Waters brothers some of the teenagers that used to have bush parties here? He drank more coffee, refusing to be pulled into a conversation he didn't want to have.

"Guess I should be going." Waters started to leave, saying, "Your week is up tomorrow. Want to extend it?"

"I'll let you know by the end of the day."

"Okay. Tourist season kicks in soon."

Will resisted looking around at the otherwise empty campground. He watched Sam head back to the office, then dumped the rest of the coffee onto the grass and checked the time. He could just make the drive to Essex, use a pay phone to call Andrews and still get back to the apiary by nine something.

Of course, he could ask to use the office phone, where Waters could listen. Or wait and call from Annie's place, where she could listen. Neither option appealed to him. Besides, he wanted to ask Andrews a few things about the job. As he drove by the office ten minutes later, he saw Sam sitting at his desk, hunched over the phone.

CHAPTER TWELVE

ANNIE DRUMMED HER FINGERS on the kitchen table while she waited for Shirley to return to the phone. She'd purposely made her daily call to Charlotte early, so she could be ready and waiting at the barn by the time Will arrived. Somehow the casual familiarity of the kitchen no longer seemed like a good place to meet.

It was almost nine. If Will came while she was still on the telephone, she would direct their conversation to the latest news from Charlotte. Otherwise she might blurt out something about yesterday afternoon. She just wished she could turn back the clock.

"Hi, Annie, I'm back," Shirley said. "Jack's being transferred to the rehab center today and has some other heart test booked for tomorrow."

"Should I come back to Charlotte?"

"I don't think so, dear. He'll be busy for

the next couple of days and then he'll be discharged." She sighed. "My cousins have a beautiful house but Jack keeps insisting there'll be nothing for him to do." Annie detected exasperation. "Nothing to do! Can you believe it? I told him what about relaxing for a change? He looked at me as if he'd never heard the word before."

Annie bit back a giggle. "Shirley, I wish I could help you with that but—"

"I know, I know. The word doesn't exist in his personal dictionary."

"Exactly. So what does this heart specialist have to say about Dad's arrhythmia?"

"He doesn't seem to think it's that serious but Jack will have to make regular visits to him at least two or three times a year to monitor the condition."

He'll love that, Annie thought. "And what about working?"

"The doctor says he can go on doing what he does, but to avoid heavy lifting—you already heard that—and to basically take things easier."

"Right."

"You said it."

"I know this isn't really your concern,

Shirley, but the harvest this summer is going to be big. I'll need to get some other full-time help in place before Dad comes home. Maybe you could start priming him for that."

"I'll try, Annie. What about that fellow you've got? The one who came by to buy honey."

And stayed to work his magic on the beekeeper's daughter? "He's still here but I'm not sure how much longer he'll...uh...be able to stay."

"Hopefully till the honey is all collected."

The end of the summer? Annie closed her eyes, hardly able to imagine the state of affairs between them by then. Not to mention the state of her libido. "Uh... maybe, but he's a bit vague about his plans."

"Oh. Well, I'll give you a call later today and leave the phone number for the rehab place. Perhaps *you'd* better discuss all this with your father. You know how he hates people to make plans for him."

"Give him a kiss for me and tell him to be a good boy about his physio."

"I will, dear."

Annie hung up and checked the time. Nine-fifteen and no sign of Will. She took her mug to the sink and rinsed it, then headed for the barn to do a quick inventory and make a list of the day's priorities. Trying to act casual would definitely be number one on the list.

She hadn't got very far with the other items when Will drove into the yard. She heard the door slam and hoped she'd got her greeting down pat. Not too businesslike, but with enough formality to let him know things were going to be different. Annie didn't glance up until she heard him in the doorway.

He looked as uncertain as she was. Not detached as he'd been yesterday, but hesitant. That touched her. She guessed he'd had the same miserable sleep she'd had. She forgot her well-rehearsed greeting.

"Hi. Thought I'd get started in here. We need to extract all the frames we collected yesterday and top up the settling tank."

He nodded and walked into the barn. "Sorry I'm late," he said, heading for the extractor and beginning to set it up.

So they were talking, Annie decided, but not about *the kiss*. She started inserting frames into the extractor. Helping her, he accidentally brushed his hand against hers.

"Sorry," he mumbled, as if the hand had committed some other more serious transgression.

Like touching my breast, she thought at once and silently swore at herself. *Mind on the job.* They worked side by side for the rest of the morning. By noon, they'd scarcely spoken more than half a dozen words to each other and when Will announced that he was driving into Essex for lunch, Annie wasn't surprised.

She sat alone at the kitchen table and wondered if she ought to try to explain what she'd meant when she'd referred to him as an employee. Or would that merely make the whole thing bigger than it was? Annie pushed away her half-eaten sandwich. She hadn't imagined days ago that asking Will Jennings to work for her would lead to such complications.

The telephone rang as she was cleaning up and she rushed to it, thinking it was Shirley. The male voice on the other end was friendly but crisp. He introduced himself as a vice president of Sunrise Foods and could he have a minute of her time?

Annie hesitated, feeling her father's presence at her shoulder telling her to hang up. But recalling her earlier conversation with Shirley, as well as the heart specialist's warning to her father to slow down, she said yes.

It took fifteen minutes, actually, and at the end Annie agreed to show him the property and the business. No pressure to sell, he'd insisted. Just wanted to look around. Impulsively, she set a date in three days' time. When she hung up, she rested her head in the palm of her hand for a long moment. She'd just complicated her life even more.

She returned to the barn to finish pouring the honey into the settling tank and was stacking the last of the frames into the extractor when Will returned. He didn't offer an explanation for his trip to town, but simply joined her at the extractor. After almost half an hour, when Annie was beginning to think the silent treatment had surely run its course, he spoke up. "I talked to Scott Andrews today about his job offer."

She looked up sharply.

"I'm supposed to meet him at the volunteer fire hall around four if I'm going to take the job."

Annie clenched her teeth. *Get on with it.*

"The thing is," he continued, "I'm interested in it but I'll need something else to do here in the valley to...you know...make enough money to stay on. So I thought I'd better pass it by you first, to make sure you still want me as your...uh...*employee.*"

Before her blood pressure hit the top of the chart, she noticed his grin. He was teasing her. "Look," she said, "about yesterday..."

He raised a hand. "No, no. My apology. I made a big deal out of nothing."

"You're not just an employee. I mean, it may sound crazy but even though we've known each other hardly a week—"

"A week today," he said.

"Oh. I was going to say that I've come to think of you more as a...well, as a friend. So if we can continue to be friends while you're working here, I...uh...I think that would be good."

In spite of her stammering, she saw that he got the message. This time his eyes didn't shutter down so much as squint, as if he were staring at a bright light. He shrugged. "Sounds like a plan," he said and went on with his work.

When they finished extracting all the

frames, Annie was exhausted. She wanted to shower, phone her father and most of all, avoid thinking of how their day might be ending had yesterday's swim not been interrupted.

Would we go back to the pond? Maybe have dinner or a movie in town? She couldn't recall the last time she'd had a date. Unless she counted going to a local sports bar with Mike Waters the first month back home, last year. She'd found out very quickly that night that high school crushes usually fizzled out for a very good reason, and had declined any more dates. Mike, she'd heard, had since become engaged. After that, she'd weathered a long dry spell, as her father might say. Which likely accounted for her heated response at the pond.

"Guess I should leave soon," Will said, as he finished pouring the last bucket of honey into the settling tank. "I need to clean up before I meet Captain Andrews."

Annie had been mopping up stray drops of honey off the floor. "So then you're going to take the volunteer job?"

"Guess so. If I can keep on here until your dad's made a full recovery."

"For sure."

There was a slight hesitation, as if he wanted to add something but changed his mind. He held up an index finger as a farewell gesture and left the barn. Annie blew out a mouthful of sour air. That was that. He was coming back after all. And although she wasn't certain if she ought to be relieved or not, her step was light as she went into the house to shower.

WILL MET WITH Captain Andrews at the fire hall about ten miles from Essex. After signing some papers and having a tour of the hall, Andrews suggested dinner in town, surprising Will.

"Guess this means you've crossed the line from tourist to part-timer, Jennings," Andrews said over beer and chicken wings at the local brew pub. "I managed to find some money through a bit of creative bookkeeping and the county officials have agreed."

Will wiped his mouth with his napkin and said, "I appreciate that. I just hope you don't regret the offer."

Andrews looked across the table at Will. "I hope I don't either." After a slight pause, he added, "I'd like to keep the money part between us. Don't want to stir things up with the other men."

Will knew exactly what he meant. "Is it difficult to get volunteers in the valley?"

Andrews shook his head. "They're easy to recruit but hard to keep. They can't really help it," he explained. "Most of them have full-time jobs, not to mention the usual family responsibilities and all that. Getting called out in the dead of night or during some family celebration is a drag, especially when you're not making any money."

Will thought at once of Sam's defensive bluster about not being available the other night, but said nothing.

"I've been trying to get the county to approve hiring at least one part-timer for the hall, but until this spate of barn fires, there'd been some reluctance. Frankly, I was surprised they went for my proposal to hire you. I told them it might be for the duration of the summer. Hope that's okay with you. There's no commitment on your part and the contract is loosely worded as to time frame, so not to worry if you decide to up and leave. Though please tell me you're not going to."

Will smiled and assured him he could at least stay for the summer. At the back of his mind though, he was wondering about Annie's reaction. After yesterday, how happy would she really be about his staying on?

It was late by the time Will returned to Rest Haven. He slowed down at the junction leading to the campground and as he made the turn, noticed an orange-red glow in the sky. Will stepped on the gas. At the second road that would take him directly to Rest Haven, he saw that the flickering light was framed by wafts of smoke. He kept his eyes to the right and the column of smoke towering over the trees. Forest fire?

But another three miles down the road, his headlights picked out the leaning mailbox at the end of Henry Krause's driveway. Will took in first the box, then the deep red glow beyond it. The fire wasn't at the campground, but at Henry's place.

He gunned the van up the gravel driveway, careening on the uneven surface. Will suddenly hit the brake as the silhouette of a figure dashed between his headlights and the fire and then disappeared.

Henry? Please let it be Henry running

around out there, rather than lying unconscious somewhere.

He flung open the van door, then remembered the cell phone Andrews had given him. He pulled it out of his shirt pocket along with the fire alert card and punched in the number.

The call was relayed to a central dispatcher. "Fire at Henry Krause's farm! Next to Rest Haven Campground," Will shouted.

The dispatcher calmly asked for a name.

"Will Jennings. I'm a volunteer."

She assured him the alert was going out as they spoke and he ended the call, tucking the phone into his jeans. He ran toward the blazing barn, shielding his eyes from the smoke. A noise rose above the flames, and he heard the crash of timbers falling inside. The frantic squawking of terrified birds. Henry's pigeons. Will raced for the pigeon coops and found Henry aiming a garden hose at the one closest to the barn. When Will reached his side, Henry clawed at his arm. "My birds! My birds! You've got to save my birds."

"Have you got another hose?"

"Round the other side of the house."

"Go get it. I'll take care of this."

The old man hesitated before running into the shadows. Will wanted him at a safe distance, afraid he'd try to go into the coop. He must have already opened the coop farthest away because pigeons were swooping, panic-stricken, in circles above the yard. The door to the coop that was ablaze was still closed.

Will couldn't even get near enough to try to unlatch it. He aimed the hose on it and as soon as the plume of steam dissipated, tried again. No use. Henry came back, dragging another hose behind him. One look told Will it wouldn't help—the stream of water barely reached the fencing around the coop.

"The heat's too intense! I can't get near the door. Turn the hose on me while I try again."

"You want me to soak *you?*" Henry looked confused.

"Yes," Will shouted over the blaze. He dropped the hose and ripped his shirt off to use as a glove. "Forget that," he said, jerking his head at the hose in Henry's hand. "Take mine."

Henry bent to pick up the other hose.

"Okay, spray me now. Quickly."

Will pivoted so Henry could cover him. He

wrapped the drenched shirt around his right hand and grabbed hold of the handle on the pigeon coop door. Steam sizzled at his touch and in spite of the soaking, Will could scarcely grasp hold of the latch. He gave one fierce pull and the handle gave. Will yanked the wire door loose.

A few pigeons flapping against the mesh walls of the coop shot out the opened gate, but Will knew he was too late for most of the birds. The wooden housing unit inside the coop was already engulfed. There was nothing they could do now except keep the one coop wet and cool until the trucks arrived.

"When did it start?" Will hollered.

"I was asleep on the couch. Heard the birds squawking. Maybe ten or fifteen minutes ago."

More than long enough for the barn to become fully involved. If Henry hadn't awakened, the house itself might have caught fire. Will shuddered at how close the old guy had come.

"What about that one? Can we save it?"

Will looked over at the flames licking out from the roof of the birdhouse inside the coop. He shook his head. "I'm sorry. It's too late for that one. We need to keep the hoses on this one here."

"But my birds!" He started to lunge forward.

Will clamped a hand on the man's bony forearm. "No, Henry. Too late for the birds in there, but I think they've all escaped from this coop."

Henry swiped at his nose with his free arm. When he raised his smoke-blackened face to Will, his eyes were red. "Thanks anyway, for opening the gate. I couldn't even get near it, it was so hot. At least some of them had a chance." He stretched to look over Will's shoulder.

Will craned around to see clusters of pigeons sitting on the roof and eaves of Henry's house. Their silent silhouettes against the backdrop of smoke and sky, eerily lit from the fire, reminded Will of a scene from some horror movie. He guessed that many had flown into the woods.

The headlights of vehicles coming up the driveway suddenly bounced off the side of the house. Relief flowed through him. The unit was here and hopefully the second coop and the house itself, could be saved.

The engine pulled up next to Will's van, followed by the tanker truck. They'd made great time. A little less than ten minutes since his phone call. He saw Captain Andrews emerge from the engine and shout orders to the firefighters leaping down from both vehicles. Seeing Will and Henry, he walked over.

"Looks like a replay of the Lewis fire," he shouted to Will. "There's extra gear in back of the truck. Why don't you suit up?" He squinted down at Henry. "Mr. Krause, would you prefer to sit in the cab of the engine or Will's van?"

"I'm happy right here," insisted the old man.

"Not a good idea, sir. I don't want any of my men to knock you down while they're setting up the hoses." He placed a hand on Henry's elbow, took the hose from him and led him toward the engine. Will dropped the garden hose and followed them. Andrews closed the cab door, leaving Henry sitting in the dark interior, then showed Will where his gear was.

"When I heard you'd made the call, I brought it along." He gestured back to Henry.

"Poor guy. He loved those pigeons. I see a lot of them made it out. You open up the coops?"

"One of them. Henry got the other," he said as he shoved his feet into the heavy-duty steel-toed boots. They were a bit snug, but safer that way than too big.

"Any sign of Waters? His wife said he was on his way but we had to leave without him."

"I wasn't at the campground. I spotted the fire from the road."

"Again?"

Will shrugged. He picked up the canvas fire-resistant bunker coat and began to fasten it. Andrews studied him for a few seconds before rushing off to supervise his men. On his way back to the group, Will glimpsed Henry hunched over in the engine's cab, staring at the blaze. There wasn't time to say anything—even if he could have eased the man's grief.

He tugged on the balaclava that covered his head and neck beneath his helmet. The fabric was fire-retardant and offered some protection from the heat and sparks that could fly up under the rim of the helmet. Though Will knew all too well that even the best safety equipment could fail.

"Jennings! You coming or not?"

The shout roused Will. He blinked twice before he realized where he was, alive and well in Krause's backyard. Taking a deep breath, he forced his legs forward. Andrews was beckoning to him, pointing in the direction of the first pigeon coop, now totally engulfed.

"Get an axe and see if you can knock some of that down before the flames fly across to the other one. I'll get Waters to keep a hose on the first while you're doing it. Signal to him where you want him to spray. It looks like it just might burn itself out if we can narrow the perimeter."

Waters? When had he turned up? Will glanced sharply to the second coop and saw Sam helping a firefighter with another hose.

He checked the strap on his helmet one more time, grabbed the axe out of the bracket on the side of the engine and headed for the coop. His heart pounded erratically and he could hardly breathe. He made himself wait thirty seconds to catch his breath and let the adrenaline ease up.

Then a shout from behind. Waters. He couldn't hear what the man was hollering but figured he was asking him what was wrong. Will raised the axe and began to hack away at the burning wood.

Much later, as the firefighters stood around the engine after mopping up, talk got around to the cause of the fire. Although there was no way to tell yet how it had started, everyone was thinking it had to be the arsonist again. Everyone except Waters, who suggested Henry might have set the fire himself, maybe accidentally.

That postscript irritated Will. "Anyone with half a brain should be able to figure out that Krause would never harm his pigeons."

"Maybe he wanted to collect some insurance money. It's damn easier to burn a barn down than to raze it. Cheaper, too," Waters retorted.

Andrews took a wait-and-see attitude. "I'll send a team out in the morning to start the investigation." He turned to Will. "Can you meet us here, about eight?"

Will thought about Annie waiting for him at the apiary but remembered he now had a cell phone. After a few more instructions from Andrews, plus a belated introduction of

Will to the other members of the volunteer unit, the men began to pack up the equipment.

"Poor old fellow," Andrews muttered, watching as Henry tried to coax the freed pigeons into the remaining coop. "Leave that, Henry. Get some sleep. The birds will go back into the coop when they've calmed down."

"I don't want to leave them free at night. Too many predators about."

"I'll spend the night in my van right next to the coop, Henry," Will said. "When they've gone back in, I'll shut the door behind them." He doubted he'd notice a fox or owl hunting but his proposal appeased Henry enough for him to agree to go back inside the house.

Andrews clapped him on the shoulder. "Thanks. I think he'll sleep easier knowing you're out here. Besides, the perp might just come back to finish the job."

"You believe that?"

"I don't want to, but you never know. This is the first loss of life we've had, you know, since the fires began." He paused. "Sure hope the record holds there." He waved a hand

and headed to the engine where his men were waiting.

He didn't have to explain what he meant to Will. He was thinking the same thing himself. Nobody wanted to see this go to the next level—human loss.

When the roof had collapsed, trapping him, Frank and Gino in the blazing warehouse, part of a roof truss had knocked Will's helmet off. The balaclava had somehow twisted over his face mask, dislodging it enough to block his vision. Frank was lying under a beam, his PASS motion alarm shrilling loudly. Will knew instantly the beam was too heavy to move. Somewhere behind him, Gino was crying for help, his voice muffled under his mask and the din of the fire.

Will made a snap decision and turned back to find Gino, pinned beneath some rubble. He bent to start clearing the debris but his mask and balaclava slipped again, blinding him. He tore off the mask and was lifting a huge chunk of burning wood when something fell on him. All he remembered was the sharp pain before everything went black.

CHAPTER THIRTEEN

WILL AWOKE TO BANGING. He sat up, groggy and disoriented. He was in the van, which was a good thing. But when he brought a hand up to rub his eyes, he stared down at the black soot folded into the creases of his fingers. *The fire.* He was at Henry's. The banging persisted and he stumbled to the door.

Henry was standing at the foot of the door, holding a tray of what looked like breakfast. "Thought you'd be hungry," he said. "Where do you want it, in or out?"

Not quite awake, Will hesitated. "Have you eaten?"

"Yep."

"What time is it?" he asked, remembering the eight o'clock meeting.

"Seven-thirty. Want to shower inside first?"

"Do you mind? The captain is coming in about half an hour."

"C'mon then. I'll take the tray back to the kitchen."

Will grabbed a towel and change of clothing. He'd fallen onto his bed last night fully clothed. As he followed Henry across the yard to the kitchen door, he sneaked a glance at the pigeon coop. The gate was closed now. He hoped nothing had made off with the remaining pigeons while he was passed out inside the van.

He paused in the doorway to the kitchen. He'd noticed the other day that the windows at the rear of the house hadn't been shuttered, which explained the airiness of the kitchen. The house was much tidier and cleaner than he'd expected. He'd assumed—and he felt guilty about this—that it would be littered with the type of debris that recluses seemed to collect. Granted, the appliances were right out of the fifties and the linoleum on the floor had not worn well. Paint was peeling from a ring of rust on the ceiling. Sign of an old leak, Will guessed. But the man's dishes were stacked neatly in a rack and the room was filled with the aroma of bacon and eggs.

Henry took the plates off the tray and popped them into the oven. He turned around, almost surprised to see Will. "Oh. Thought you'd gone upstairs."

Will smiled. "I'm not sure where to go, Henry."

"Of course. Foolish of me." He led the way along a dark hallway to a staircase at the front of the house. Will glanced into the living room where, except for a small television on a bookcase and a shabby reclining chair, pieces of furniture were shrouded in sheets. His face flushed when he realized Henry had caught him looking.

"Don't spend much time in there," he said. "I'm usually in the kitchen or out back with my birds."

Will wanted to ask why the windows were shuttered but hesitated to pry.

"Bathroom's upstairs, second door on your right. The hot water takes a few seconds to get going, so be careful. And don't worry, there's lots of light. I didn't close up the bathroom."

"Oh."

"I put shutters on the other rooms about sixteen years ago, when my wife—Ida Mae—got sick. She couldn't bear the light. Had terrible migraines with her condition. Just never got around to taking them off."

"Keeps the place cool in summer, I bet," was all Will could think to say.

"Go get your shower then." The old man gestured to the top of the stairs. "Breakfast won't keep warm forever." He shuffled back to the kitchen.

Will found the bathroom as antiquated as the kitchen, but likewise, as clean. The tile floor was spongy in places, where water had overflowed, perhaps from the tub. Stripping down, Will sneaked a peek out the small window. No one had arrived yet. He pulled the cracked plastic shower curtain around the old-fashioned tub and turned on the faucet. A spray of rust-colored water shot out and, after a few seconds, Will tested it before stepping into the tub.

He soaped himself liberally and had to stand patiently while the thin stream of water trickled all over. Knowing that the captain might arrive any time, and that Henry would be disappointed if he didn't eat breakfast, Will decided to forego a shave. He toweled dry and changed quickly, bundled up his dirty clothes and took the stairs two at a time.

Henry was sitting at the table, sipping a cup of coffee. He started to get to his feet when he saw Will.

"No, no, I'll get it." Will took the plates out of the oven and set them across from Henry. The eggs had slightly congealed and the bacon was no longer as crisp. But he was starving and polished off everything, including two pieces of cold toast and two cups of coffee.

Henry beamed. "Glad to see you enjoyed it."

"Yes, sir, I did. And thank you very much for going to the trouble. I wasn't expecting you to do that."

"Least I could do after you saved my birds last night."

Henry's watery blue eyes confirmed how much that had meant to him. *Hard to believe that mere days ago this man was holding a shotgun on me.* "I'm sorry we couldn't save them all," Will said.

Henry looked down. "Me too."

"What about the ones that flew off? I noticed that some went up to the roof, but others headed into the woods."

"They'll come home when they're no longer spooked."

"Come home?"

"Pigeons home, Will. They find their way eventually."

The sound of vehicles coming up the driveway interrupted them. "Guess that's Captain Andrews," Will said.

"Guess so."

"Mind if I ask you something, Henry? I know the captain will anyway."

"Go ahead." The old man's face sobered.

"Do you know anyone who might want to hurt you? Get even with you for something?"

Henry pursed his lips in thought. "I haven't been exactly hospitable—if that's what yer thinkin'—for a long time, but I doubt I've offended anyone enough to warrant a fire. Still, there've been some strange goings-on lately."

"How do you mean?"

"I've seen flashlights in the yard from my bedroom window, at the back of the house. Thought it was kids again, but now I'm not so sure. Then a few weeks ago someone must've opened the door to one of the coops. The pigeons were okay and those that flew off came back, but some predator could've got in after them. That was distressing."

He'd been lucky the old guy hadn't shot first and asked questions later, the afternoon he'd wandered onto the property.

When Henry didn't say anything more,

Will stood. "Thanks again for the breakfast, Henry. And by the way, I thought I'd come back after work today to discuss rebuilding that pigeon coop."

Henry's face lit up. "You mean that?"

"I sure do."

"I can't believe a stranger's willing to do that for me. Thank you, son. I surely do appreciate the offer."

Will had his hand on the kitchen door to go outside when Henry added, "And bring that young Annie Collins with you again sometime. She's a corker, that girl. Just like her mama."

Annie. He'd almost forgotten. Will closed the door behind him and went to get the cell phone from the van.

ANNIE REPLACED THE RECEIVER. Another fire and even closer to home. For the first time since the fires had begun, she was starting to worry about the apiary. There seemed to be no particular pattern to the blazes either. Certainly the few people in the valley who'd been hit so far had no obvious connection to one another.

She'd have thought that if the arsonist was

a problem teenager, the Krause place would've been one of the first targets. Henry was legendary for his pigeons and his avoidance of people. The fact that he didn't allow residents of the valley to use his pond could be reason alone for some kid to want revenge. And the ramshackle outbuildings on his property would have been irresistible.

She sighed. Enough speculation. Your big problem now is whether to tell Dad or not. She ought to, but if he detected trouble in the valley he'd be home in a shot, which would ruin Shirley's plans.

She went upstairs to finish getting dressed. No rush if Will was going to be late. She could pour off some of the honey from the settling tank and get the Essex bakery order ready. But as she went about her tasks, part of her was attuned to the sound of Will's van. He might be able to give her some advice about her father. Annie saw the irony in that immediately. Seeking advice from someone who'd been in the valley all of one week and who hadn't even met her dad?

Midmorning, with no sign yet of Will, Annie returned to the house for a cold drink. She'd finished the order and, after pouring a glass of iced tea, picked up the phone to call the bakery to arrange pickup. There was a voice mail message and she quickly tapped in the password. *Maybe something's come up with Dad.* But the voice she heard—unexpectedly high and slightly tremulous—belonged to a young girl. Annie's damp hand clutched the receiver as she listened to the message, then replayed it.

"Hi, this message is for Annie Collins. Um, my name is Cara Peterson and I got your phone number from Sister Mary at Saint Anne's Adoption Agency in Charlotte. Sister Mary called a few days ago to tell me that you said it was okay to get in touch with you. I guess you know who I am….and…uh…I sent you an e-mail right away after I heard from Sister Mary but never got an answer."

Annie closed her eyes. She hadn't checked her computer in a week things had been so nuts.

"I'm really looking forward to seeing you whenever we can arrange something. My mom—her name is Devona Hall—says we can drive there anytime that's okay with you."

Annie forced herself to ignore her rising panic.

"Anyway, I'll send you another e-mail with some information about me in it. Mom says it's better to do it that way first. I'm really looking forward to meeting you and I hope you are, too. Bye."

After replaying it, Annie saved the message and slowly hung up the phone. She'd had a sense of unreality listening to the call, as if it were happening to someone else, not her. The voice could have belonged to any young girl and Annie hadn't felt much more than a strong sense of disbelief as she'd heard it. But partway through the second play, realization struck. *This is your daughter.*

Dazed, she went immediately to the spare bedroom that served as a den and booted up the computer. Sure enough, there was the e-mail. It was almost word for word the same as the phone call and Annie wondered if the girl had written the message down first. Somehow that touched her more than anything.

She had no idea what to say to her. Not *her.* Cara. Cara Peterson. *Your daughter.* Annie sat and stared at the monitor. Finally she began to type.

Dear Cara,

Thank you for your phone message. I'm glad you called because I haven't had time to check my e-mail since I saw Sister Beatty in Charlotte. She gave me your photograph. Thank you for that! I can see that you have a lot of your birth father in you. You are tall like he was and have his coloring. I am sorry to admit that I never had an opportunity to tell him about you—or even that I was pregnant. I have had no contact with him at all, but I think you may get some information about him from the University of North Carolina. At least, perhaps they have an address on record. Now let me tell you something about myself.

ANNIE KEPT IT SIMPLE, giving a general summary of the years after Cara's adoption. She knew that Cara would want to know about her father, too, but didn't want to overwhelm her with information in the first message. Not that she had a lot of information about the tall, good-looking young man she'd dated briefly that year. She also didn't want to tell her just yet that she had a grandfather. Best to let the grandfather know first.

Dad. Annie pressed her forehead against her fist, overwhelmed by guilt. She could summon up convincing excuses for not telling her father thirteen years ago. First, she hadn't realized she was even pregnant until ten weeks into her first trimester. Because she'd only been intimate that one time with Adam, she hadn't made the connection, little dreaming she could get pregnant her first time. *I was another statistic there, too.*

The days following the positive pregnancy test had been frantic, tormented. Adam had already left university to be with his family after his father's sudden death. She didn't expect to hear from him again and she hadn't. When she finally confided in her aunt, the two spent long hours discussing Annie's options. Adoption came out at the top of the list, allowing Annie to finish university and start a career. Once the decision was made and Auntie Isobel began making inquiries about where and how to place the unborn child, Annie had immersed herself in school work. Success was now more important than ever. Not telling her father had never been a plan—more a fallout of the mental and emotional chaos she was experiencing at the time.

The last trimester had coincided with the apiary's busiest time of year. Annie knew her father would leave for Charlotte right away, had he known, but their hired man would never have managed on his own.

After the birth, Annie was out of commission for a few weeks. Post-natal depression, without the joy of a baby to help pull her through. Once again, Isobel came to the rescue and by the time classes resumed in the fall, Annie was ready to start over. More or less. She'd made it—but not unscathed.

Her thoughts leapt to Will. They were alike in some ways, though his scars were both tangible and invisible. Annie checked the time on the computer monitor. He'd said midmorning at latest and it was eleven already. She didn't want to greet him in an emotional upheaval a second time. She ended her e-mail to Cara and promised to write again in a few days.

After washing her face and a quick change from T-shirt to tank top, Annie jogged downstairs and into the kitchen just as Will's van pulled into the yard. Although they'd smoothed out the rough edges of their misunderstanding, she still felt awkward. *As if my life isn't complicated enough. Now you're going to stir it up even more, in true Annie fashion, by falling for this complex, mysterious man.*

She found him in the barn, inspecting the buckets for the bakery order. When he turned at her footfall, his smile disarmed her. The other day at the pond might never have happened.

"You've been working hard this morning," he said. "When is this lot going to be picked up?"

"About three this afternoon. You look like you've been working hard, too."

"Things have been hectic."

"I can imagine. Look, I need to check the new hive we set up from the swarm at the Vanderhoffs. Why don't you tell me about the fire on the way?"

"Sure. Want me to load a few supers into the truck and the rest of our gear, in case we need to take off some more honey?"

He was learning fast. If Danny could help out when he finished summer school, they might manage to bring in the whole harvest without depending on her father at all.

"Yes, please. I'll run back into the house

for some cold water. It's getting hot and if we have to stay longer, we'll need to cool off." Annie blushed as soon as the words were out. She was describing the very situation that had led to the swim at Henry's pond.

But if he made the same connection, he didn't indicate it. He simply nodded and began to pack up the equipment.

Annie made her escape. When she walked into the kitchen, she noticed the red light flashing on the phone. She hesitated. Was it Cara again, or some message from her father? She picked up the receiver and waited for the voice mail to activate.

It was the man from Sunrise Foods, asking if he could reschedule their meeting to tomorrow afternoon, instead of the day after. Annie had forgotten about the meeting and now wished she hadn't agreed to it. The summer harvest was no longer in immediate trouble and she no longer felt a sense of urgency to make a decision about the business. She tapped in the number and was immediately transferred to voice mail.

"Hi, this is Annie Collins from Ambrosia Apiary returning your call. Look, I've changed my mind about discussing a possible sale at this time. Sorry for any inconvenience," she said and quickly hung up. Then she collected the water and a couple of apples and headed for the barn.

Will was loading the back of the pickup in the yard. "I've got everything," he said when she approached.

She peered into the pickup. "Okay," she said, glancing up to find him studying her. "What?"

He looked away. "Nothing. Have I missed anything?"

"No, you haven't. I'd say you're becoming a beekeeper, Will."

He was walking toward the passenger side of the truck as she spoke, but she caught a glimpse of his satisfied smile.

"How's Henry?" she asked as she pulled out of the driveway. "You said he wasn't hurt, but he must be upset about the birds he lost."

"He was a bit emotional this morning, but I think he's beginning to realize it could have been a lot worse."

"How bad was it?"

Will's expression was serious. "He came that close—" he put his thumb and index finger an inch apart "—to losing his house and maybe even his life. If the wind had shifted at all, we wouldn't have been able to save anything."

Annie shivered.

"Are you worried about your place?"

She shot him a look. "Should I be?"

"This person—male or female—is either mentally unhinged or has some kind of hidden agenda. I don't think Andrews knows a lot yet. We gathered some evidence this morning, but it wasn't quite what we were expecting."

"What's Henry going to do? Does he have insurance?"

"He said he has an old policy from years ago. He was searching for it upstairs when I left."

"Did you go into his house?"

"Yeah. I spent the night in my van in his yard, then went in for a shower and breakfast."

"You were in Henry's house and he made breakfast for you?"

"Yeah. Is that so weird?" He sounded amused.

"Well, Henry Krause isn't exactly known for his social skills."

"They're a lot better than some I've witnessed this week."

What did that mean? Was he referring to her? Spotting the Vanderhoff place ahead, she tightened her grip on the wheel, grateful not to have to pursue the topic.

After she parked the truck, Will placed a hand on her arm. "Henry's a harmless old man who shut out the world in grief," he said. "But I will admit I was surprised myself when I saw that his house was as normal and tidy inside as...well...as yours."

Annie's eyes held his. As far as she knew, Will was the first person to actually step foot in Henry Krause's kitchen in fifteen years. Certainly not since the days after Ida Mae's funeral, when neighbors were still bringing casseroles and cookies. "You're a good man, Will," she finally said.

His face flushed and he turned his head. "Not really. I just don't have a history with Henry." Then he opened the truck door and got out.

Judging from the way he'd stressed Henry's name, Annie suspected there was definitely history with someone—or something—else. She watched him as he collected their gear. He *was* a good man. But also a man with a mass of contradictions. Dry sense of humor yet dead serious. Vulnerable but closed. *Maybe by the end of the summer, I'll begin to understand him. Just as he's about to leave.* That sobering thought in mind, Annie climbed down out of the truck.

MUCH LATER, after they'd checked the new hive and found it thriving, they took a break before placing bee excluders in some of the hives. Annie stepped out of her bee suit and kicked it aside. Her face was red from the heat and physical labor and damp crescents drooped from the armpits of her tank top. Will got out of his suit too, watching her sprinkle water on her face and guzzle the rest down, greedily.

That was something else he liked about her. She seemed to hold little regard for how she looked. What you saw was what you got. Of course, he knew that a lack of attraction to him could easily account for her nonchalance about her appearance. Though the feverish kiss at the pond told him otherwise.

He left his suit on the grass and walked over to get his water, drinking the whole bottle in one go. Then he sank down under a tree a few feet from Annie, munched on an apple and leaned his head against the trunk. Except for the hum of the bees as they flew in and out of the hives and distant bird calls, the orchard was silent. The perfect summer day, he was thinking as he closed his eyes.

Waking up was a long slow journey through a landscape of bizarre images. Flames licking at shapes in the night. The silhouette of flapping birds rising soundlessly against a red-tinted sky. Smoke, black and acrid, billowing into the atmosphere in a towering column. Teasing at his nostrils, seeping into his lungs. Will shot up, heart racing and gasping for air.

He must have called out, because Annie, suited up and holding the smoker in her right hand, turned sharply toward him. She set the smoker down on the grass beside her and took off her hat. "Are you okay?"

Had she been working the whole time he was snoring away under the tree? Embarrassed, Will just nodded. He rose clumsily to his feet, holding onto the trunk for a second while his dizziness subsided. He hadn't dreamed about the fire for a while and last night was the obvious trigger. He hoped the dream didn't signal another cycle of the flashbacks that had tormented him since the accident.

"Are you sure you're okay, Will?" Annie was frowning at him.

"The heat." He picked up a water bottle and poured some into the palm of his hand to wash his face. "Have you been working long?"

She looked sheepish. "I fell asleep, too. I woke up about fifteen minutes ago."

He walked over to where he'd dropped his suit and began to climb back into it.

"We can call it a day, if you'd like," she said. "It's really hot."

"Yeah, but it's a good one for disturbing the hives. Right?"

"Right."

"Okay," he said, pulling up the zipper and stepping into the boots. "Let's get at it."

They spent another hour checking which hives needed honey extracted. When they ran out of excluders, Annie stuck a piece of red electrical tape on the covers of the hives that were left. "We'll get these tomorrow," she said.

Will set the last super into the back of the truck and eagerly removed his suit. They loaded everything up and sat in the shady interior of the cab for a few seconds, panting. "Now I know what the expression dog days of summer means," he said.

Her laugh thrilled him. His head lolled against the back of the seat and he half turned her way, grinning. Her cheeks were bright red and her hair dark with perspiration. A tendril clung to the side of her neck and Will reached out to loosen it.

"Hair," he explained when she looked surprised. She didn't move. He slowly drew her toward him. Shifting onto his side, he brought her face close. There was a slight resistance and he paused long enough for her to pull away. If she wanted to.

Then she smiled. Will held her face between his two hands and lowered her mouth to his, closing his eyes. Unlike the kiss at Henry's pond, this was a slow, gentle roll. Exploration without urgency. He felt a rise of excitement, but forced his mind to stay on her lips. He kept his hands on her cheeks, not trusting them to stray. No way did he want a repeat of the pond. But God, she tasted good.

Warm and fruity, like the apples they'd eaten earlier. Crisp green ones. Her hair draped over his face and it smelled of apples, too.

Her fingers were digging into the back of his head and he knew that the kiss could lead to something else. Right there, in the cab of the pickup. In the Vanderhoff orchard. His passion ebbed at that. He could feel it draining right out of him as he pictured Ted Vanderhoff coming along to check his orchard. His sigh fanned her cheek. The same thought must have occurred to her. She lifted her head and gave a small giggle tinged with embarrassment.

"That was a great kiss," she said, "but maybe this isn't such a good place for it."

"Yeah," he said, watching her adjust the straps of her tank top and smooth it over her breasts. Beautiful, round, plump breasts. Will forced his eyes away. "Sorry," he started to say but was cut off by her index finger on his mouth.

"Don't say that," she whispered. "We both enjoyed it. It was a kiss. That's all."

Yeah, but that's not all I wanted. His reassuring smile felt a bit weak.

Annie, on the other hand, seemed energized. She started the truck and flashed a smile at him. "How about a cold drink?"

"I'd never turn down a cold drink on a hot day," he said.

He leaned back against the seat as the truck bumped and jostled out of the orchard. Out of the corner of his eye, he watched the determined way she drove. Her long fingers wrapped loosely around the wheel. The toned but slender arms, golden-brown, glistening with perspiration.

She's had one bad experience from an impulsive, short-term affair. He wasn't going to be the man to give her another. Will repeated that to himself all the way back to the apiary, where a large white truck was parked on the driveway. Someone was waiting for them.

CHAPTER FOURTEEN

ANNIE SWORE UNDER HER BREATH.

"The bakery?" Will asked.

She pulled a face. "I forgot all about it. I guess we'll have to postpone the cold drink."

"Probably just as well. I promised Henry I'd help him rebuild his pigeon coop and we'll have to go to town for the lumber."

Was there no end to the thoughtfulness of this man? she wondered. She parked the pickup and got out to greet the delivery man.

"Hi, Joe. Hope you haven't been here long."

"Just pulled in, Annie. How's it going?" His eyes drifted with interest to Will.

Annie introduced the two and led Joe into the barn. They loaded the truck in minutes and it was heading down the driveway when Will asked, "Is there something pressing to do tomorrow morning? Henry wants to get the remaining pigeons in their own coop as soon as possible."

"I have to go into town anyway. I ordered a couple of new queens and they might be in. Plus I need a few supplies."

"You can order new queens?"

"A couple of hives at the McLean beeyard didn't survive the winter. Dad and I never got around to starting them up again. We ordered the queens from a bee supply company."

"They *mail* them?"

"Well, express and registered, so they arrive quickly. I'll show you tomorrow." She paused, then impulsively asked, "Feel like staying for dinner?"

"Tomorrow?"

"Unless you have other plans."

"That would be great, thanks. I'll come by after lunch or before, depending on when we finish the coop."

"Okay. If I'm not back from town, you could start decapping the frames we took off today. Shall we unload the truck, then?"

"Of course."

Annie headed into the barn, sensing a sudden awkwardness between them. Less than half an hour ago they'd been kissing passionately in the pickup, like teens at a drive-in. Now it was business as usual, with both of them pretending it had never happened. We can't continue with this charade anymore, Annie realized, as they worked with the supers. She had to decide what kind of relationship she wanted to have with Will, talk it out with him and make sure they both followed whatever decision was made. *Sounds easy enough. If only we can synchronize mind with body. Resolve with impulse.*

After Will left, Annie locked up the barn and went inside to forage through the fridge for something for dinner. She'd been picking at food the past few days and ought to make herself a decent meal. But remembering her invitation to Will, she decided the meal could wait until tomorrow. She popped two pieces of bread into the toaster and fried some bacon for a BLT sandwich. While it was sizzling, she browsed through a few of her mother's cookbooks for inspiration. Cooking had never been her thing, but she'd watched her mother at work in the kitchen and since coming back home, had taken over from her father.

She turned a few more pages and came upon

a handmade Valentine's Day card she'd made in primary school for her mother. The paper doily border was frayed, but the scrawled message—TO THE BEST MOMMY IN THE WHOLE WORLD—was still vivid. Annie's eyes filled with tears. What was it like to receive such unconditional love? The love of a child for a parent.

Whenever she'd allowed herself to wonder what had become of the daughter she'd given up, she'd never thought about missing out on hugs or cards like this one. The small daily pleasures of child-rearing were unimaginable to an eighteen-year-old. She'd thought only of gossip and the surrender of her dreams.

Now there was a possibility of some kind of relationship with her daughter. Not as a mother—she was sensitive enough to know that—but perhaps as a special friend. It wouldn't be the same, but it would be something.

Annie closed the book and put it back on the shelf next to the stove. The bacon was ready and she quickly put together her sandwich. She'd just sat down at the table when the phone rang. She stared at it, almost afraid to pick it up. But on the fifth ring, she dashed for it before the voice mail came on. It was Shirley.

Disappointed and relieved at the same time, Annie said, "Hi, Shirley. How're things?"

"Fine, Annie. Your dad's here and is itching to speak to you so I won't be long. Could you do me a favor and drive over to my place sometime in the next couple of days to check my mail? I'm waiting for my credit card statement before I…uh…make a purchase I'm thinking about."

"Sure, no problem. So, how's Dad? What did the doctor say about the heart test? Or can you talk right now?"

"I'll let your father tell you all about it. Thanks, Annie. Hold on a second, he's not moving very quickly."

Annie prepared herself for the onslaught of questions she knew her father would fire at her. She heard the sound of him fumbling the receiver and then, *"Annie?"* It came out like a bark. He's in fine form, was her immediate thought.

"Hi, Dad! Good to hear your voice."

"Humph. *Not moving very fast.* I'd like to

see *her* get to the phone a week after a hip replacement."

Uh-oh. Things weren't good if Dad and Shirley were quarreling. "What did your heart test show?"

"Lotta fuss over nothing, that's what. *Watch your diet. Take it easy,*" he said in a mimicking falsetto. "Save that advice for a seventy-year-old. I'm not there yet."

"But the idea is to get there, Dad. How's the physiotherapy?"

"Don't get me started."

"I guess you're almost through, then," Annie commented, searching for a safer topic.

"Darn right I am."

There was a pause, followed by muffled speech as if his hand was covering the receiver. He was answering some question from Shirley. When he came back on the line, he asked, "How's that fella doing? The one you hired to help out."

The afternoon kiss popped wickedly into her head. She felt her face heat up. "Fine, Dad. He's picked it up very quickly."

He made a doubtful grunt. "What're we paying him?"

Not nearly enough. "Minimum wage."

"Huh. That's what I don't get. How come a grown man is content with that kind of money. He's not…you know…one of those transient types?"

I have a feeling he might be, Dad. Unfortunately. "Does it really matter? He's only here for the summer."

"*Summer!* I thought he was there till I came home."

Uh-oh. Big mistake. "Well, he can stay on longer because he's got a temporary job with the volunteer fire hall."

"What? *How come?*"

Another very big mistake. "Uh…I think they're a man short and Will is a firefighter from New Jersey. Did I tell you that?"

"I don't know if you did or not, Annie. What does it matter? What I want to know is, are you filling the orders in time? What about that swarm? Did it take to the hive or move on?"

Her head was spinning. "It's fine, Dad. And the bakery picked up their order today."

"What about the gourmet food shops here in Charlotte? How many jars do they want this year?"

"A hundred each. And they asked for some honeycomb."

"I don't know if we have enough containers for comb. Can you go check?"

Annie had had enough. "Dad, I will take care of it, okay? Relax. I can practically hear your veins popping from here."

"What's that? What did you say?"

"Nothing, Dad. Just that everything's fine. Don't worry. Get better and have a bit of a holiday."

She held the phone away from her ear at his response, counted to ten and came back on as he finished. "Okay, Dad, got to go now. Give my love to Shirley."

"What? Hold on—wait a minute."

"I've got something on the stove," she lied. "Call me when you've set a date for coming home. Bye. Love you." She hung up before he could say anything more and stared blankly for a long moment, calming down.

She'd discovered in her teens that a long hot bath was the perfect antidote for too much Dad and, although it was barely seven o'clock, decided to have a luxurious soak and then catch a flick on TV. While the bath water was running, she checked her e-mail again but there was no reply yet from Cara. She shut down the computer, wondering how she could tell her father about Cara if she had trouble communicating with him about the everyday business of the apiary.

The bath wasn't quite as effective as usual, but then, Annie had a lot more than just her father on her mind. Restless, she prowled the house looking for any diversion. Television stations were already into summer repeats and after a few listless clicks of the remote, she turned off the set. She went back to the kitchen for a glass of water, locked up and headed upstairs to read in bed.

Dusk had fallen by the time she'd finished in the bathroom. Walking in the darkness back to her bedroom, she paused to look out the window at the end of the hall. It had a commanding view of the long driveway, the road passing their property and the distant hills. When Annie was a little girl, she used to run to look out whenever they were expecting guests, wanting to be the first to announce that the company had arrived. She leaned forward, pressing her face to the glass, exactly as she'd done then.

That was when she noticed the flicker of

car headlights enter the driveway. Will, dropping by as a surprise? A thrill shot through her. Annie waited for the car to continue up to the house, but after a few minutes, it reversed onto the road. Probably someone using the driveway to make a U-turn. She waited but the car didn't move away. She frowned. Should she do something?

Like what? Storm down the driveway in your nightwear?

If it was Will, how funny would that be? And if it wasn't...well, her mind shied away from other possibilities. The car slowly drove away. Annie went into her room, feeling somewhat foolish. Valley paranoia about the arsonist was getting to her, too.

WILL LOOKED UP as the screen door slammed shut. Henry was coming his way with two glasses of iced tea, a plate of cookies and a huge grin. They'd been at it since seven in the morning and now, three hours later, the new pigeon coop was actually taking shape. He just hoped they'd bought enough chicken wire yesterday and wouldn't have to make another trip to Essex.

He and Henry took their iced tea and cookies to a bench under an ash tree adjacent to the kitchen door. They ate in silence. Will was content to cool down in the shade and listen to the gentle cooing of the pigeons. He thought of Annie's story about how the locals used to use Henry's pond.

"Was it your wife's illness that made you close off the pond to the community?"

"It was all the noise. Not just cars driving back and forth, throwing up gravel and dust everywhere, but the shouting and screeching. When the windows were open we could hear them as if they were right in the yard here. Then there was the drinking and tossing empty bottles into the bushes. After a while, I just had enough. So I put barbed wire around it and blocked off the end of my driveway. There was no way to the pond, unless they walked along the stream from the campground. They did that, too, at first, but it wasn't convenient. Couldn't take a car." He'd said this last word with a sneer.

"I'm surprised Sam Waters hasn't tried to buy the pond from you."

"Guess you haven't heard the story."

"What story?"

"All that land where the campground is

used to be mine. I sold it to Sam Waters's pa about seventeen years ago, after Ida Mae was first diagnosed."

"I didn't know that. What happened?"

"We ran out of medical insurance and the bills were piling up fast. Sam's daddy wanted the whole thing but Ida Mae loved that pond. Loved to walk around it and watch the wildlife. After she died, I still couldn't bring myself to sell it. Besides, her ashes are scattered in the bullrushes on the far side." Henry looked off into the distance. After a while, he said, "Scotty Andrews told me in confidence that he actually hired you to replace one of his men. You must be good at your job, if the county's willin' to pay you a wage."

"Guess the county's worried about all the fires." Will watched Henry out of the corner of his eye for his reaction.

But he was staring at the new pigeon coop, obviously thinking of other things. Will wondered how much Andrews had told Henry about the arsonist. The evidence they'd collected from the ruined barn—a dented old jerry can and burnt plastic container of cleaning solvent—had been traced to Henry himself. He'd told them the stuff had been in the barn but he hadn't used them in ages. Will had no reason to doubt the old man, but Andrews wasn't so sure.

Henry suddenly asked, "You get that injury in a fire?"

Will nodded. He didn't feel like explaining and didn't think Henry was looking for a long story.

"You going to be okay fighting fires again?"

Will smiled. "I hope so, Henry."

The sound of an approaching vehicle ended the conversation. When the red fire hall SUV rolled into the yard, Will got to his feet. Scott Andrews climbed out wearing his standard issue uniform. So it was business, rather than social.

"Morning, Henry, Will." He paused to survey the new coop. "Been doing some building, I see. Looks great." His eyes cut back to Will. "You're a man of many talents, Jennings. Henry, I wonder if I could ask you a few more questions. The fire marshal will be visiting you soon and maybe the sheriff, too."

Will frowned. Obviously the sheriff had been investigating the fires and would have interviewed all the other victims. He glanced quickly at Henry, who seemed unperturbed.

"Have you had the forensic reports yet?" he asked Andrews.

"Nah. The evidence has to go to Charlotte. It'll be a few days." Andrews looked at Henry. "Mind if we sit down, Henry?" He pointed to the bench they'd just vacated.

Henry shrugged and took his seat again. The rest of the iced tea and cookies sat on the table next to the bench, but Henry didn't offer anything to Andrews. Will hesitated, wanting to stay but uncertain whether he was welcome.

Andrews glanced up at him and said, "If you want to go on with your building, that's okay."

He waited for some signal from Henry that he wanted him in on the questioning, but when none came, strolled back to the pigeon coop. The talk yesterday after the morning meeting had inevitably swung back to Henry as a possible suspect. Mainly because the evidence collected from the other fires hadn't belonged to the victims. Although the official report was out, Andrews had implied the

Krause fire might not be the work of the valley arsonist.

Will resumed hammering the chicken wire in place, but every now and then his gaze shifted to the two men on the bench. At the first sign of Henry appearing upset, he'd counsel the old man to call a lawyer. But after a few minutes, he saw Andrews pat Henry on his shoulder, get up and walk in Will's direction.

"I suggested Henry call himself a lawyer."

Will set down the hammer onto the frame of the coop. "Yeah?"

"I know the report's not ready yet, but I talked to the marshal this morning. He agrees there's something different about this one. The ignition source was Henry's own jerry can."

"Could be a teenager," Will countered.

"We haven't ruled that out."

"But you don't believe it."

The captain shrugged. "I don't know what to believe." He lowered his voice. "And in spite of what you may think, I find it hard to believe—damn hard—that Henry would torch his own barn, risking his pigeons like that. No way. But—" he heaved a sigh "—all we've got is the gasoline can. If his are the only fingerprints on it…"

"That means nothing," Will said angrily. "Of course his prints will be on the can. The perp could've been wearing gloves."

"And he does have a motive."

"What? Insurance?"

"He still owes money for his wife's medical bills. According to the bank that covered the loan, he's been making regular but small payments over the last fifteen years. A few weeks ago they gave him a deadline for the balance. He's got three months to pay or they'll collect his collateral. This place." He ducked his head closer to Will's. "And between you and me, I doubt the guy's old age security is going to cover the balance. Unless he's got a fortune hidden under a mattress in there."

"He told me he sold land to the Waters family to pay his bills."

"I think the cost of treatment came to more than what he got for the land."

"Captain, as you said, there's no way Henry would endanger his birds. You've got to consider other possibilities."

"Such as?"

"Such as maybe someone set the man up."

Andrews frowned. "What would be the motive? I was only kidding about the coins under the mattress thing. The bank told me all Henry owns is the house and the property. He's living from month to month on his security. I mean, unless someone around here covets his pigeons…"

"You think you've got enough evidence to have the sheriff lay a charge?"

"Not yet."

"So why call him in?"

"I just wanted to see his reaction. The sheriff will probably come around in a day or two as part of the investigation, but right now his office is too busy to make the valley arsons a priority."

He sounded bitter, which might explain his negative attitude. But it wasn't a good enough excuse for Will. "So you were trying to intimidate him? An old man?"

Andrews's gaze turned cool. "I've lived my whole life in this valley. My father went to school with old man Krause. Please don't assume you've got things figured out here after a week or so. I wanted to give Henry a heads-up that things are serious. If he has anything to confess, better he does it to us than to someone from the sheriff's office."

"He's got nothing to confess, Captain."

After a long moment, Andrews looked away. "Let's hope not." He headed for his vehicle, waving to Henry on the way. The SUV made a dust-raising three-point turn and sped down the driveway.

ANNIE KNEW SOMETHING WAS WRONG the instant Will stepped out of his van. His face was tight and his eyes grayer than a November day in New York. It was just past noon and she'd only returned from town minutes ago.

"Hi," she said uncertainly. She watched him stand by the van, as if catching his breath. Or calming down. Then he walked toward her, managing to conjure something that resembled a smile.

"Did you pick up the queens?" he asked.

She nodded, realizing he wasn't going to talk to her about his problem right away. "Come and see them." She led him to the worktable in the barn and pointed to a wooden box the size of a small chocolate bar. He gingerly picked up one of the boxes and brought it close to his face for a better look. There were three small cavities covered with a fine mesh. At each end of the flat box was a tiny cork.

"How does this thing work?"

"It's called a queen cage. There's a piece of sugar at one end, on the other side of that cork. I'll pull out that tiny cork just before I put the box upside down in the hive. The worker bees will start to eat the sugar candy and will eventually release the queen and her attendants."

"Her attendants?"

She had to smile at the incredulity in his voice. "That's what we call those other bees in the box with her. There are about eight or ten of them. They look after her in transport."

Will shook his head. "She really is a queen in every sense of the word."

"For sure."

"Why not just dump the queen into the hive?"

"Because the bees already there won't accept her. They'd probably kill her. This way, by the time they've eaten the sugar, they're used to her smell. When she's free in two or three days, they've accepted her."

"When will we put them in the hives?"

She liked the way he used that word, *we*. "Tomorrow, if the weather's right. It's kind of an involved procedure and I don't have time today."

He put the queen cage down on the table. "So what's the plan for today? Are we setting excluders in the other hives at the Vanderhoffs'?"

"No, there's no rush on them yet. I have to fill some orders. We need to pour off honey from the settling tank into those jars." She pointed to boxes stacked on shelves above the table. "Then we pack the jars and send them to a couple of specialty food shops in Charleston. They want a hundred each so we'll be—"

"Busy."

He'd warmed up since his arrival. But still no hint about why he was upset. He'll tell me in his own time, she figured. "Have you eaten?" she asked.

"Had lunch with Henry."

"Oh? Did you finish the pigeon coop?"

"All done."

"Henry must be thrilled."

"Happy as a pig in...you know, the proverbial."

Annie laughed. "Okay, well shall we get started?"

They worked steadily for more than an hour, seldom speaking except to ask for something to be passed. When Annie mentioned she was thirsty, he went to get sodas from the fridge in his van. She paused to watch him, straight-backed and confident. He was the kind of man her father would like and for some reason, she found that reassuring.

She sealed up the box she'd been working on and made for the barn door. Will was taking a bit longer than she'd expected. When she stepped outside, she saw him talking to a man in a khaki-colored suit. Both men turned her way.

Will's face was flushed and his eyes flicked coolly across her as she drew nearer. The stranger, a pleasant-looking thirty-something business type, beamed at her as he extended his right hand.

"Miss Collins? Tom Farnsworth."

She frowned.

"From Sunrise Foods."

"Oh." She shook his hand and asked, "Did you not get my message?"

His brow furrowed. "Message? Did you call the office?"

"Yesterday."

"I've been on the road and haven't got around to checking in today. Are we still on for the tour?"

Annie glanced quickly at Will. "Um, I guess so… since you're here. But you should know that I…that is, we…haven't made a decision yet."

"About selling the apiary? No rush, Miss Collins. As I explained when I first spoke with you, we're on a fact-finding mission. Just to check things out, see your operation and make an assessment to determine if it's the kind of asset we can use."

Will interrupted. "Still want that soda, Annie, or do you have other plans?"

She turned his way. His eyes were darker than ever. "Uh, I guess not. I should show Mr. Farnsworth around."

Will shrugged indifferently. "Then I'll call it a day," he muttered, climbing behind the steering wheel. Before he started the engine, he stuck his head out the window and said, "See you in the morning."

He'd forgotten she'd invited him to dinner. Or had he? Annie wondered, watching his van disappear down the driveway.

CHAPTER FIFTEEN

PARTWAY THROUGH HIS MEAL with Henry, Will remembered Annie's dinner invitation. He almost choked on a piece of chicken and had to fumble for the water.

"You all right?" Henry asked.

Will could only nod and gasp. After leaving Annie's, he'd headed for the campground and a shower. But en route, he'd spotted Henry's pickup parked in his driveway and dropped in to see if he needed any help transferring pigeons to the new coop. Then Henry had asked him to stay for dinner.

What to do? Henry ate early, so presumably Annie might still be preparing their meal. Or was she? Maybe she was relieved he'd forgotten. He'd left angry. When the agent had said he was there to view the property, Will had known right away what that meant.

How could she consider selling the family business? On the way back to the campground, it occurred to him that perhaps Jack Collins didn't know about the visit either. Will doubted he was the type to sell out to a big conglomerate. Another apiary, perhaps, but not a food giant like Sunrise.

All through his meal with Henry, the more he thought about it, the more it rankled. But if the old man suspected something was amiss, he didn't let on. He was preoccupied himself, probably from Andrews's visit that morning. The only reference he made to the fire investigation was his comment, while they watched the pigeons swooping about their new cage, "I'd never hurt those birds." And Will believed him.

After helping wash up, Will asked if there was any heavy work around the place Henry would like him to do. Henry hesitated and looked at the ruined shell of the barn. Will knew what he was thinking. The debris needed to be removed, but it would be expensive to hire the job out. He thought about what Andrews had said about Henry's financial state.

"If you're not in a rush about cleaning that up," Will said, "I could probably haul away a few pieces every day. Is there a dump around here?"

"They won't take that, but I can use some of the boards for my woodstove. The rest could be taken out to the back of my field over there." He looked back at Will. "Sure you wouldn't mind?"

"Hey, nights are long with no television in the van. I'll come by tomorrow after I leave the apiary."

"Any word when Jack will be home?"

"Not that I'm aware of," Will said. He realized he didn't know a lot about what was happening in the Collins household. *Witness the Sunrise Foods visit today.* What irked him most, though, was his reaction to being left out. As if he had some entitlement to the family.

It was dusk when he got back to the campground and the place was deserted. Waters kept saying people were going to start showing up any day, but Will had yet to see anyone but the workmen applying the finishing touches to the laundry facility. He'd thought Waters would be pleased when he made a down payment for the duration of the summer on his campsite—considering he was the only paying customer. Instead, the man had almost questioned his sanity about staying on in the valley.

At the moment, Will was inclined to agree. If he'd been able to maintain an appropriate working relationship with Annie, he wouldn't be having such doubts about staying. Problem was, the longer he hung around the more difficult it would be to leave. That was where the sanity issue came in. Even if Annie was as attracted to him as much as he was to her—and he had little doubt about that—where would that take them?

The end to his brief marriage had left him feeling he was no good at long-term relationships. *You never talk to me. You never share things. You never open up.* His ex-wife's breakup mantra. At the time, he'd thought he had been doing all those things. But in retrospect, he knew some part of himself was always held in check, as if he'd sensed all along that she wasn't really interested. When he learned about her affair with a friend of his—*make that former friend*—he'd been almost relieved that he no longer had to pretend the marriage was a happy one.

After parking and setting up the van for the

night, he lit the kerosene lamp, made a cup of coffee and sat outside on his folding aluminum lawn chair. It was a clear, warm night and the sky was filled with stars. He leaned back, staring up at the canopy directly overhead. It was a perfect night for stargazing. A perfect night for romance. He wondered what Annie was doing.

Annie. He liked saying her name in his head. And he'd liked her, too, right from the start. Of course there'd been that instant physical attraction, but he also simply liked being around her. He liked the efficient, quiet way they worked together. She wasn't the type who needed to have empty space filled with talk. Silence didn't make her feel uncomfortable.

She had a strong sense of place, too. He admired that most of all, not ever having felt a particular connection to any one spot until the day he drove up to the apiary. Leaving Garden Valley and losing that sense of belonging frightened him. Losing *her.*

Will poured the last of his coffee onto the grass. He was restless and needed to be active. Anything but to sit and ponder a future without Garden Valley and Annie Collins.

Maybe he'd drive into Essex to check out the flicks at the only movie theater in town. He was closing the van's side door when headlights traveling up the long gravel road into the campground caught his eye.

He paused, wondering if it was Waters coming to see him about something. The lights suddenly veered his way, holding him in their glare like a moth at a screen. He held a hand up, shielding his eyes, and the headlights extinguished. As the vehicle came closer, a warm calm eased through him. Annie's pickup.

The truck stopped a few yards from his van. He walked toward it, heart racing. If she'd arrived even ten minutes later, he might have been gone. The door swung open and she leaned over to pick up something from the seat beside her. Will reached her just as she climbed out, holding a plastic container.

She was wearing loose cotton trousers and a filmy, Indian-style top with bits of mirror that sparkled in the light spilling out from the interior of the truck. Her hair shimmered, and bounced against the top of her shoulders when she turned her head to him.

"You forgot about dinner," she said, holding out the plastic container, "so I brought dessert. Brownies. Made them myself."

Her beauty lit up the night, leaving him speechless. He closed the truck door behind her, took the brownies and set them on the roof. Then he gently drew her to him, tilted her chin slowly upward and kissed her. It was a tender and forgiving kiss.

"That thing about the Sunrise Food man—"

"Just a big misunderstanding," she murmured, nibbling at his lower lip.

"Would you really think about selling?" he asked.

"Can we talk about this another time? It's distracting me from what's really important here." Then she pulled his head down, parting his lips with the tip of her tongue.

"I love brownies," he whispered, tasting her lips, "but I think they can wait."

He clasped her hand, picked up the brownies and led the way into the van. She stood in the doorway while he swiftly pulled the fold-down bed onto the tabletop.

"These things are quite compact," she said, then laughed. "I can't believe I said that."

She looked nervous, one hand at the base of her neck while the other grasped the edge of the banquette seat, now transformed into the end of the bed. Will pressed down on the foam mattress, securing it into its frame. Then he reached out and gently pulled her close.

"I think this is how we both want the day to end." He stared down into her eyes. "Isn't it?"

Her breathless *yes* was the sweetest sound he'd ever heard and he lowered his lips onto hers, wanting to sear every sensation into his memory. He couldn't remember when—or even *if*—he'd felt such abandon making love. From the way she responded, he guessed it was the same for her, too. And when she came, clinging to him, her eyes were alive with passion—and something else. He wasn't certain what, but he hadn't seen it in a woman's eyes for a long time.

Later they crept out of the van whispering and giggling like teenagers. The balmy air cooled their bare skin and Will spread the heavy comforter on the grass. They made love again, more boisterous this time. There was one breathtaking moment when she ran her fingertips along the ridge of his scar, tracing its outline with her lips.

Will tensed, unaccustomed to being touched there, until her mouth left to explore other parts. He closed his eyes, giving himself up to the exquisite sensations of her body on his, her round full breasts and smooth satin skin.

"Tell me about it," she whispered afterward as they lay, spent, gazing up at the sky.

He knew at once what she meant. He also knew he wanted to talk. So he began, halting at first, until it all came back—the sounds and smells, the cries for help.

She listened in silence and then rose on one elbow to lean over him, her hair across his chest. She studied his face. "You couldn't have done anything more, Will."

"Maybe not. I just wish one day I could really believe that."

"You will."

Her eyes burned with an intensity he wished he could match. He wasn't certain he could ever share that kind of optimism but he sensed that if healing was at all possible, Annie was the person who could make it happen.

He tucked her into his arms and stared up at the night sky until he fell asleep.

Much later when he awoke, he lay still, listening to the wind rustling the trees at the stream. Will tightened his arm around Annie's sleeping form and figured his world was pretty much perfect. But when he rolled onto his side, he thought he caught a movement across the flat stretch of land between his site and the office.

He narrowed his eyes, trying to penetrate the dark. A large shape was moving slowly toward the campground office. He carefully extricated his arm from around Annie and sat up. Some kind of vehicle. It stopped and Will waited for the interior light to come on, but it didn't. Perhaps some teenage couple seeking a lonely place for a bit of romance.

He smiled and looked down at Annie. A faint metallic noise drew his attention back to the vehicle. Was it a door, opening or closing? Not teenagers, Will suddenly decided. They might coast in quietly, but they'd leave the headlights on. The campground was usually deserted until later in June. They'd have no reason to expect someone else to be there. Will carefully folded back the sleeping bag and tucked it around Annie. He tiptoed into the van and felt around in the dark for his jeans.

Barefoot, he set out across the grassy field. As he got closer, he could see it was a pickup, but he was still too far away to identify anything else about it. Something wasn't right. He started jogging. The vehicle suddenly lurched forward, made a wide semicircle and headed back to the road. Will watched it disappear into the shadows.

Puzzled, Will noticed a small flicker of light behind the new laundry shed. He stood absolutely still, reading the dark for sounds that had meaning for him. And then he found them. Crackling and hissing. *Fire.*

He ran toward the van.

SHE WAS FALLING. More like floating, actually. Somewhere in that suspended state between sleep and wakefulness. Annie burrowed deeper into the warmth, remembering, then reached out a hand to feel him. Except he wasn't there. She was raising her head, groggily, when Will suddenly loomed over her. Annie smiled up at him.

"Get dressed," he said, his voice urgent.

He looked far too serious for someone

who had just been making love with her. Annie sat up and the sleeping bag fell away, exposing her breasts. His smile was quick, tight with disappointment.

"What is it? What's happened?"

"A fire. Someone drove up seconds ago and set fire to the place. I have to get my cell phone and call it in."

He dashed into the van and she heard crashing inside until Will emerged, now wearing running shoes and a T-shirt. He stood in the doorway with a flashlight in one hand and the phone in the other, using the light to punch in the numbers. "Get dressed, Annie. They'll be here soon."

She brushed past him, fumbling in the dark for her underwear and the gauzy outfit that now, in the dead of night with a fire raging, was not only impractical but ridiculous. By the time she stumbled out of the van, Will had disappeared. She strained her eyes against the darkness and thought she saw someone running. A flare of crimson burst skyward and Annie started to run, too.

The sight of the flames licking up the end of a shed near the office stopped her cold. She'd never seen a fire blazing out of control and the awful beauty of it both fascinated and terrified her.

"Will!" she cried.

He appeared from the other side of the building, pulling what looked like a garden hose. "Get back," he hollered. His face was taut, almost angry. Not at her, she knew, but at the person who'd started the fire.

She moved toward him. "What can I do?"

"Nothing except stay back. I don't know what's inside that shed. The workmen could have left acetylene tanks or God knows what. Go back to the van. If something happened to—"

The expression in his face conveyed what he couldn't. She moved backward, keeping her eyes on him, ready to do whatever he needed. The rumble of an engine distracted her and she moved farther out of the way. Headlights streaked across the road, bouncing up and down as a black Chevy Blazer roared up. The door flew open and Sam Waters jumped clear.

"What the hell?" He stared, confused, first at Annie and then at the blaze.

She pointed to Will, frantically spraying the office and the building adjacent to the shed. Waters ran over to Will, gesticulating madly. She couldn't hear what he was yelling over the fire. Then the wail of an engine sounded from the road and Annie began walking back to the van. She wrapped her arms around her to ease the shakes. When she reached the van, she pulled the sleeping bag close and sat on the picnic table to watch.

Silhouettes of men dashed back and forth in front of the fire engine's headlights. Another truck arrived with more men. Shouts filled the air. After a long time, when the column of smoke seemed to have dissipated, Annie went inside the van and lay down on Will's bed.

She didn't sleep, of course, but forced her mind to things other than the fire—hardly a romantic end to an unbelievable night. Annie shivered, recalling the touch of Will's hands on her skin, the taste of his mouth. He'd made love to her slowly the first time, as if every second counted. She could have lain there forever in his arms.

So what happens after tonight? After the summer? In her ideal world, he would definitely stay in Garden Valley, working at the apiary with her and her father. *Her father. Cara.*

Annie sighed. Life was suddenly getting

too damn complicated. Still, she wouldn't have traded tonight for anything.

Much later, she was awakened again by Will, brushing strands of hair away from her face. "Rise and shine, sleepyhead."

Annie stretched and held out her arms. He grinned, shaking his head. "I can't believe I'm saying this, but I think you'd better go home. The place will be crawling with people at daybreak and there is that Garden Valley Grapevine."

She remembered Sam's surprise when he saw her. "I think it may be too late for that anyway. I mean, my pickup with the apiary logo is sitting right next to your van."

"Yeah, guess you're right. But I still think—"

"I know, but first tell me about the fire. I couldn't see much from here, but it looked as though most of the building's frame was still standing when they were packing up their gear."

"Waters was lucky. We were able to contain it quickly. Lucky for him he happened to be on his way home when he spotted the flames." Will fell silent.

"What is it?" she asked.

He hesitated. "I shouldn't really be talking about this to you, but Waters will probably be doing plenty of that himself so…"

"What?"

"He said just before he got to Henry's place after the turn at the junction, he saw a pickup roaring up Henry's driveway."

"And?"

"He said it was Henry's."

"What would Henry be doing out at this time of night?" Then she got it.

"Oh no. He doesn't think Henry had something to do with…that's crazy. He's a harmless old man."

"There's more." Will sagged onto the edge of the bed. "We think the fire was started by a Molotov cocktail. You know, kerosene in a bottle with a wick? We found part of a bottle—the kind people use for homemade wine. There was a partial label on it with the name *Krause Fine Wines*. Apparently Henry bottled his own wine for years…?"

"But it doesn't make sense, Will. What would his motive be?"

"Try a longtime feud between Sam's father and Henry, so I'm told."

"Sam's father died more than a year ago

and I think the hard feelings about the land sale ended long before his death."

"Well, I don't know all the history, but I agree that it doesn't make sense for Henry to set fire to this place, much less his own place."

"What do you mean? Wasn't that the work of the arsonist?"

Will looked at her but said nothing.

"Don't tell me you think Henry Krause—a man well into his seventies—has been running around the valley setting fires? Oh please, that's too ridiculous to even contemplate!"

"I don't think it, Annie. But Sam does and he's doing a damn good job of persuading Captain Andrews and the other men that the idea is plausible."

"Poor Henry," she said. "You've got to help him, Will."

"Help him? I'm in a bit of a jam on this one, Annie. I'm a newcomer to the valley and I think Andrews is starting to wonder about my friendship with Henry. All I can do is suggest he contact a lawyer, in case the investigation turns serious."

"But what about the fire marshal's report?"

"He's talked to Andrews about both fires but apparently hasn't had a chance to see Henry yet. Since there's been no loss of human life, Andrews said the cases here are a low priority. So most of the investigation has been left to the captain. He's had some training in gathering evidence and so on, but in the end, he has to hand it all over to the marshal for his analysis."

"Whenever that happens," she said.

"Exactly." He yawned. "It's almost four in the morning and our day starts in about five hours."

"Sleep in," she said. "I plan to. Besides, I have to drive to Shirley's to pick up her mail. She lives just outside Essex so I might as well do some banking while I'm there."

He nodded, rubbing his eyes, red-rimmed from smoke and soot. "Sleep would be good."

Annie lowered her legs off the bed and sat up, smoothing her hair back with her hands. She caught him staring at her. "What is it?"

"You're so damn beautiful. I just can't begin to tell you what tonight meant for me."

Annie grinned. "I think I have an inkling."

He grasped her hand and pulled her to her feet, drawing her against his chest. He smelled sooty and sweaty, but Annie could have stayed there for hours. Finally he kissed the top of her head and said, "Come on, let's get you home."

"I can manage on my own."

He tilted her head up to his, his eyes serious. "No way, Annie. I'm not letting you go home alone at this time, after what's happened tonight. I'll follow you in the van and make sure you get in the house safely."

She was tempted to make light of it, but the seriousness of the night's events were beginning to register. Returning to a dark and empty house was not something she wanted to do. She waited, perched on the picnic table, as he rolled up the blanket and sleeping bag and popped them in the van. After he slid the door closed, he came to her and touched the end of her chin with his finger.

"This isn't the way I thought the evening would end."

"No," she said and glanced away. There was so much she wanted to say but nothing that didn't seem corny or ring false. They'd made love and both enjoyed the experience. But she'd had a one-night stand once before and didn't want another. *Maybe you ought to have considered that before jumping into bed with him.*

"No regrets, I hope," he said, his voice low.

Annie took a deep breath and turned back. "No regrets," she echoed. *Not yet anyway.*

Daybreak was peeking above the distant hills when she drove up to the apiary. Will's van rolled to a stop behind her, but he didn't cut the engine. Guess he's not coming in to finish the night here, she thought. Disappointed, she snatched the key from the ignition and climbed out of the truck.

He insisted on checking the barn doors and came into the kitchen with her, pausing in the doorway while she turned on the lights upstairs. He was still standing there when she came back down. She had a feeling that if she moved close enough—kissed him—he would follow her upstairs in a heartbeat.

But she didn't.

"Good night, Will," she said. "Thanks for coming with me."

He didn't speak for a long time and Annie

knew any move from either of them would break the spell. They'd be falling all over each other again, the way they had on the blanket at the campground. She knew, too, that he was thinking the same thing.

"Good night, Annie," he replied. "Lock the door behind me." Then he was gone.

Annie walked quickly to the door, hand on the knob, ready to call him back. Finally she locked the door and went up to bed.

HE LEFT BEFORE the investigating team arrived. Last night—or rather, that morning—he'd lain sleepless till dawn, wondering how to help Henry. Then he'd fallen into a deep slumber for almost an hour, in which nightmare visions of the fire vied for attention with memories of Annie—her long slender legs wrapped around him, her full, luscious lips on his. By the time he rolled out of bed, he knew it was going to be a long day.

Fifteen minutes later, after a cold shower as a result of the power outage precipitated by the fire, Will drove up Henry's road. The first thing he noticed was that Henry's pickup was not in the same spot it had been when he left him after dinner last night. As he walked by it, he ducked his head to check the tires. There were chunks of mud clinging to the treads, but Henry could have picked that up anywhere. More damning were the clumps of grass.

Will surveyed the gravel driveway and the gravel road at the end of it. No grass there and not much around Henry's yard, except for under the ash tree. He looked inside the cab. The key was still in the ignition. He wanted to reach inside and grab it, but knew he'd be in big trouble if it came out he'd been helping Henry conceal evidence. Then he thought to hell with it. He opened the door, took the key, slammed the door shut again and headed for the house.

The screen door to the kitchen was ajar. "Henry!" Will called.

There was no answer but he could see a plate and coffee cup still on the table. Maybe at the pigeon coops. He walked around the corner and saw Henry inside one of the coops, cleaning out the bird house. A wheelbarrow loaded with fresh straw was parked at the closed door of the coop. He didn't hear the van drive up, Will thought. So he might not have heard someone drive away with his truck last night, either.

Henry happened to look his way and waved. "Come on in, but watch where you step."

Will pushed open the wire door and gingerly stepped around the piles of droppings and soiled straw that Henry was shoveling out. The stench was almost overpowering, though it didn't seem to bother Henry. Will breathed through his mouth.

"What do you do with all this?"

"I've got my own little landfill site out in the back field, but don't let on to the authorities," Henry said, winking.

Authorities. Yes. Get to the point, Jennings. "Look Henry, I came by to tell you there was another fire last night."

"Oh yes?" He didn't look up, intent on forming another pile with the shovel.

Will waited for him to show some interest, but when he didn't, quietly said, "At Rest Haven."

Henry's head came up sharply. He narrowed his eyes and repeated, "Rest Haven."

"That's right."

"Huh."

Will gave the old man another few seconds

before asking, "Did you hear or see anything unusual about two this morning?"

"That the time? Nope. I was up in my bed sawing logs, as Ida Mae used to complain."

Will wondered how to begin. Of course, he could just come out and ask Henry if he'd set the fire. But the small, frail man leaning wearily on the shovel looked incapable of making a fire in his own woodstove, let alone tossing a Molotov cocktail from a pickup. As Annie had said, the idea was absurd.

"I, uh, happened to notice your truck isn't parked in the same place it was when I left here last night."

Henry's eyes darkened. "You think so?"

Will shrugged, sensing he was now in over his head metaphorically. "Look, Henry, I shouldn't be telling you this, but I have to. Someone saw your truck—at least a truck very much like yours—leaving the campground right after the fire started."

"Why would I be driving around there in the dead of night?" Understanding crossed his face. "Ah. Someone thinks I set the fire myself. How? With my own jerry can, the way I was supposed to have set fire to my barn and pigeon coop?" His voice was angry.

"No, not a gasoline can this time. A Molotov cocktail."

"A what? People still make those things?"

"I'm afraid so and this one was made with a wine bottle." He paused. "A bottle used for homemade wine."

"With one of my labels on it?"

The sadness in Henry's voice made Will want to hug the old man. "That's why I asked about the truck. I noticed you left the key in it." He held out his hand, with the key in the center of his palm.

Henry took the key with trembling fingers and tucked it into his overalls pocket.

"Do you always leave your key in the ignition?"

"Sure. Why not, way out here in the country? Saves me looking for it in the house every time I want to go into town."

"Does anyone know you do that?" Will asked.

"Who could? It's not as if I have any visitors here. 'Cept for you, of course." He frowned at Will. "You don't believe I set that fire, do you?"

Will swore under his breath, regretting having raised the matter at all. "Not for a second." He hesitated a beat. "Do you have a—"

"Lawyer? Used to, years ago." He kept his gaze fixed on Will. "Maybe I should get to Essex and look one up."

"The sooner the better," Will said. He took the shovel from Henry's hand. "You go in and wash up. I'll finish this and we'll drive into town together."

The old man didn't say a word, but turned and shuffled toward the house. Will drove the shovel blade into the pile of straw.

CHAPTER SIXTEEN

ANNIE WAS ALMOST OUT the door the next morning when the telephone called her back. She hesitated, knowing she was already running behind schedule, but picked it up on the third ring.

When she heard her father's voice, she sighed. This wouldn't be a phone call she could handle in a few seconds. She wished she'd let the voice mail pick up.

"You answered pretty quick," he said. "Thought you'd be working. It's almost ten o'clock."

"What's up, Pop?" She made herself sound cheery, and knew he hated to be called Pop.

"Heard there was another fire last night."

Sheesh, Annie thought, the grapevine is better than I thought. "How'd you hear that?"

"I was talkin' to Arnie Harris this mornin'

and he told me. How come you didn't tell me about old man Krause's fire?"

Old man Krause indeed. He's only ten years older than you are, Dad. "There wasn't really much to tell. The fire marshal's official report hasn't been filed yet."

"Official report!" He snorted. "A child could figure out that Henry Krause wouldn't set fire to his own pigeon coop. Got to be that arsonist again, only this time he's working too damn close to us. I'm coming home."

The pulse at Annie's temples drummed loudly. This was exactly what she'd feared. "Look, Dad, that's ridiculous."

"Ridiculous! You call looking out for my own property ridiculous?"

"Dad, the fires might not have been set by the same person. That's why Captain Andrews hasn't made a public announcement. He's still collecting evidence," she said, repeating most of what Will had told her last night.

"All the more reason to come home. Things are going haywire there in the valley. What's happened to people these days?"

"You promised Shirley…"

"I don't recall doing any such thing."

There was a muffled sound and Annie

could hear Jack talking to someone in the background.

He came back to the phone and, in a slightly mollified voice, said, "I'm working on that. I'll talk to you in a couple of days."

Mystified, Annie had to ask, "What are you saying, Dad?"

He heaved a loud sigh. "Apparently I did make some foolish promise—*when I was under the knife.*"

Annie grinned. That dig was obviously for Shirley, likely standing nearby. "I'm shipping off that order to Harvey's today," she said, referring to the fine food shop in Charleston.

"Good, good. And what about that young fella?"

Young fella, as in Will? Annie felt a wickedly delicious thrill.

"Well?"

"He's working out just fine, Dad," Annie said. Her face heated up at the memory of last night. "Tell Shirley I'm on my way to her house to get her mail."

"Yeah, okay. She said to open up the credit card bill and call her back to let her know the balance. I don't know what she's got up her sleeve," he complained.

"Okay, Dad, will do. And you be nice to that woman, you hear? She's a saint."

"Humph. Talk to you later."

Annie was shaking her head as she replaced the receiver. She hoped Shirley was going to buy something outrageously luxurious for herself.

On her way out to the truck, she paused at the door. People seldom locked up in the valley, but since the arsonist had moved closer to home, Annie decided not to take chances. She locked the door, checked that the honey barn was also locked and got into the truck. If Will arrived before she returned, he knew where to find the spare key.

She drove down to the main road, thinking of the previous night. Not the fire at the campground, but the fire Will Jennings had set. She'd tossed and turned in four hours of attempted sleep after he left. His lips and fingers everywhere, his husky exclamation as he climaxed. Annie shivered at the mere recollection.

Annie turned onto Dashwood Side Road in the direction of Essex. When she reached the junction that would take her to Rest Haven, she braked and waited. Would she have time for a quick visit with Will? To test the post-coital waters, so to speak. She grinned. Who was she kidding? She just wanted to see the guy, to be next to him, breathing in his masculinity.

On the other hand, the place would be busy with some of the unit helping Captain Andrews search for evidence. Maybe Will would be one of them. She pictured his embarrassment if she drove up. The girlfriend dropping by the workplace thing. God, do you have it bad.

She cranked the steering wheel right, toward Essex. Her first stop was Shirley's pretty bungalow, about half a mile out. The bungalow sat on land that used to be owned by Shirley's parents. After they sold the family farm, they built the house as a retirement home, where they lived for several years. At the time, Shirley and her husband were living in Charleston. When he died, she moved back to her parents' place.

Annie remembered very well the first time her father brought Shirley Yates home after they'd been seeing one another for a few weeks. She was home on spring break in her third year of college and had actually been pleased that her father was involved with a woman, having seen his loneliness whenever she was home on vacation.

Over the past few years, she'd often wondered why the two hadn't married. But recently she figured living apart might be the trick to the success of their relationship. They each had their own separate lives but still shared one together. Not for me, she thought. I want a man who's going to be around all the time.

The involved process of paying the apiary's bills and updating bankbooks absorbed Annie's morning. By the time she finished at the bank, it was almost noon and she was starving. She dropped into the new café in town for a salad before heading for the post office.

"You've got a parcel," the postal clerk told Annie after she finished unloading the boxes of honey. "Just came in this morning. I'll get it for you."

Annie finished applying the address labels and was taking her wallet out of her purse when the clerk plopped a large brown padded envelope in front of her. "All set, then? I assume you want the receipt for these boxes."

"Oh yes, they'll be handy at income tax time." Annie handed over the money, examining the envelope while waiting for change. The address was unknown, some place in Raleigh. But the name of the sender froze her to the spot. *Cara Peterson.*

"Anything else?"

Annie looked up, dazed. The clerk was smiling politely. "Uh, no thanks. That's it for today."

She tucked the envelope under her arm and made for the door.

HENRY HARDLY SPOKE all the way back from town. Will kept glancing at him out of the corner of his eye, not wanting to fuss over the old man but worried about him all the same. He'd been subdued ever since leaving the office at the Legal Aid agency, but the lawyer had assured him he'd nothing to worry about. *So far.*

The way he'd repeated those last two words was some indication of Henry's state of mind. Or so Will figured. He'd waited in the reception area. The wait stretched to an hour. Once, bored with the limited selection of magazines, Will paced back and forth in front of the plate glass window of the agency on the main street of Essex. He thought he saw Annie's head in a sea of others and felt his heart pound.

She'd said she had to come to town on business. He hoped he'd bump into her later, maybe go for a long lunch somewhere cozy. But by then, he'd be driving Henry back.

The old man hadn't wanted to stop for lunch in town, so Will drove up to a roadside hamburger stand. The guy needed some nourishment. They ate in silence, though once Henry looked slyly at Will and asked, "So you like Garden Valley?"

"Love it," Will said over a mouthful of burger.

"People here are good people," Henry said. "Salt of the earth. This arsonist—that's an aberration. You gotta believe that."

Will frowned. What was he getting at? "I can see that," he said, waiting for some clarification.

But the old man just stared out the windshield, hamburger half-eaten on the wrapper in his lap. After a few minutes of waiting in vain, Will gathered up his garbage, packed the rest of Henry's meal in the paper bag for his supper and started the van. By the time they pulled into Henry's driveway, the man looked exhausted.

He helped him into the house. "Sure you don't want me to stick around a bit longer? I could finish cleaning out the coop."

Henry shook his head. "Too tired, son. You go see that girl of yours. Maybe she'll persuade you to stay in the valley."

He had a bad feeling about leaving the old man. When Henry insisted, Will quietly slipped out the kitchen door after promising to look in on him later in the day. Henry's remark about going to see Annie—*your girl*—was the best advice he'd had in a long time.

He found her in a mess. An emotional one, he realized after a heart-stopping second. He saw her through the kitchen screen door sitting at the table. She must have heard the van drive up, but the fact that she hadn't come to greet him was the first clue that something was wrong.

"Annie?" he asked, hesitating to simply walk right in.

She raised her head and managed a wobbly smile. "Hey," she said.

It came out like a throaty croak. His hand rested on the doorknob. "Hey yourself." He paused. "Can I come in?"

"Sure."

He gently closed the door behind him and walked over to the table.

There was a brown envelope lying on the table. Next to it, Annie had her hands on what looked like a scrapbook. It had a deep blue leather cover, which was closed.

Will sat in the chair beside hers. "You okay?"

Her smile was stronger now, though he saw the remnants of tears on her face. "I…uh…I got this in the mail today. From Cara. My… my daughter."

From the way she choked it out, he could tell she wasn't used to saying that word.

"Looks like a scrapbook."

"It's the most amazing history of her life. Well, from when she was about ten or so. Here's the letter that came with it." She handed him a single piece of typed paper.

Will's eyes held hers. "Sure you want me to read it?"

"Yes, I do."

Dear Annie,
My mother said you might be interested in seeing my scrapbook, so I am sending it to you on loan. *(underlined, Will noted)* Mom said that it might give you an idea of what kind of person I am, so that when we meet you'll already know a lot about me. We started keeping this scrapbook when I was in Grade Five because that year I won the Track and Field First Place Ribbon at my school. It was for the Hundred Yard Dash. My picture was in the school yearbook and Mom said we should keep track of important events in our lives. So we started this scrapbook. There are all kinds of things in it—all about me, of course—but I am not a conceited person. I hope you like it. Maybe you have something similar? It doesn't matter if you don't. You can mail this back or give it to me when we meet. Whenever that happens. Bye for now, Cara

Now he understood. Will set the letter down next to the book. "She sounds like a neat kid."

"Very. Her parents obviously did a great job."

"Did you pick them, or what? How did that go?"

"No, Sister Beatty—she's the nun at the adoption agency—picked them, but I told her the kind of people I'd like."

"Then she followed good advice," he said. He wiped a tear off her cheek with his index finger.

Annie dug into the breast pocket of the checked cotton shirt she was wearing, took out a tissue and loudly blew her nose. "I'd show you the book, but I don't think I could take another look at it right now. Maybe later."

"Later is okay. Do you feel like working today? If you want to…you know…have a rest or something, I can manage on my own."

Her laugh made him want to drag her off the chair onto his lap. "I may be emotional," she said, "but I'm not sick. I'll be okay, Will. But thanks."

If she keeps staring at me with those eyes, I may drag her onto my lap anyway. He cleared his throat. "Did you mail off the jars to Charleston?"

"Yes. That's when I got this."

"Oh." He peered down at the book, then back up at her. "Maybe we could *both* take a nap," he suggested softly.

"Maybe we could." Her eyes locked onto his.

He could see the desire in her eyes, but also turmoil and confusion. It wouldn't be right to make love now, when she was feeling so vulnerable and mixed-up about the book, her daughter. Everything. "Or maybe we should—"

The chime of his cell phone solved the problem. "Damn," he said. "Knew there was a reason I never bought one of these myself." He was only half joking and he saw relief in her face.

He stood up to extract the phone from his jeans. Caller ID told him it was not the fire alert line, but Captain Andrews himself. "Just a sec," Will said to Annie. He moved away from the table to lean against the counter, where he could still look at her.

"Yes, Captain."

"Wonder if you could meet me at Henry Krause's place in about half an hour. I know you have a special relationship with the old man, and he might want to have a friendly face when we talk to him."

Will's mind raced. "We?"

"The sheriff and I."

Uh-oh. "What's the problem?"

"Well, we found quite a cache of those empty wine bottles in one of the sheds. The sheriff wants to interview Henry."

"Have you considered the possibility that someone else found them, too?"

"Yeah, we've talked about a lot of possibilities. But we also need to talk to Henry again. You coming or not?"

"I'm coming. Half an hour?"

"Right."

Will ended the call. Half an hour. It was five now. He stared at Annie, absently tapping the phone against the palm of his other hand. Finding the other bottles was merely confirmation of what they already knew—that the Molotov cocktail had been made from something that belonged to Henry. It didn't mean he'd made it or thrown it. So far the evidence was all circumstantial.

Except for Sam Waters saying he'd seen the pickup on the road, just before the fire was discovered. Eyewitness testimony made the case a lot more serious.

"Trouble?" Annie asked.

"The captain found some of Henry's empty wine bottles."

"That doesn't mean anything!"

"Not a whole lot on its own, but together with what Waters said, about seeing the pickup…"

She was shaking her head in disbelief. "There's no way he did that. No way."

"They're having a meeting at Henry's in half an hour. With the sheriff."

She rose to her feet. "You're going to be there with him, aren't you?"

"Oh, yes." They stared at one another silently for a long moment, both knowing that the afternoon siesta was scrubbed. Finally, Will said, "I should go. I'll call later when I get a chance."

When he closed the door behind him, his last glimpse was her pale face, set with worry, looking out through the screen mesh. He'd have given anything to go back for one more kiss.

AFTER WILL LEFT, Annie thumbed through the scrapbook one more time—*a sucker for punishment*—had another cry and made herself a cup of tea. The perfect antidote, Auntie Isobel always said, for any upset.

There were certificates of merit for swimming, more track and field ribbons and lots of photographs of Cara on teams or in clubs. She was obviously a kid actively involved in life. Annie liked that, even knowing she had nothing to do with it. Other than donating a few genes. And she could see those genes in small, subtle ways. The tilt of Cara's head toward the camera or the slight frown puckering her forehead in some of the photos. Her father's coloring, along with his height and lankiness.

Annie closed the book. It had only whet her appetite for more. That's when she knew for certain she was going to meet her daughter. She had to see that grin for real and hear the sound of her laughter. She took her cup of tea upstairs to the computer, booted it up and logged into her e-mail. There was a brief message from Cara asking if she had received a surprise in the mail. Annie smiled and began to type.

When she was finished, having sent the

longest e-mail in her life, she sat back in her chair, rolled her shoulders to ease the knots and felt an enormous sense of relief. She'd made a decision. It was too late now to change her mind. The next hurdle of course, was her father.

She wouldn't tell him on the phone. No way. So a meeting with Cara—promised in her e-mail with a date yet to be decided—wouldn't take place until after Jack was home. Fortunately, when she'd called Charlotte with the information Shirley wanted about her credit card bill, she'd reached voice mail.

The one person she could tell about the scrapbook—and her decision—was her aunt.

"I'm so very happy for you, dear," Aunt Isobel said after Annie told her. "You've made all the right decisions every step of the way."

"You know, Auntie Isobel, I never really believed that until today. After seeing that book, I now know that Cara has had a wonderful fulfilled life. It made me feel good about my decision—for the first time."

"And well you should. Now, what's the latest about your father?"

Annie gave her a quick summary of the most recent phone call and, after a promise to let her know when the meeting with Cara would occur—*"we all want to meet her"*—hung up. She checked the time on the kitchen wall clock. Almost six-thirty. Will had been gone for about forty-five minutes.

Anxious and restless, she decided to go out to the barn to make a list of jobs for the next day and see what materials needed to be ordered from the supplier. She picked up the keys from their hook near the kitchen door and went out into the yard. It seemed empty and lonely—almost deserted. She paused midway and scanned the area. Everything looked the same, but suddenly felt very different.

You're seeing this place through different eyes now, Annie. It won't ever be the same. Not after finding Cara. Not after Will. That must be it, she realized as she unlocked the door. There was no Will inside or walking back from the kitchen with cold drinks. No Will suited up to move supers or collect honey frames. She had a vivid picture of what life at the apiary would be like after he left. And she didn't like it.

Dust beams streaked across the shadowy interior of the barn, lit from the side windows. It was eerily silent and Annie shivered. Overactive imagination at work, she told herself. She went to the long counter and checked the supply of plastic packaging for the honeycomb she and Will would be taking off in the morning. *Unless he's still occupied with Henry Krause.* Poor Henry, she thought, having to endure such stress at his age.

After counting up the packages she had on hand, she took a pen and piece of paper to make up her order. But where was the catalogue? She checked all the drawers and cupboards beneath the counter. Then she remembered seeing it on the desk her father used, in a corner at the end of the barn.

Annie was surprised to find the desk covered with shards of glass and the window above it with a gaping hole in the center. Sometimes birds hit the windows, but this had to be a very big bird. Like an owl or hawk. She bent to check the floor and noticed something lying in the gap between the desk and the wall.

Getting down on her hands and knees, she

stretched to feel for it. Her fingers latched onto something sharp. Glass. Broken. She swore at herself for being so stupid and pulled her hand back. Blood oozed from a thin slice across her fingers.

She got to her feet and sat down in her father's chair. Her hand was beginning to throb and she wrapped a tissue around the cut. When she felt steady, she got the sturdy commercial-size broom hanging on the opposite wall to sweep under the desk.

Blood was starting to seep through the tissue as Annie used the broom to drag out a large rock, with a piece of paper held in place around it by an elastic band. Her hands were shaking as she snapped the elastic off the rock and unfolded the paper.

YOU'RE NEXT.

CHAPTER SEVENTEEN

WILL'S CELL RANG just as the sheriff was attempting to ask Henry the same question he'd already posed twice. Will was getting sick and tired of the whole farce. Henry was gray with frustration and stress, though bravely refusing to buckle.

Glaring at the sheriff, Will said, "Hold that a minute, okay?" He walked a few feet away to talk to Annie, whose number had popped up on call display.

Her voice came across as shrill and insistent.

He listened, trying not to let his face reflect what she was telling him because the others were right there, sitting at Henry's kitchen table. She was upset, but more worried than frightened. He wanted to ask her some key questions but didn't want to say too much within earshot of the others.

"Stay right there," he said. "I'll be back as soon as I can."

When he ended the call and put away the phone, he glanced up to see Captain Andrews's quizzical expression. He knew he had to tell him about the threat, but hesitated in front of the sheriff. He was certain if he did, the sheriff would insist on taking Henry into town. Perhaps even lay a charge. There was no way to tell exactly when the rock had been thrown into the barn. They'd been working there yesterday and would have noticed the broken window. It had to have been in the night or sometime that morning. He'd been with Henry since nine in the morning and through the lunch hour. But he knew that Henry was an early riser. So the perp could possibly be Henry. At least, that's how the sheriff and maybe Andrews might spin it.

"Everything okay?" Captain Andrews asked.

Will gave a casual shrug but didn't say a word.

The sheriff made one last try to get Henry to confess, but the poor man simply repeated what he'd been saying for the last half hour. "I haven't seen those bottles for years. I put them away in my shed when I stopped making wine and haven't seen 'em since."

The sheriff, a heavyset man in his late fifties, heaved a sigh that seemed to shout, *I hate to have to do this but...*

Will quickly spoke up. "Henry contacted his lawyer yesterday in town and frankly, I don't think he ought to have been talking to you gents at all. But he wants to be up front about everything. He's got nothing to hide, right, Henry?"

Henry kept his gaze on the tabletop, but nodded.

"So rather than have this go on any longer—you can see he's tired and it's getting near supper time—I suggest I bring Henry into town tomorrow—with his lawyer—and continue any questioning there. Okay?" He crossed his arms and stared unflinchingly at the two pairs of eyes focused on him.

The sheriff turned to Andrews. "He's one of your men?"

"A damn fine firefighter. We're lucky to have him. And he's perfectly right, Sheriff Johnson." Andrews got to his feet, placed a hand on Henry's shoulder. "Sorry about all this, Henry. We have to take those bottles with us, but otherwise, we'll let this go until tomorrow."

Will walked the men to the door and watched them drive off. Then he turned and looked at Henry, still staring blankly into space.

"I don't suppose you have any of that wine tucked away, do you?"

Henry cracked up. "Got something much better. A bottle of rum Jack Collins gave me for Christmas a couple of years ago. I think there's even a cola in the fridge. Unless you want yours straight?"

"I'll get the cola, you get the rum."

After a few sips, Will decided the time was right to tell Henry about Annie's phone call.

Henry was shocked. "I can't think of anyone in this valley who'd want to harm the Collins family. I don't understand what's happening here. Take those empty wine bottles—I can see how some kids might've come across them and taken a few. But threatening Annie? I don't get it." Henry shook his head.

"Can you think of anyone who knew you had them?"

"I don't know. I mean, no one's been around

the farm much at all since Ida Mae died. And that was fifteen years ago."

"Were you making the wine then?"

"Heck, yes. Ida Mae loved it. We had a glass every night before supper. Right up to the time when her medication was increased and she couldn't take alcohol anymore. That's when I stopped drinking it, too." He averted his face. "Wouldn't have been fair."

Will waited a moment, then asked, "Did you ever give it to people?"

"All the time. For Christmas, mostly, 'cause we didn't have a lot of money for expensive gifts."

"And did the people you gave wine to give you back their empty bottles?"

"Some did, some didn't."

That really narrows the field, Will thought. "So you probably gave wine to Annie's father."

"He loved it!"

"Anyone else you can think of?"

Henry frowned. "Lots of people. Back then."

The loneliness of Henry's life tugged at Will. He peered down into his drink, not trusting himself to speak.

"'Course, there were more neighbors then,"

Henry added. "Ed Waters—Sam and Mike's dad—and his wife were still alive. They liked my wine. And there were some people who rented the farm a few miles farther north of the Waters place. A few people in town, too."

"Where did the Waterses live?"

"Two miles north of the campground. That's why Ed wanted that piece of land. He was thinking of getting into raising goats, but nothing came of it. Don't know why."

Will mulled that over. "And who lives there now?"

Henry gave him a "who do you think" kind of look. "Sam Waters and his wife. Plus their three kids. Thought you knew that."

He probably had been told that Waters lived nearby. It made sense, the way he appeared at the campground early morning or late afternoon. On his way back and forth to town, he guessed. Something turned over in Will's mind. He needed to think.

"Look, Henry, I told Annie I'd be right over and I think I should check on her. Make sure she's okay."

"Of course, son. She'll be worried."

"Are you okay here, on your own?"

"Son, I been on my own for the last fifteen years." He smiled up at Will.

Will managed a smile, patted him on the shoulder and left. Before he got into the van, he pulled out his cell and called Annie.

"Are you okay?"

"I'm fine, but definitely ticked off. Someone has a lot of nerve."

"Listen, I've decided to camp out in your yard tonight and every night until your father comes home."

"You don't have to do that."

"Oh, yes, I do," he said, in a tone that preempted any argument. "But will you be okay for a while longer? I want to drive by the campground and pick up the rest of my stuff. I'll leave a note for Sam to let him know I won't be around for a bit."

"Are you sure you want to do this? I mean, I doubt the creep who threw that bottle in my window is going to come back."

He wished he could agree.

"You don't think so, do you?" she asked when he didn't answer.

"Annie, if I thought so would I plan to stay there?"

"I thought maybe it was me you were

coming to stay for," she said, almost plaintively.

He laughed. "You're a tease."

"Teasing is only one of my many strengths."

"If I had time, I could list some others," he suggested. Her laugh thrilled him.

"Maybe we'll have time tonight."

"Maybe. Hey, you know what? I'll come over right now and go see Sam later."

"Sounds like a plan."

"See you in five," he said, pressing the end button. As he backed the van out of Henry's driveway, he realized he hadn't been this impulsive in years. If ever.

She was waiting for him in the yard and was in his arms the instant he stepped out. The first thing he did was inspect her bandaged hand.

"Should I take you into town to get stitches or something?"

"It's not deep. I put antibiotic cream on it. It's fine."

He kissed the bandaged area tenderly, then raised his lips to her mouth. "Why do I feel like I haven't seen you in weeks?" he asked when he came up for air.

"Well, it's been at least an hour. Might as well be a week."

He hugged her, breathing in Annie Collins. When she pulled away and suggested they clean up the barn first, his disappointment was slightly eased by the wink she gave him.

"I cleaned up the glass from the window," she said when they were inside.

Will stared down at the note. He felt a combination of anger and fear rise in his gorge. "I'll have to give this to the sheriff."

"Will it be bad for Henry?"

"Unfortunately, they've only got one suspect and even if it's an old man in his seventies, they're not ready to look anywhere else. Maybe this note will actually help push them in another direction. I doubt even the sheriff would believe Henry could toss rocks through barn windows. And besides, what would his motive be?" He walked over to the broken window. "Let me do something about this." He took one of the empty cardboard boxes from the counter and flattened it with his foot. "This'll do for now."

As Will taped it over the window, Annie said, "Want a glass of wine? We could have it…you know…before dinner."

He turned his head. "Dinner?"

She merely grinned and walked out of the barn.

Will finished as quickly as possible, stowed the rock and note in the van and headed into the kitchen. He stopped abruptly in the doorway, the screen door flapping against his back. Music from a portable CD player on the counter filled the room. There was a small vase of flowers on the table, along with a plate of cheese and crackers and two wineglasses. Annie was nowhere in sight.

Will smiled. Nibbling on a piece of cheese, he opened the refrigerator to look for the wine, eventually finding it in the freezer. After another search through drawers for a corkscrew, he uncorked the wine and poured two generous glasses. He was sipping his when Annie came into the room.

She was wearing something clinging and filmy that looked more like lingerie than a dress. She'd had a quick shower, he guessed, from the damp tendrils at the base of her neck. The rest of her hair was swept up into a fancy knot.

"You should have told me it was formal

wear," he said. "I'd have put on my pressed jeans."

"You have pressed jeans?"

"Well, I did once."

"I thought maybe we could have a drink and then go to town for dinner."

Not possible, he thought. Unless it was a very late dinner.

He passed her a glass and raised his own, sipping without taking his eyes off her. Finally, he set his glass down and moved closer, gently removing her glass and putting it next to his on the table. Then he leaned down and kissed her behind her ear.

She sagged into him. Her hands reached up to draw his head down. "Maybe we can skip dinner."

"Hmm." He was intent on the nape of her neck, when he felt her stiffen.

"Supper break?" a gruff voice behind him said. "And who's this? Not the hired help?"

Will closed his eyes and prayed he was hallucinating. Ever so slowly, he turned around, still holding onto a speechless Annie.

A tall, stooped gray-haired man leaning on a cane hovered just inside the screen door.

The door, Will thought, that perversely did not slam shut for once.

Annie managed to find her voice first. "Daddy."

He shuffled to a chair and sat. The screen door opened and closed again behind a pleasant-looking woman in her sixties, smiling.

"Hi, Shirley," Annie said as she extricated herself from Will's arms. "This is a surprise."

Jack Collins snorted. "Guess so."

"Sorry, Annie, I tried to talk him out of it but ever since Arnie called, he's been obsessed about coming home."

"Obsessed! Makes me sound like a kook instead of someone who's concerned about his property.... Aren't you going to introduce us?"

Annie's face reddened. "Oh, sorry. Dad, Shirley, this is Will Jennings."

"You the firefighter?"

Will nodded. And the hired help, he wanted to add.

"Heard you saved the Lewis place."

"Helped. The volunteer unit did all the work."

Jack gave him an appraising look. "I think you're modest."

Will tried not to smile when he caught Annie winking at him.

"Don't talk too much, either. Guess that's what makes you a good worker." He turned to Annie. "Or is it?"

The redness in Annie's face deepened.

Then Jack gave a funny barking kind of laugh and pointed at the wine. "Are you sharing that with us, or do Shirley and I have to open our own?"

"I suppose you'll want our cheese and crackers, too?" Annie asked, grinning, her hands on her hips.

"Guess so." Jack motioned for Shirley to sit.

Will found the interplay between Annie and her father fascinating. They almost had a routine. Banter with an edge, but coming from strong affection. Patterned out of living alone together for a few years. Annie had hinted at a turbulent period after her mother's death.

After Annie had found two more glasses and set them on the table, Jack reached over to pour. Asserting his place as head of the family, Will thought. And rightly so. If it were me walking in on my daughter in a stranger's embrace, I might not have responded so well.

There was a brief interlude of small talk, mainly between Shirley and Annie. Will was aware of Jack's eyes on him the whole time. He tried to act nonchalant, but realized he wasn't much of a match for the old guy.

"How did you convince Shirley to bring you home?" Annie suddenly asked, turning to her father.

Jack frowned, obviously nettled by the question. He made a noncommittal sound and glared at Shirley, who smiled smugly.

"Your father and I are going on a Caribbean cruise," she said.

Annie had a coughing fit. She plunked her wineglass on the table, tears running from her eyes. Will stared at her, alarmed, but no one else moved. He was about to jump up and pound on her back when she sputtered to a stop.

Shirley and Annie laughed together then, ignoring Jack's baleful expression. "Good one, Shirley," Annie said. "That's a fair trade. When does this happen?"

"In November. Two weeks. That's why I needed my credit card balance. As soon as I got your message, I booked the cruise. Then I told Jack we could come home."

Will sneaked a look at Jack, whose glare had mellowed into a half-smile.

The talk slowly died as they ate the cheese and crackers. Annie filled Jack in about the fires, omitting what had happened in the barn. Probably waiting for a better time. She also left out the suspicions about Henry Krause, though Jack himself muttered at one point, "Henry would never endanger his birds."

When Will realized it was getting late—his plans to spend the night in the yard now moot—he pushed back his chair. "Guess I should get going. Will you need me in the morning?" He didn't know where to direct this question, so kept his gaze fixed between Annie and her father. He did catch the expression on Annie's face and knew she felt as let down as he did.

Before Jack had a chance to speak, Annie said, "Will was going to sleep in his van in the yard tonight, Dad. In case the arsonist happened to come by."

Jack shot Will an incredulous look. "Yeah?"

Will knew that without an explanation about the rock and note, the reasoning sounded lame. He started toward the door when Annie said, "I'd like you to come back, Will. Okay? I think it's still a good idea for you to stay here tonight."

He knew she was sending him a message—that she was still worried the creep might come back. Her father would be of little help.

"Sure. I'll go get some things and maybe check on Henry, while I'm at it."

She walked him out to the van. "Don't be put off by Dad," she said. "He's gruff and grouchy, but if you give it right back, he'll bend a bit."

"He seems okay. I've known crankier, believe me." He ran his fingertip along the curve of her cheek. "I just wish—"

"Me, too," she said, snuggling into him. "You can't imagine how much."

"I think I can." They stood locked together for several minutes until Will dropped his arms. "I'll be back in about half an hour."

"And I'll be waiting," she promised.

As he drove down the lane, he kept his eyes on the rearview mirror. There was enough light from the kitchen to see her wave goodbye, her dress shimmering in the shadows.

When he passed Henry's, the place was in darkness. He slowed, debating whether to disturb the poor guy or not. No doubt he was enjoying a much-needed sleep. On the way back to Annie's, he'd drop by and check out the pigeons and the yard. Make sure things were okay.

He was surprised to see Sam's SUV parked in front of the office. There weren't any lights visible inside, but perhaps he was in a back room. Now would be a good time to let Sam know that, although he was packing up his things, he'd likely be back. Somehow he didn't think Jack Collins would be happy about a prolonged camp-out in his farmyard.

He left the van next to the SUV and knocked sharply on the office door. It was unlocked, so Will stepped inside.

"Sam?"

Silence. Will thought he saw a crack of light beneath a door at the end of the office area and headed for it. He knocked. "Sam? You in there?"

He pushed it open into what appeared to be a storage room. Shelves lined three sides of the small area, filled with an assortment of tools and containers of what looked like nuts, bolts and screws. He stood still, listening for any sounds that would suggest the man was even on the premises. Has to be here somewhere, he thought. His SUV was still warm and he wouldn't go home without it. He walked farther into the room and that was when he noticed it. The faint but unmistakable odor of gasoline.

Frowning, he followed his nose to the end of the room, where he found a red metal gasoline can. Two green bottles lay next to it. Heart pounding, Will turned one of the bottles over in his hands to read the label. *Krause's Fine Wines.*

He stared in disbelief, thinking at first that the arsonist had been interrupted in the act of making up another Molotov cocktail. But images and snippets of conversation flooded his mind. Sam appearing magically on the spot at his own fire here. The laundry shed that was insured. Sam mysteriously absent at some of the other fires.

Will dropped the bottle and ran.

ANNIE WAVED goodbye to Shirley and, wrapping her arms around herself against the unexpectedly cool night air, went back into the kitchen. Shirley had helped her get Jack upstairs to bed before she left. In spite of his protests, they could both see he was tired. There'd been a rush of whispering on the way down to the kitchen afterward, as Shirley recounted the events that had brought them home.

"Basically he felt cooped up staying in someone else's house," she said. "My cousins watch a lot of television and Jack couldn't stand that. Anyway, I've been wanting to go on a cruise for ages and, seeing a window of opportunity—isn't that what they call it?—I took it."

"Good for you," Annie said, hugging the other woman.

But the problem of having her dad home again sank in with full force the instant Annie returned to the kitchen. She'd have to temper the new relationship that was developing between her and Will. And of course, she could no longer defer telling her father about Cara. Maybe tomorrow morning. Get it over with right away. For some reason, the thought of doing it while Will was there made it less daunting.

Will. She was glad she'd insisted he come back, though heaven only knew if she'd have the nerve to creep out to the van to him. Still, just knowing Will would be there was reassuring. She checked the time. He'd been gone more than an hour. Perhaps he'd visited Henry. She called him on his cell phone and let it ring more than a dozen times. Annie knew he kept it on all the time, in the event of a fire. Had something happened?

She paced the room, considering all the plausible explanations. But an inner voice nagged her. He'd answer the cell phone. Wherever he was and whatever he was doing, he wouldn't let it ring. Knowing she'd never get to sleep anyway, she grabbed the keys to the pickup and was on the road in less than five minutes.

As she drove by Henry's place, she slowed to see if Will's van was there. Things looked quiet and the house was in full darkness. She headed for the campground. The first thing she noticed was Will's van parked in front of the office. And the office door was ajar.

She waited a moment, half hoping Will

would come sauntering out. Then she cautiously stepped down from the truck. Pausing at the van to peek inside, she noticed something on the floor. Reaching down, she picked up the cell phone.

Her heart pumped harder. She forced herself to stay calm as she walked to the office door. "Will? Are you in there? Will!"

Some inner sense told her he wasn't. Not with the phone in the van. *Lying on the floor, as if someone had tossed it there.* Something was wrong. She went back to the truck and waited a few more seconds. Panic started to rise inside. She didn't know Sam Waters's phone number, but the cell phone had the fire alert and Scotty's number programmed.

The phone rang several times before the captain finally picked up, his brusque greeting making her wince. God, she hoped she wasn't imagining things.

"Scott, it's Annie Collins. Sorry to bother you but I'm at Rest Haven and I can't find Will. He was supposed to check on Henry Krause and then return to the apiary. But he hasn't shown up and when I got here, his van was here with his cell phone in it. That's what I'm using to call you and—"

"Whoa, Annie! You've lost me. Why are you worried about Will?"

Annie clenched her teeth. "He wouldn't go anywhere without his cell and I've been trying to call him on it. But it was here in his van the whole time and he is *not* here. Do you understand?"

"And what do you want me to do?"

"I'm not sure but I think he might be investigating or something."

That got his attention. "Investigating what?"

She told him about the rock and note.

"Damn it, Annie, you should've told me about this right away! Does Will think Henry did it?"

"Of course not, but he might have gone back to talk to him. Maybe I should go there."

"Maybe you should just go straight home. If you're really worried, I'll drive out to Henry's myself."

"Okay," she said and ended the call. She got back into the truck, taking the cell phone with her, then—ignoring his advice—gunned the truck toward Henry's.

There was something different about the place, she thought as soon as she climbed out of the truck. She hesitated in the dark yard. No sign of Will and it looked as though Henry had already gone to bed. Suddenly she froze.

Crackling sounds emanated from the back of the house. She ran along the side, past the kitchen door to the rear. Flames were licking out from a basement window. She stared in disbelief. Something crashed inside, breaking her trance and she dashed to the side door, pushing it open and flying inside.

Smoke was seeping up from the basement and the floor was hot beneath her feet. "Henry!" she screamed. Where did he sleep? Upstairs? Or down, where Ida Mae had spent her last days?

If only she could remember the layout of the house, but she hadn't been inside it for fifteen years. She ran down the hall leading from the kitchen. The smoke was thicker now and she started coughing, holding a hand over her mouth as she scrunched up her eyes, trying to find the staircase. There.

She moved forward but her foot bumped against something soft. Her eyes were streaming and her chest heaving so rapidly she thought she was going to pass out. She leaned down to feel what was obstructing the way and heard a soft heart-stopping sound. Like a moan.

CHAPTER EIGHTEEN

WILL FELT HIMSELF BEING pulled up. His head was pounding and when he opened his eyes, neon lights swam across his vision. He blinked several times, trying to figure out where he was until he realized the fog was smoke and the pale face hovering over him was Annie. He shot up, only to sag back against what felt like Annie's knees. How did she get behind him? He thought he heard someone groan. Was it him, or her? Then he heard a voice in his ear, pleading.

"Will, you've got to help me. I can't lift you on my own. Come on! You've got to get up. The house is on fire."

That got the adrenaline pumping. He tried to talk but his tongue was stuck to the roof of his mouth. He pointed up.

"Henry? He's upstairs? I'll get him." She pushed him forward and rose to her feet.

He grabbed her arm, clutching it as he levered himself off the floor. Stood panting like an old man, catching his breath. His mouth was dry, lips swollen. He passed his tongue tentatively over them and tried to talk again. "No," he whispered as she began to shake loose. "Me. You. Outside. Call."

She gave him a look that made him want to laugh. *She thinks I'm out of it.* He tried once more. This time, filling in the gaps. "Call in the alarm. Now. Go." He pushed her away, pointing to the front door of the house. She hesitated and he was afraid he'd have to use force to get her out of the house.

"Henry!"

"I'll get him."

She spun around and made for the door. The smoke roiled out when she opened it, giving Will a dose of air before he started up the stairs. He prayed Henry was in his bedroom, because he had a rough idea where that was. He didn't know how much time he had. Maybe not enough to search every room.

The smoke was thicker up there, rising on the waves of heat. He hunched over and crawled, feeling his way along the wall. The second room on the right, or on the left?

Think Jennings, think! You've done plenty of searches before, stay calm.

His back was killing him but he continued on, hugging the floor.. He strained to see but it was almost impossible in the thick acrid smoke. Passing the first room, he trailed his fingers along the wall. It was already warming up, as was the floor. Not a good sign. How much time did he have? When exactly had the blaze started? He didn't remember much. Walking into the kitchen and calling out to Henry. Then nothing. Someone—Waters?—must have knocked him out.

What was that? His ears strained against the loud roar of the fire. He crawled faster, following the muffled sound. Second door on the left. That was it. He rose higher and edged through the doorway, trying to find Henry. His eyes stung from the smoke and the tears streaking down his face.

"Henry!" he hollered. "Henry!"

No one on the bed that he could feel. He leaned over it, realizing he was touching the covers. Then he heard what could've been a cough. Will edged around the foot of the bed, feeling his way to the other side. There he found Henry, wrapped in a cocoon of sheets.

He was barely conscious, but seemed to recognize Will.

Will scooped him up into the firefighter's carry, wrapped over his shoulder head-first and staggered out of the room. Running now, because the heat had intensified. He heard beams falling below him. God, please don't let the stairs be cut off. He reached the top and ducked his head down, careful not to smash Henry into the walls. If the man had been any bigger... The memory of trying to drag Gino out from under the beam flashed in his mind.

Taking the stairs two at a time, he tried not to rush. Can't afford to fall. May not be able to get us both up. Tendrils of flame were licking into the kitchen now. He could feel the heat radiating out from the back of the house. It was slowly collapsing beneath them. The open front door was only feet away, but his lungs were heaving, scorched from the smoke and heat, and burdened by the extra weight he carried.

He kept his eyes on the doorway, trying not to let the horrifying crashes behind distract him. His legs were rubbery and seemed to carry him in slow motion, as if in a nightmare. Running but getting nowhere.

Suddenly part of the floor gave way to his right, the floorboards falling inward, consumed by the flames beneath. Will glanced into the gaping maw of fire and, using all he had left in him, shot through the opened door to fall in a heap onto the grassy lawn. He lay there, fighting for air, cradling Henry's still form as if he were holding onto a baby.

The cool night air rushed around him. From far away, he thought he heard men shouting and the loud hum of the tanker as water poured into the portatank. He propped himself up on one elbow, pulling the sheets away from Henry to uncover his face and let the air get at him, too. "Henry?" he croaked.

The soot-covered face creased in what might have been a smile or a grimace. Will couldn't be sure. But the old man's breathing was shallow and he needed oxygen right away. "Getting help for you. Stay there." As if Henry was going anywhere.

Will stumbled toward the corner of the house where all the action was taking place. Men were hauling hoses and spraying the house, but once he saw the back of it, Will knew there was no hope. His eyes filtered through the hissing steam and the spewing smoke, finally spotting Andrews's red helmet.

"Jennings!" Relief broke across the captain's face. "Thank God. Where's Henry?"

"Out front, on the lawn. He needs oxygen."

"I'll get a tank from the truck. We called an ambulance. It's on the way from Essex." He turned to leave but Will grabbed hold of him.

"Where's Annie?"

Andrews patted his hand. "She's safe. Sitting in her truck. I hope."

Relieved, Will ran back to where he'd left Henry and was feeling for a pulse when Andrews came with an oxygen tank and mask.

"Is he breathing?"

"There's a faint pulse."

"Put the mask on him, keep him warm if you can. You know the drill. I need to get back."

"Can you save the house?"

"It doesn't look good. There must've been a lot of junk in the basement."

"Was it another Molotov?"

"Won't know till we get down there. Maybe not for a day or two."

Will attached the oxygen and covered Henry with the sheet. Andrews turned to go.

"Cap," Will said. "Something I need to tell you. Before I came here, I went to the office at Rest Haven. I found gas cans and a couple of those wine bottles. I think—"

"Save it. I called the sheriff as soon as I got here." He paused, shaking his head. "I couldn't raise Waters on his cell again. It's not the first time. I've no doubt he'll come roaring up here any minute with a lot of explanations."

"I think he'll be surprised to see me."

Andrews pursed his lips, sadness washing over his face. "He was a good man…once upon a time." Then he swung around and headed back to the fire.

Will looked down at Henry's chest, moving slowly up and down as the pure oxygen filled his lungs. He wanted the old man to live, though he wasn't certain how grateful Henry would be now that he'd lost everything. Will pulled his sweatshirt over his head and tucked it around Henry. In the distance, he could hear the faint wail of the ambulance.

TWO DAYS. The longest forty-eight hours Annie could recall since, well, since the day she went into labor thirteen summers ago. She hadn't seen Will since the night of the fire after the ambulance had taken Henry to the hospital in Essex. She'd overheard one of the paramedics congratulate Will, saying another ten or fifteen minutes and... She'd missed the rest, but not the grimness in Will's face or the dampness in his eyes when he'd turned to find her standing nearby. Then she was in his arms.

Work at the apiary had been put on hold since the fire at Henry's but it couldn't wait any longer. She suspected the hives were brimming in all the beeyards and decided to call Danny McLean to see if he could spare a few hours every day.

"Can Danny come or not?" her father asked as she hung up the phone.

"He can come," she said.

"Is that Will fella going to be helping, too?"

Annie smiled. "Yes, that Will *fella* is coming later this afternoon. He's been staying at Henry's, helping with the investigation and the cleanup. And at the hospital visiting Henry whenever he can."

"Busy man." Jack stared down into his coffee and muttered something Annie didn't quite catch.

"Pardon?"

The edge in her voice brought his head back up. He looked embarrassed. "Nothing. Well, I, uh…just said that he was busy here, too."

"He has been busy here, Dad. If you've noticed, we've managed to do a lot in the last ten or twelve days."

He cleared his throat. "I did notice, Annie girl. But…well…was it all *bee* work?"

Annie girl. She hadn't heard him use that childhood pet name in years. She held his gaze, searching his face. He'd been an easy person to read in the past. His emotions flared and played out in his face on a regular basis. Except for his silences, he'd never been a man to keep his thoughts hidden. Or so she'd always thought.

"Daddy," she said, "I need to tell you something."

She sat in the chair across from him at the kitchen table. "When you were away, I realized how much work the apiary is. Too much for one person."

"I'll be up and working in no time," he said.

"I know Dad, but the thing is—"

"And I can do twice the work of a man half my age."

Annie smiled and patted his hand. "I know that, too. But I started to worry about the future of the business. I wasn't certain how long I'd be here to help—remember I told you when I came home last year that it was temporary."

"Annie, I never expected you to give up your life for me."

She blinked back tears. "Of course you didn't, Daddy. I'm just trying to explain why I…well…why I gave a representative from Sunrise Foods a tour."

He jerked back his head. "What?"

"The vice-president came and had a look around. In the end, I told him we weren't interested in selling. That's all that happened." She took a deep breath. "But I'm sorry. I shouldn't have done this behind your back—when you weren't home. I wasn't thinking."

He didn't speak for a moment. Finally he said, "I guess you just did what you thought was best. I can't blame you for that, Annie."

He smiled. "Maybe it's about time I started to plan for the future of the apiary, too." His smile turned sly. "I have a feeling you might be here a bit longer than we both expected. Are you in love with him?"

The question startled her. It wasn't what she expected him to say. "Yes, I am."

He nodded. "He seems a decent man, Annie. Though I wonder...does he have a shady past? You know...that scar and all?"

She burst into laughter. "I'll tell you about the scar later, but there's something else.... I want to tell you what happened to me, thirteen years ago."

When she finished, he didn't speak for a long time. Neither did he drop his eyes from her face, but the whole gamut of emotions flashed in his as she told her story. None of them, she realized gratefully, had anything to do with anger or disappointment.

"You could have told me," he said, his face twisted with regret. "I wouldn't have let you down, Annie. I know I can be tetchy but—"

"Dad, I know you'd have been there for me but...it's hard to explain...there was this silence between us—ever since Mom died." As soon as she'd said that, she realized it was the very first time in years either of them had directly referred to her mother.

"All my fault," Jack said in a low voice. "Isobel tried to tell me, but I couldn't...I didn't want to accept what happened. Working the bees kept me sane. It was the only world left for me and I...well, I guess I cut you out of it. I'm so sorry about that, Annie." His eyes filled with tears.

She didn't trust herself to speak for a long moment. Wiping the corners of her eyes she said in a shaky voice, "I'm sorry, too, Daddy. If I'd been less focused on my own guilt and grief, I'd have noticed yours."

"Honey, I was the parent and you, the child. It was up to me. I let you down." He stopped again, taking a deep breath. "What do you mean, *guilt?*"

"It was my fault Mom went to town that day. I wanted a pair of winter boots I'd seen. I bugged her about them for days."

"You think that's why she went? Honey, she went out because she was mad at me."

"What do you mean?"

"We'd had an argument. I'm not the easiest man to live with, you know that. Even back then. She said she was tired of never going anywhere or doing anything. It was our usual quarrel. I wanted to stay on the farm and she liked to get out and see people. Some friends of hers were in town that day and had invited her for lunch. I told her she shouldn't go, the roads would be bad because of the storm the night before. She said I always tried to stop her from seeing friends and having fun. Finally I shouted that she damn well better go or I'd never hear the end of it." He stopped, his breath catching. "She slammed out the door and...and I never saw her again until I...until I had to go to the hospital morgue."

Speechless, Annie watched as her father lowered his head and sobbed.

WILL PASSED Danny on the drive up to the house and when he pulled up in front of the barn, Annie was standing there, waiting for him. He felt a lump swell in his throat. It was a sensation that had come and gone frequently over the past two days. Like when he'd curled up to her the night of the fire, his ear pressed against her back, feeling the light beat of her heart as she slept. Or when the doctor told him Henry was going to be all right. And especially whenever he thought of that night, how they all could've been trapped inside the house. Then his anger rose and he knew, no matter how sorry he might feel for Sam and his family, he'd never forgive the man for what could have happened.

"Hey," she said as he stepped out of the van.

Warmth surged through him at that one little word. *Hey.* Not to mention the smile that came with it. He wanted to fold her into his arms, but something held him back. Maybe the thought of Jack watching from inside the house. Maybe the sudden inexplicable shyness he felt in her presence. When had that begun? he wondered.

"So...did you and Danny finish up?"

"Oh no. We barely started."

"Do you want to keep at it, or are you tired?" She didn't look tired but something had changed. There was an air of contentment about her, as if she'd found what she'd been seeking. He felt a faint hope that he was a part of it.

"You can borrow my father's suit again but I think we'll have to get you one of your own." She grinned up at him and his hope grew. "Come on into the barn and I'll show you what we took off today."

He followed her inside and was amazed at the number of stacked supers. "Danny's coming back in the morning to help extract them," she said.

"What about his summer school?"

"He said he can spare one or two hours a day for the next week. After that he'll be busy with tests and essays." She paused, looking from the supers to him. "I…uh…I'm hoping you'll be able to stay."

"I'm not going anywhere."

She caught her lower lip between her teeth and blushed. "Great. Well, shall we suit up? We need to put excluders in the hives in the clover field out back, so we can walk it. That okay with you?"

She sounded nervous. *Having second thoughts about us?* He prayed not. Not after what he'd been thinking and planning for the past two days. He wondered if she'd had a chance to talk to her father about Cara. He wanted to ask her, but knew she'd get around to telling him.

"Fine," was all he said and they suited up quickly. He thought back to the first time he'd tried to get into Jack's bee suit and how funny he must have looked. Was it really less than two weeks ago? His life had shifted so dramatically in such a short time.

"All set?" she asked from beneath the black mesh of her bee hat. "I'll take the smoker if you can carry the excluders." She led the way out of the barn.

A maroon Buick was pulling into the yard. "Shirley's taking Dad to his physio in Essex."

"Does she need help getting him into the car?"

"No, she can manage. I helped him get downstairs and he's been waiting at the kitchen table."

So I wasn't just imagining his eyes on me. He hadn't quite figured out Jack Collins yet, but suspected Annie's father would need time to adjust to Will's presence, too. And, as he'd just told Annie, he wasn't going anywhere. If all turned out the way he'd planned.

As they tramped in silence along the lane, Will thought how exotic everything here had seemed when he'd first arrived. Now he was filled with a sense of familiarity. He knew that the grove of poplars on the right ahead signaled the turn to the buckwheat field and the clover beyond it. He knew the stump from the old beech tree that Annie said fell down in a lightning strike ten years ago was a few feet farther on, to the left. That the blackberry patch to the north of the stump would soon be swelling with fruit and she'd promised him a pie.

"My mother's recipe," she'd said, when he'd called her from the hospital the first night after the fire. When they wanted to talk about anything but what had just happened.

They reached the first row of hives. It was a bright sunny day and Will knew the bees would be active. He smiled. Two weeks ago, he wouldn't have known that. Annie didn't have to tell him what to do anymore, either. He put on his gloves and headed for a hive to remove its cover. She brought the smoker over and puffed smoke into the top super. For a frightening split second he flashed back to the other night and his frantic scramble to get Henry. He waited for his heart rate to slow down, then lifted the super gently onto the ground.

Annie got the next one, and they alternated until five supers were resting on the ground around the hive. Will picked up one of the excluders and set it down over the super where the queen and her brood were in residence. He and Annie restacked the rest of the supers and headed for the next hive. He was about to remove the cover when Annie placed her gloved hand on his arm.

"Dad told me that Sam Waters has confessed to all the fires. He was trying to get Henry off his land?"

"Yeah," he said. "Apparently his brother didn't know what Sam was up to. He was desperate to make the campground work. He thought that if there were other fires in the valley, everyone would assume the last one—which was going to be Henry's place—was the work of the same arsonist. He chose sites where there'd be minimal damage—"

"But why try to put the blame on Henry?"

"A last-ditch idea, which only shows how far gone he was. Things accelerated when I joined the unit. My staying at the campground and making friends with Henry made him paranoid. He was afraid I'd figure things out."

"So setting fire to his own place was just a distraction."

"Yes. He found some empty wine bottles at his place—Henry had given his father the wine years ago. He knew the old grudge with Henry was common knowledge in the valley and figured everyone would assume Henry was the culprit."

"And of course he conveniently identified Henry's truck."

"He even drove the truck there, in case I happened to see it. Which I did."

"But that night, when you went to the campground to get your things?"

"When I realized he'd been there minutes before, making up a Molotov cocktail, I knew he was going back to Henry's."

Will closed his eyes. He didn't want to think about what might have happened if Annie hadn't come looking for him. When he opened his eyes again, she was staring at him. Her face was bright red and her eyes damp.

"What?" he asked.

"I just…I was thinking about what—"

He leaned over and kissed her. It was a deliciously slow kiss. Will let himself fall into it for a few tantalizing minutes—the minty sweetness of her mouth on his, the sun beating down on his back and above it all, the pervasive scent of honey in the air.

He raised his head and smiled. "I love you, Annie."

Her face lit up. "I love you, too, Will." She laughed, then caught her lower lip in her teeth.

He held her gaze, his heart full. Speechless.

Annie shifted her eyes to the hive they'd been working on minutes ago. "You know, when I was a little girl I never really understood how bees could find their way home. Everyday they travel—long distances sometimes. See that?" She pointed to the bottom entrance to the hive where a cluster of bees hovered.

Will looked, but didn't know what he was seeing. "Yeah," he said doubtfully.

"They're new bees, just hatched. They're moving up and down and sideways in a kind of dance."

"Why are they doing it?"

"They're about to make their first flight out of the hive and they're memorizing their home."

"Say again?"

"Every bee returns to their own hive. They memorize what it looks like so they won't mistakenly try to enter another. That would mean death. To survive, they have to know instinctively where their home is."

He knew exactly what she was talking about. Coming home again. To Garden Valley.

"Let me tell you about my plan," he said, taking her hand.

EPILOGUE

"You ready?"

Annie pressed her lips together for the third time, patted a few strands of hair in place and stood back from the mirror for one last look. She'd deliberated for hours over what to wear. Nothing too casual, nothing too dressy. In the end, she settled on a cream-colored skirt with a subdued flowered print. It barely reached her knees and flowed smoothly over her hips, flaring slightly at the hem. She matched it with a sleeveless periwinkle blue, scoop-necked cotton top and, at the last minute, added a pair of dangling blue and silver earrings.

She couldn't recall the last time she'd taken such pains over her appearance. *In my other life. The one before I came back home,* she thought.

"Annie!"

She poked her head out of her bedroom.

"Coming, Dad." She reached for the small gift-wrapped box on top of the chest of drawers and walked slowly down the stairs. Her stomach was making ominous noises and her underarms felt damp already. She paused outside the kitchen, took a deep breath and walked into the room.

Her father was standing at the door, cane in hand, and wearing what he called his Sunday suit. Annie smiled. The fact that she hadn't seen him in it since the day he went to Charlotte for his operation suggested there weren't many Sundays in her father's week. Certainly not if the day signified one of rest and contemplation. She and Shirley had managed, however, to limit his hours in the barn during the past six weeks since the fire.

Six weeks. So much had happened since that night. Sam was in custody and awaiting trial in Raleigh. Annie had heard that the family's farm was up for sale and that Sam's wife and children were living with her parents in Charlotte. She'd met Mike Waters once, in town. He'd summoned a curt hello and passed on by. One more connection to the past cut forever.

"You look beautiful," her father said, breaking into her thoughts.

"And so do you."

He colored slightly, muttering a humph, but she knew he was pleased. She'd seen him ironing his shirt that morning and he'd even changed his tie at her subtle hint.

"I think I hear a car coming now," he said, tilting his head to the side nearest the screen door. "Are you nervous?"

"Scared stiff."

"Me, too. I've never been a grandfather before."

Annie bit her lip. She'd vowed not to cry. "You'll be an amazing one."

"Think so?" His smile vanished for a second. "But I'll be number three."

"But the best one," Annie said. She kissed him on the cheek and took his arm through hers. "Come on, let's go outside and see if it's them."

She didn't feel the slightest disappointment when Will's van drove up in front of the barn. So, he'd made it on time. She felt only a rush of gratitude.

He'd been a busy man since the fire at Henry's. He'd rented a trailer, which was parked in Henry's backyard, and Henry was living in it while Will stayed in the van. But what had astonished and warmed Annie more than anything, was how Will—through Captain Andrews—had gathered together a crew of firefighters from the whole county. They were spending all their free hours rebuilding a home for Henry. It was part of the plan he'd concocted during the long hours waiting for word of Henry's recovery. There was something else too, he'd hinted, that he was saving for the right time.

She waved as he got out of the van and saw at once that his shopping trip into Essex the other day had been successful. He was wearing tan chinos and a short-sleeved striped cotton shirt. He'd even bought new shoes.

"Isn't he the dapper one," Jack remarked.

Annie turned sharply and caught the warm smile in his face. Who was he kidding? Everyone in the valley was already commenting on how much Jack liked the newcomer at the apiary. "You be good," she whispered, removing his arm from hers so she could greet Will.

Will leaned into the van and came out with a long white box. He carried it awkwardly. "I got some roses," he said. "The woman in the flower shop said you can never go wrong with roses. Even for a thirteen-year-old."

Annie stretched to kiss him lightly on the lips. "That was very thoughtful."

"First impressions are important," he said.

She recalled what he'd told her after the first time they'd made love. That she was one of the few people he'd met since the accident who had noticed his face first, and the scar last.

"So, is today going to be the right day?" she asked, teasingly, reminding him of their conversation weeks ago. She was aware of her father's questioning face turned her way, but kept her eyes on Will.

"Oh I think it's going to be," he said. "Later. After."

If eyes could write songs, Annie was thinking, his are sending me a ballad right this moment.

"There they are," Jack piped up, looking down the driveway.

The three of them watched as a red station wagon drove into the yard. Annie's stomach lurched, but she knew she was going to be all right. Her two favorite men in the world were beside her.

The car stopped behind the van. Annie squinted against the sun and managed to catch a glimpse of a bright glow of flaming hair and a freckled face. She grasped Will's hand and walked forward to greet her daughter.

SILHOUETTE® Super ROMANCE™

THE PROMISE OF CHRISTMAS
by Tara Taylor Quinn

Shortly before Christmas, Leslie Sanderson finds herself coping with grief, with lingering and fearful memories and with unforeseen motherhood. She also rediscovers a man from her past—a man who could help her to move towards the promise of a new future...

THE PREGNANCY TEST by Susan Gable
9 Months Later

Sloan Thompson has good reason to worry about his daughter —and that's before she tells him that she's pregnant. Then he discovers his own actions have consequences. This about-to-be grandfather is also going to be a father once again!

BIG GIRLS DON'T CRY by Brenda Novak

Reenie O'Connell has plenty to cry about when she discovers her husband has betrayed her. Isaac Russell is merely the messenger, but it's hard for Reenie not to blame him. Still, Reenie's initial resentment of Isaac begins to change into admiration and attraction...and maybe something more.

THE DAUGHTER HE NEVER KNEW
by Linda Barrett

Guilt and anger made Jason Parker turn his back on his home and family after he lost his twin. Now, after nine years, he's returned to discover that nothing and no one in Pilgrim Cove is the same—and that he's left behind more than he had ever guessed.

On sale from 20th October 2006

Available at WHSmith, Tesco, ASDA, Borders, Eason, Sainsbury's and most bookshops

www.silhouette.co.uk

From No. 1 *New York Times* bestselling author Nora Roberts

Atop the rocky coast of Maine sits the Towers, a magnificent family mansion that is home to a legend of long-lost love, hidden emeralds—and four determined sisters.

Catherine, Amanda & Lilah
available 4th August 2006

Suzanna & Megan
available 6th October 2006

Available at WHSmith, Tesco, ASDA, Borders, Eason, Sainsbury's and all good paperback bookshops

www.silhouette.co.uk

To Be a Fine Lady
ELIZABETH JEFFREY

A vivid recreation of 1850s Yorkshire, packed with romance, drama and scandalous family secrets…

Abandoned as a baby and brought up by the cruel farmer who found her, Joanna dreams of a rich family and a better life. As a potential marriage and a forbidden attraction develop, the truth about her real family lurks just around the corner—and is getting ready to reveal itself on the most important day of her life…

On sale 15th September 2006

www.millsandboon.co.uk

All you could want for Christmas!

Meet handsome and seductive men under the mistletoe, escape to the world of Regency romance or simply relax by the fire with a heartwarming tale by one of our bestselling authors. These special stories will fill your holiday with Christmas sparkle!

On sale 6th October 2006

On sale 20th October 2006

1106/XMAS TITLES b

On sale
3rd November
2006

On sale 17th November 2006

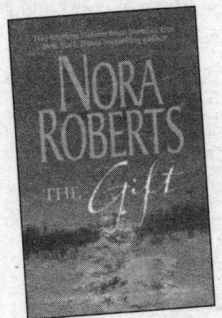

On sale
1st December
2006

Available at
WHSmith, Asda,
Tesco and all
good bookshops

www.millsandboon.co.uk

M&B

2 FREE

BOOKS AND A SURPRISE GIFT!

We would like to take this opportunity to thank you for reading this Silhouette® book by offering you the chance to take TWO more specially selected titles from the Superromance™ series absolutely FREE! We're also making this offer to introduce you to the benefits of the Mills & Boon® Reader Service™—

- ★ FREE home delivery
- ★ FREE gifts and competitions
- ★ FREE monthly Newsletter
- ★ Exclusive Reader Service offers
- ★ Books available before they're in the shops

Accepting these FREE books and gift places you under no obligation to buy, you may cancel at any time, even after receiving your free shipment. Simply complete your details below and return the entire page to the address below. You don't even need a stamp!

YES! Please send me 2 free Superromance books and a surprise gift. I understand that unless you hear from me, I will receive 4 superb new titles every month for just £3.69 each, postage and packing free. I am under no obligation to purchase any books and may cancel my subscription at any time. The free books and gift will be mine to keep in any case.

U6ZED

Ms/Mrs/Miss/Mr .... Initials ....

BLOCK CAPITALS PLEASE

Surname ....

Address ....

....

.... Postcode ....

Send this whole page to:
UK: FREEPOST CN81, Croydon, CR9 3WZ

Offer valid in UK only and is not available to current Mills & Boon® Reader Service™ subscribers to this series. Overseas and Eire please write for details. We reserve the right to refuse an application and applicants must be aged 18 years or over. Only one application per household. Terms and prices subject to change without notice. Offer expires 31st January 2007. As a result of this application, you may receive offers from Harlequin Mills & Boon and other carefully selected companies. If you would prefer not to share in this opportunity please write to The Data Manager, PO Box 676, Richmond, TW9 IWU.

Silhouette® is a registered trademark and under licence.
Superromance™ is being used as a trademark.
The Mills & Boon® Reader Service™ is being used as a trademark.